"Lyrically brilliant and deeply memorable, *The Woodsman's Daughter* is a heartfelt tale of sadness and suffering contrasted against hope and redemption. Jeni Swem Edmonds' expertly drawn characters practically leap off the page in this superb story of the indelible links between the past and the present that will remind many of Joyce Carol Oats and Judith Guest. She works the keyboard like an artist, painting broad strokes that bring richness and life to her beautifully fashioned world. A major debut and sparkling new voice."

- Jon Land,
bestselling author of STRONG JUSTICE.

The Woodsman's Daughter

"One must be so very careful as to what comes out of their mouth, for it may cause one to lose their head."

Jeni Swem Edmonds

Order this book online at www.trafford.com
or email orders@trafford.com

Most Trafford titles are also available at major online book retailers.

Printed in Victoria, BC, Canada.

ISBN: 978-1-4269-3342-4 (sc)
ISBN: 978-1-4269-3343-1 (e-b)

*Our mission is to efficiently provide the world's finest, most comprehensive book publishing
service, enabling every author to experience success. To find out how to publish your book, your
way, and have it available worldwide, visit us online at www.trafford.com*

Trafford rev. 07/14/2010

Trafford
PUBLISHING® www.trafford.com

North America & international
toll-free: 1 888 232 4444 (USA & Canada)
phone: 250 383 6864 ♦ fax: 812 355 4082

Chapter one

Jennifer had no idea that July 20th would be the last time she ever hiked with her father. She was three days shy of her eleventh birthday, and all she had on her mind were the binoculars her father had promised to get her. However, this particular Saturday would end tragically with his death.

Thomas Martin had been the class clown in his youth. He was a prankster—one of those men who thought he was funny, but his jokes were told at very inappropriate times. Do you know the kind?

During his early childhood his passion had been gourmet cooking. His dream was to serve his country and be the personal chef to a famous general, but an unfortunate accident had rendered him unable to pursue his passion. His right hand was partially mangled during one of his escapades in the woods, and this kept him from serving a general or anyone else!

Thomas liked playing tricks on campers, hikers, and anyone unfortunate enough to trespass on his property, and this meant anyone he saw as a threat to his privacy. His "privacy"—now that was laugh! The few "No Trespassing" signs he had were put up when it suited his purposes, and they were taken down when it didn't. He enjoyed misguiding hikers down the wrong path just to watch the looks on their faces when they realized they were lost. He was very amused by it all.

His "woodland," as he called it, was a rolling landscape of beauty. It encompassed over five hundred acres of untouched forest that pushed up against the Smoky Mountains. No one ever pushed back. Part of the acreage was so steep that not even the most talented of hikers would venture onto it. To make things worse for the campers, Thomas had an agreement with the local rangers that he would keep an eye out for any stragglers. Unfortunately for them, there was one local ranger that had no scruples and let Thomas do as he wished with the stragglers he "rescued." Although he called this acreage "his," the deed was titled in the name of his wife, Eileen Thorpe Martin. It was a thorn that always stuck in his side.

He was a very frustrated man, and he took his frustration out on Eileen. Many times he would not let her out of the house, much less off the property! He was a verbally abusive husband although he had never laid a hand on her. His words cut deep, and they left a wound on Eileen's soul that would never heal. Mostly due to his obsessive behavior, she had become a recluse, and one thing for sure, she loved her daughter more than any sunset or sunrise, and certainly more than life.

Jennifer didn't like the tricks her father played on the campers either. It made her sick to her stomach, but she went along with it anyway thinking he might change his ways, but he never did. If things didn't go as planned, she hoped he would direct his anger to her and not at her mother. She was strong in spirit and had a quick wit about her when it came to her father's antics. She loved the outdoors. When she wasn't helping him, the natural beauty of the place she called home helped her escape the reality of an unhappy childhood.

~

"Daddy, are you sure you won't get caught?" Jennifer asked, looking over her shoulder. It was the beginning of fall, and the trees had just started to change color. This was Jennifer's favorite time of the year. She thought each leaf to have a purpose, and sometimes she would stare off into the tree tops and would swear to anyone that she saw the face of God in every canopy of red, purple and orange.

"Are we men or mice?" Thomas whispered. He paused for a moment and then whispered again, "I am the Woodsman."

Jennifer giggled. "I'm a girl, Daddy. If the rangers ever catch you, I won't bail you out!"

Thomas was not worried about the forest rangers. "I worked very hard on this fake bear head," he replied, beaming with shallow pride, "If it doesn't scare the life out of him, nothing will!"

Jennifer stepped back into the shadows and pulled the rim of her homemade camouflage hat down past her eyebrows. "Do I have to look? I don't like it when you scare them. Sometimes they look like their eyes are going to pop out of their heads. It's scary. I'll admit you have mastered the skill of scaring the crap out of the city folk!" There was a pause as Jennifer thought. "Do they put kids in the same cell with their fathers? I don't think I would do well locked up, how about you? The thought of no trees, no wild berries, and nothing to do—it would certainly drive me up the wall! What about you?"

Thomas smirked and shrugged his shoulders. "Are you turning into a 'fraidy-cat? Prove to me that girls are not sissies. You pull the string! If you do it precisely when I tell you to, I might let you in on some of my secrets."

Jennifer frowned. "I am not a 'fraidy-cat, but sometimes I think it's mean. That's all. I...I don't want to pull the string. Mama told me..."

He grabbed her arm and squeezed it, causing Jennifer to wince in pain. "You never mind about what your mama tells you. I am the one who takes you to picture shows, or have you forgotten who pays the bills?"

"I...know, Daddy, but it was Mama who wanted you to take her to the picture show, not me! It was her birthday, and you took me instead. Why did you have to hurt her feelings like that? I didn't like dressing up like an old lady, and it was dark in there. The theatre smelled like olive oil!"

Thomas obviously did not like his daughter arguing with him. "You're doing it! Stop whining, or I will shove this bear head on your shoulders, and you can be the one who makes me laugh! I take you everywhere. I am the one who pays for all those toys, and I am the one who pays attention to you," he said, jamming his thumb against his chest. "Your mama doesn't like anyone going hiking with her, and that is why you are with me, alright? So, just sit there and keep quiet, or I will trade you in for a boy. God Almighty child! Don't you know it was a miracle you came out of her on time?"

"What do you mean by that?" she asked shyly.

"Your mama would have let you grow inside of her until you were an old lady if it hadn't been for me! Like I ever wanted a girl, anyway! They had a heck of a time getting her into the ambulance."

"Stop!" she insisted. "You're just making up another story! I know all about the birds and the bees, Daddy. You're only saying that about the ambulance because you know she doesn't like to be cooped up! You're just trying to make up something so I will run and tell her, and she'll get upset. Here, take your old bear head! And while you're at it, go jump off Shallow Grave!"

He took a deep breath as he removed his goggles and wiped his forehead. "Your mama has always loved you more than anything—or anyone!"

Jennifer glared at him. "...are you jealous? That is the way it is supposed to be in regards to anyone lucky enough to have a woman like Eileen to be their mother." Thomas glared back and then grinned at her. "I wish she paid more attention to my needs, that's all. Keep quiet now. The trespassers are getting up, and then, maybe if you're a good listener, I *will* jump off Shallow Grave!"

Jennifer's jaw tightened. "You should be grateful I don't tell on you! Don't say bad things about Mama. You know she's been sick, and it's not her fault I'm a girl. It's not my fault either!" She paused. "I still want you to take me to see *The Mask of Zorro*. Please, don't forget."

Thomas Martin took out his knife and dug the tip of it into the bark of the hickory tree. "You fell asleep in Pinocchio, and yes, it is your mama's fault you're a girl. She promised me a boy." He closed his eyes for one second and then opened them again and said, "I am the Woodsman, and you are the Woodsman's daughter. Don't ever forget it."

He looked away and snidely said, "I don't want to carve the date on the tree today. Whose initials should I carve instead?"

Jennifer folded her arms and did not answer at first. Finally she said, "I would think someone as smart as you would not put any sort of initials on any tree. Someday, it might lead back to what you've been up to."

Unexpectedly he said, "...W.D. it is then, and I was never sorry that you were a girl. You are the Woodsman's daughter. Don't ever forget it."

Jennifer was touched by his admission. "Sorry, Daddy," she said, holding back the tears. She changed the subject, not accustomed to the emotions his words had stirred. "If I thought you would stop this nonsense, I would ask the Lord to change me into a wooden boy. How would you like that?"

"Why I hadn't thought about it!" pausing as though he intended to think about it right then. Suddenly laughing he said, "You're a real card, girlie. What would I do with a wooden boy?" He paused again and shot

4

a glance at her that made her think twice about what she had said. "…I am way too fond of carving up wood, Jennifer, so I don't think your idea would work at this time." He looked away and continued talking. "You're a real card girlie. That was real funny coming from you, Jennifer. You might make a comedian one day. Oh, and I'm not worried one little bit about anyone figuring out who carved the dates on all those trees. That is one thing that will never happen. I can promise you that!"

"How can you be so sure?"

"I'm retiring from all these antics soon enough," he replied. He looked at her teasingly. "Don't you want to carry on the tradition of being the Smokey Mountain Prankster?"

Jennifer kicked at the leaves and said quietly without emotion, "I never want to be like you. I like me just the way I am."

Thomas almost snorted at her. "You *are* just like me. You are here with me, right? You have watched what I do. You have walked with me when I did these things. You are more like me than you will ever know."

Thomas turned to her and smiled. "Dry those tears, Mama's girl. You are my special girl. I did not mean what I said. I'll make it up to you. I promise."

There was a moment of silence. "We could take a trip to New York City again. *The Thief of Baghdad* is scheduled to have its premiere at Christmas. Doesn't that sound great? We can see those big city lights and eat at one of the diners where they have waiters with shirts and bowties."

"I would hope they have pants on, too."

Thomas giggled and slapped his knee.

Jennifer swallowed the lump in her throat. "I won't go unless you take Mama. I missed her too much the last time. Don't you want her to come with us?" she pleaded. "I think it would be a wonderful idea to take her! Maybe if she got out more often…"

His reaction cut her off before she could get out another word. He stiffened like someone had stuck a rod up his backside. She saw the twitch in his lip that told her she had just said the wrong thing at the wrong time in the wrong place, and for one second she wished God would turn her into a squirrel, up the tree she would go!

It only lasted as long as the bat of an eyelash. After the twitch disappeared, Thomas slurred his next words. "Can you f-f-find your w-w-way back to the house, smarty pants? Maybe if w-w-we took her she could run out in the middle of the street again. M-m-maybe she could scream like she did last time. And if I didn't think me screaming the answer out loud would wake up the dead, I would tell you—NO! It ain't happening! Your mama is a lunatic, enough said girlie."

A chill ran down Jennifer's back. "...and she still married you, but I think I can find my way home, and I think you had better lay off that homemade wine from now on," she paused, thinking she might have said something she shouldn't have, "If I have to, I can find my own way back," she said struggling not to show her fear. Once again she quickly changed the subject, but this time because the emotion was all too familiar. "Have you gotten me a birthday present yet? You only have two more days to buy me a pair of binoculars, and that is all I want from you, nothing else."

Then as if someone had tickled his funny bone, he replied with a grin. "Not yet. Not today. You're too much of a good sport! You will get the binoculars. Sit tight, and wait for the finale. Could be I'll take a leave of absence from doing these silly things and then your life would be pretty boring."

Jennifer stood up. "I'm going to leave, Daddy. I feel sick to my stomach. Maybe I shouldn't have come with you."

Ignoring her, he turned his attention to the object in the burlap bag. "This is one of my finest..."

Jennifer had stopped listening. She whispered the words her father would never hear her say aloud. She turned and started to walk away from him. "I will make it up to you someday, Mama," she promised.

With sudden sternness Thomas said, "You had better get back here." A sound interrupted him. "What?" he started. "Hush, they will hear you," he finished as he reached for her arm. "Get down, and don't make a sound."

"I don't have to make a sound," she retorted. "When he sees the bear head, he will wake up everyone on the mountain." She crossed her arms defiantly. "When are you going to grow up?"

He started to close the space between them but stopped abruptly, turning his attention back to the prank.

Jennifer bit her lip as she watched her father pull the fishing line attached to the fake bear head. Thomas had set up a pulley device that ran alongside of three trees, hanging over the area where the campers were. It had taken Thomas two days to put the bear head together. It was made of squirrel hide, rabbit fur, and burlap. Two hand-carved wooden eyeballs completed the "masterpiece." It was held together with glue made from flour. It was crudely crafted, but it was a sure-fire way to stop someone's heart!

He dropped into position and waited. Jennifer prayed she would not throw up again like she did when the woman fell head first into a bucket of deer intestines. Then there was the time when the park ranger found the maggoty squirrel head sitting on top of his steering wheel. And what about the time Thomas threw a hive of yellow jackets into a tent of sleeping cub scouts!! Thomas had found that one particularly entertaining, but for Jennifer it was very distasteful. Actually, it was the maggoty squirrel head that had originally tipped the scales. Jennifer had thought the prank was funny, but when the ranger tripped and hit his head rendering him unconscious, she started wondering if they put kids in the same jail cell as their parents.

"Daddy, what if they find out who does this? Won't they arrest me, too?"

Thomas grinned. "They will never find out...unless your mama tells on you. Now, wouldn't that be something?"

"Mama would never tell on me," Jennifer asserted.

Thomas' grin never wavered.

Chapter two

Eileen Martin was a strong woman for her size. Her petite stature had nothing to do with being submissive or shy. She deliberately wore clothes too big so that she looked like she was losing weight. Her legs were very muscular and although her arms looked thin, they were like an archer's bow, but one thing she knew, her husband was stronger.

There were times when she would not eat at all in front of him. She wanted him to think he made her feel guilty by not eating, but she stored food in the woods and would eat when she went hiking in the early morning hours. Many times she crouched by Shallow Grave and kept a careful eye out for him. If he had found her stock piling food; well, her woodland dining would be over. Still though, there were times when she was very sick and Eileen wondered if he had something to do with it but her mind always went back to when they first met. His words echoed in her brain, 'Eileen, if I ever even think of hurting you…may God strike me dead.' This was when she was young and stupid.

Every morning had been the same since she married him. She loved to hike and take long walks in the woods. She would hike in the early morning hours before it was time for him to get up. It actually humored Thomas at times because Eileen did not wear the ordinary clothing one would wear to hike; she wore whatever she had on when she got up out of bed. Sometimes she would hike naked, but not before smearing her entire body with mud and then roll around in leaves, but to her this was not lunacy at all. It was an escape from being sane.

Jennifer was right. Her mama did have a problem with being inside most of the time, but her avoidance of the outside world was not due to some mental problem. It was her husband and there was no question about it, she was afraid of him. Eileen's fear was that she would have to live with him until she died of some prank he pulled on her. She knew the day after she married him that she should have taken her mama's advice.

~

If she put her ear to any tree and listened real hard, Eileen could almost hear her mama, Clara Alice, talking to her. "Eileen, honey," she would say looking over her shoulder. "He's a pretty good catch for a city boy even though his right hand is a little messed up. Having two hands ain't got nothin' to do with what a man is good for. Oh, sure, he says he can cook, but is he willin' to clean and take care of the children when you are ailin'?"

Eileen's mind drifted back to a happier time. Sitting at the kitchen table watching her mama busy at the stove was a pleasant memory for her. They were in her mama's kitchen, a place where mother-daughter talks like this were common. "We love each other, Mama," Eileen replied. "He loves the outdoors most of all, and he has a wonderful sense of humor! Really!"

Clara Alice's concern for her daughter showed on her face.

"I know all about men like him, honey. Yes, he is all proper when he is in the public eye but as soon as his feet hit the floor of his own domain, well, just 'cause he has a wonderful sense of humor and he is fond of the outdoors doesn't make him a good catch," she seemed more nervous than usual, and said, "I want you to be happy, I do, but there is just something about Thomas that gives me the willies. Does he know your name is on the deed to all this land your papa left you?" her mama asked. "That will spark a big laugh out of him!"

"It doesn't matter, Mama. He told me he doesn't care about any of that. He is kind, and gentle. He loves me."

Eileen looked lovingly at her daughter. "You are so smart. I thought you wanted to get off this mountain and see the world? What happened with wantin' to see what really was at the end of a rainbow?"

"Isn't it far better to see the world from here on this mountain, and do it with someone you love?"

"Hogwash!" Eileen's mama shook her head. "Silly young'un! Who in the heck put those notions in your head? I would highly recommend that you live with him before you guide him to your marriage bed. I have a feelin' about him." She saw the dismayed look on her daughter's face. "Yes, people will talk. They talk about everybody's business but their own!" She paused and looked intently at her daughter. With a deep sigh she continued, "You go on and marry him, but promise me one thing, honey."

"What, Mama?"

"If he puts a hand on you, kill him dead. If he just runs his mouth, well, then be thankful he don't put his hands on you."

Eileen sat very still and looked out the window of her mama's very modest home. She had needed to ask the question for years and decided now was the time. "Mama, did you have anything to do with Papa's death?"

Clara Alice Thorpe walked from the stove to the same window Eileen was looking out and put her hand on the window pane. With a smile she replied, "I loved him. How could I have done anything to him? He loved his business more than me…us," she added quickly and continued, "To be honest, I sure have enjoyed spending his money. I miss him at times, but there are a lot less of *those* times than the times when I don't. People said he was so mean that even the maggots wouldn't have sat on his head when they buried his sorry ass." This last sentence was said with emotions bridled by long practice.

"Mama! I have never heard you speak that way! Will you just tell me this one truth, Mama?" Eileen became very intent. "Did you ever think about doing something to Papa?"

Clara Alice smiled again. "I wanted to do many things to him, but just you hush, child. Who put those thoughts in your pretty head? I wouldn't have hurt one flea on his spiteful head!" Clara Alice turned away and whispered, "…didn't say anythin' about his spiteful ass."

"Papa put those things in my head, Mama." Eileen was silent as the surprised look on her mama's face changed slowly to suspicion. "He did! He told me just before he ran off that you might want to kill him someday for how he treated you. I might have believed him, but…"

"But what, Eileen?" Clara Alice interrupted. "You cannot be that dumb! You heard words that no child should ever have heard a papa say to her mama!"

"He showed me the bruises on his legs," Eileen said quietly. "When did you start hitting *him*, Mama?"

"Well, doesn't that settle it all then? He ran off. He belittled me over and over, and I got one good shot in…well, a lot actually." At this admission the smile returned to Clara's lips. "No one would have believed him even if he had told somebody. Imagine me, one hundred and five pounds soaking wet smacking around one hundred and ninety five pounds of meanness. I got this land and all that stands between me and those dusty roads. I got paid a pretty penny for some of those hills. His words hurt more than you can ever know. Words cut deep into your brain, and they stay there for a long time." Clara Alice sat and took her daughter's hands. "If this man ever says words like that to you, will you promise me to leave him?"

"I will, Mama, but he's a good man."

"Your papa was a good man, too," Clara Alice said. And now he is dead. I didn't get to be fifty-eight by being stupid. I've got friends that are the same age as me and they look to be a hundred," she took a deep breath and held her chest, "I took advantage of this wonderful mountain air every chance I got. I have hiked every path, every road, and if I had to I could find my way back blind folded." Eileen thought for a moment. "Some people say he might be living out there in the woods like a hermit. Some are saying he watches us but is afraid you will find him. Some say…"

Eileen stopped when her mother released her grip and began to rock back and forth. "Oh, he would rather be dead than live like a hermit. He liked the comforts *I* provided *for* him. He liked his cornbread just so; he liked his shirts just so…just so…just so, every little crease had to be pressed just so, and Heaven forbid if I put too many noodles in his chicken soup. He was so picky!" She mocked his words and imitated his gestures. With sudden bitterness she said, "Sometimes I wanted to shove the iron right where…" She stopped herself and looked at her daughter. "Well, you know."

Eileen stood and put her hand on her mama's shoulder. "It's alright, Mama. I do know. No one will ever find out. It's our secret. I understand. Really, I do. Do you suppose he could have fallen down Shallow Grave? Is there a chance that he really did get eaten by a bear?"

Clara looked up at her daughter with tears in her eyes. "I thought you knew," she began quietly, "but I was too ashamed." The confession began to rush out of her like water released from a dam. "It wasn't my fault! He fell! It was an accident! I saw the bear and screamed; he pushed me forward and tried to get up! He … was eaten by a bear."

Eileen cleared her throat, pulling her mama close to her. "I understand, Mama, but why would a woman as mountain-savy as you were ... scream?"

Clara became very still and made a childlike giggle. "I accidentally pushed him back ...just so. Goodness, he was a clumsy man."

"I will make some tea, Mama."

Chapter three

Eileen flinched, and then she was back in reality. She was standing by the kitchen door when she saw Jennifer coming up the path. Her only child had never taken sides, but it did not matter anymore. Eileen knew that something was going to happen. She just did not know when. It was a gut feeling. She felt like she was on the edge of a precipice. Someone was going to push her over the edge. She prayed that she landed on both feet. She knew Jennifer was always trying to keep the peace by not taking sides, but lately she had seen a change in Jennifer. A change that was not quite the daughter she had envisioned growing up and it made her feel very strange inside.

The words rang through her head. "Eileen, do this; and whatever you do, Eileen, do *not* underestimate my reactions to poor house keeping or lousy cooking. Oh, Thomas Martin, if I only had the courage! You…" She saw the worried look on Jennifer's face. Something had happened, something unpleasant.

She reached for her cane and watched Jennifer hang her hand- made pack on the rocker that sat by the kitchen entrance. "Let him stay where he is. Let her be by herself," she thought. "Let her run up to me and tell me he has been eaten by a *real* bear! No more of his words!"

Jennifer looked at her mama and said, "Mama, you look like you saw a ghost."

"Your expression coming up the path is not what I wanted to see. What happened? What did he do this time?" Eileen asked Jennifer as she came into the kitchen. "No! Don't tell me! I want to eat my dinner in peace."

Jennifer sniffed an aroma of something familiar. "Do I smell macaroni with your special cheese sauce? You know Daddy hates that, but I will take a little if it will make you happy. Oh, mama, he is not in a good mood."

Eileen hesitated at first and looked down the hallway. "…since when is he ever in a good mood?" her demeanor changed suddenly, "no, no, sliced potatoes with my special cheese sauce. No macaroni and cheese." She finally asked, "Did he scare anybody today?"

Eileen looked especially tired to Jennifer, and she decided to lie. "No, Mama. Can I get anything for you? Are you feeling better, today?" Eileen didn't answer. "It was a perfect day to go hiking," Jennifer added politely. "Maybe if you're feeling better, we can go out for some ice cream. Maybe our 'secret guest' will come by again, and we can…"

Eileen stopped her short. "A hug would be nice." Jennifer gave her mama a tender embrace. Eileen looked out the door and down the path. Wearily, she gently pushed her daughter away and asked, "Where is he? Did he stay in the woods? Did he pack for spending the night in the woods?"

Jennifer shrugged her shoulders. "He is probably laughing at what he did." Jennifer's hand flew to her mouth. "Oh, I wasn't going to tell you!" Eileen looked at her expectantly. Jennifer changed the subject. "Can I ask you something, Mama?"

"I thought you said he didn't scare anyone," Eileen responded, but then she allowed the subject change. "What do you want to ask me?"

"How come we didn't have a proper funeral for the baby?"

Eileen stared through the large picture window and became silent.

"Mama," Jennifer said. "Are you listening to me?"

"Jennifer, how do you really feel about your daddy?" Eileen started to gently sway back and forth. Jennifer started to speak but Eileen interrupted her. "It was my idea. We could have had a proper funeral, but I thought she would prefer being put to rest where she is now." Eileen became still. "Don't you think it's the most beautiful place on earth? Don't you just love the way the colors run together? It's like a quilt that was put out to dry, and all the colors have started to fade, and soon I truly believe I might see the face of God just over the hill." Her voice drifted off.

Jennifer hugged her tightly again. "Well, Mama, I cannot answer that, but I can try to answer how I really feel about my daddy." She hesitated. "I love Daddy, but I do not like him at all. I think it is time he changes his ways especially how he treats you. What do you think we ought to do about his behavior? And as far as this being the most beautiful place on earth; well, the only place I have been besides here is New York City, and there's no comparing the two!" Jennifer released her mama and moved closer to stare out the window. "I think Heaven might come in a close second." She turned back to Eileen and said with a glint in her eye, "Now, New York City was certainly entertaining, but you must know if I had a choice, the Smoky Mountains will always be my first love. Could you ever leave here, Mama?"

"…never," Eileen whispered. Eileen suddenly closed the gap between them and grabbed Jennifer by the shoulders. "But you *do* have a choice, Jennifer! You do not have to stay here once you get grown. You sound like your father! Oh, that's not what I meant," she clarified when she saw the pained look on her daughter's face. She let Jennifer go and slowly walked away. "I'm just so tired of all this. I'm tired of your father's pranks, and I'm tired of him getting you involved. I want to see New York City…someday. Sometimes I want to just go for a walk and never come back. Maybe Heaven is just over the ridge. I pray every night that when I wake up, he has packed his belongings and left. This is exactly what happens to women when they do not listen to their mamas," she paused. "I should have listened to mine, but then, if I had, you would not be born, and that, I thank her for."

"…but you know he will never leave, Mama," Jennifer said quietly. Jennifer felt sad for her mama. She knew the marriage had not been happy, but she wasn't used to seeing her mother like this. "Mama," she said, "can I ask you another question?"

"Quickly! He's coming!"

"Have you ever thought about doing something to Daddy?"

Eileen stared blankly at Jennifer. She caught her reflection in the picture window over Jennifer's shoulder and recognized the look as the same one she had seen on her mother's face over ten years ago. "Why would you ask me such a thing? '*Doing something to Daddy?*' Like what?"

"Oh, Nothing," Jennifer said quickly. "Here he comes. Be strong, Mama, for me, okay? He put that stupid old bear head on a string and scared somebody with it real bad. I did not look back. I hope the man is alright. I wish the joke had been on *him*! I wish *I* had the courage to do something to him."

"One of these days somebody is going to scare him to death, and I will laugh myself right off this mountain!" Eileen replied.

"...things have a way of getting better Mama. Just you wait and see. Things will get better," Jennifer said.

Eileen grabbed Jennifer's arm. "Do not let on that we talked about this, alright?"

Jennifer shrugged her shoulders, "Yes, Mama, I understand. I have always understood. Someday..."

Chapter four

Thomas walked in and took off his coat. He stuck his head around the corner and grinned at Eileen and Jennifer. "What are you two mountain girlies up to?" He didn't give them a chance to answer. "Turn on the radio, Eileen." Thomas pulled the curtains further apart. Music from the radio quietly drifted through the room. "Ahhh! Another wonderful day in paradise has come and gone! Don't you think this is the most beautiful place on earth?" He turned to his wife, "What did you do today, my sweet?" He did not give her a chance to answer, and continued, "…lie in bed all the live long day, pine over memories lost, hide more goodies in the forest?"

Jennifer took a deep breath and patted her mama on the hand and then whispered to her mama, "He came across the soup, I told him I put them there just in case I decided to run away." Jennifer giggled.

He chuckled. "I smell those special potatoes. I smell…is my nose playing tricks on me? Do I smell those disgusting noodles?" With a snort he continued. "Why would any human being name a noodle after a body part?" Jennifer looked confused. He cocked his head to one side. "Is it elbow macaroni with that degusting cheese sauce?" he said, with words dripping with sarcasm. "I *hate* noodles, and you *know* I hate noodles, Eileen! You are the dumbest woman on the face of the earth if you have cooked that dish!" he finished with an unmistakable threat in his voice. I'll throw it down the ravine!"

Eileen shook her head back and forth, staring at Jennifer. She mouthed her words just soft enough so that he could not hear her. "…you won't get the chance, I will shove it up your tail, and you are the dumbest man on the face of the earth if you think you're going to outlive me." Jennifer looked blankly at her mama, and whispered, "…good one, Mama."

"Did you hear me, Eileen?" Thomas shouted as he turned and glared at his wife.

Eileen cringed. She knew what was coming next and carefully formed her answer. She stuttered, as she often did under stress, and the words came out slowly, "Yes, I h-h-heard you. I-I started to…b-but I thought this time…it's potatoes with cheese sauce, a new recipe from the cookbook you gave me last month." She regained her composure. "I thought you might think it was funny. I'll just set it aside for now."

Jennifer stood wide eyed, and speechless.

"…funny? Good one, Eileen! You're learning!" he replied with obvious pleasure. "I think I will eat in the living room. It looks to be a most pleasurable sunset. Do you mind, my love? Later we can sit by the fire, and you can tell me about your day. I'll do the popcorn, and you can give me a massage." Eileen felt as if she might vomit.

He turned back around and folded his arms, staring blankly out towards his water garden. "Did you hear me, honey?"

Most women would have welcomed a chance to spend an evening by the fire with their husbands, but Eileen was not most women, and Thomas was certainly not most husbands. She had a vision of his head on a spit turning slowly over the fire. She wiped her hands on her apron. "I heard you, dear." She paused before she made her next admission. "I didn't get a chance to split any firewood today."

"Don't you think this is the most beautiful place on earth?" he asked again as though the last few minutes of conversation had never happened. "I think God himself must have lived right over that ridge. What do you think?"

Eileen's stomach felt like it had just been punched. "Yes," she answered.

"Daddy, Mama just asked me that same question," Jennifer said innocently. The only sound was Bing Crosby singing a love song. Jennifer turned to her mama. "I can help split some firewood later, Mama, and then we can go for a walk." She nudged her mama, whispering softly, "We'll make sure there is enough soup."

Eileen was starting to feel stressed again. She could sense Thomas's rage, and she wanted to defuse it. "Jennifer t-t-told me she had a good t-t-time t-today. Thank you for," she took a deep breath, "taking her," she finished clearly. Did anything happen interesting?"

Thomas turned the volume up on the radio and ignored her. Eileen put her finger to her lips and, took Jennifer by the arm, gently pushing her through the kitchen. "Go outside until dinner. Please do not come in until I call you."

Jennifer stood by the back door and waited for a moment. Opening the door she said, "I'll be out here if you need me, Mama, and *this* is the most beautiful place on earth...," her voice dropped as she whispered the rest, "as long as you are in it with me, Mama." She tip-toed back to Eileen and kissed her on the cheek. Eileen's heart sank, and she whispered into Jennifer's ear, "Yes."

Jennifer looked to see if her father was watching. He was already in his chair with his back to both of them as he stared at the deer head over the mantel. He was humming along with Bing. Jennifer pulled her mama closer to her. "What do you mean, 'yes'?"

Once again Eileen pushed her gently in the direction of the back door and spoke softly to her daughter. "Yes, I have dreamed many times of doing something to him. You be strong for me now. Go."

Jennifer winked at her mama, and just before she closed the door she said, "I thought you told me yesterday you were out of potatoes, but I think I understand." For once Jennifer thought things might change for the good. Her Mama was going to get some back bone.

~

Jennifer stepped on the back porch and drew in a deep breath. It was the most beautiful place on earth! She loved everything about it: the trees, the small creek that ran behind the house, and she especially loved the idea that someday all this would be hers. She wandered into the yard and watched an owl fly passed a large cypress. She sighed, and then she saw it, freshly cut fire wood, and neatly stacked, but one thing was very out of place, a photo of her papa. An axe was sticking right in the middle of his face. She turned and said, "Someday Heaven will be at Mama's doorstep."

The sun was setting, and for a ten-year old soon to be eleven it was more than a sunset. It was the beginning of a new life for her mama, she hoped. She had certainly prayed for it many, many times. They were not regulars at the small church in town, but occasionally she and her mama would go to Sunday service. Jennifer and Eileen always sat in the back when they did go. Jennifer was amazed how well her mama could read the preacher's lips. Eileen was partially deaf in her right ear due to Thomas's ranting and raving. He had held her down one two many times in bed and shouted in her ear about what he wanted her to do the next day. He called it 'his list.'"

Jennifer couldn't help but wonder why women stayed with husbands who made them deaf in one ear. She especially could not understand why her daddy had not caught on to eating all those 'special' ingredients in his food. Yes, she knew all about those new recipes, and her mama was delighted that her papa thought so highly of her in that way.

Although mature for her age, she had just recently begun to appreciate what her mama had endured for so many years. Why did women stay with husband's who didn't contribute to anything regarding housework or outside chores? And why in the world would her mama stay with her daddy if her mama was the one who controlled the money strings!? Yes, her mama was sick, but it wasn't like her daddy made things any easier for her! Jennifer shook her head. It was more than a little girl could fathom, and certainly was nothing she could do anything about. She was not an adult, not yet. Yet, she knew her granny; Clara Alice had known what to do with a worthless husband. Jennifer smiled innocently, "Well, things have a way of turning over a new leaf, now, don't they?"

~

Thomas leaned back in his chair and beamed at the deer head hanging over the mantel. He hadn't killed it at all! He had stolen it from a hunter three years ago. Granted, the hunter was poaching on the Martin's property, but Thomas knew the man and his family were down and out. He was just trying to feed his four kids. Thomas Martin scared the poor man to death by putting a stuffed raccoon in his sleeping bag. Now, Thomas putting the raccoon head in the man's sleeping bag is not at all what caused his death, but it certainly put it motion. It wasn't the raccoon that did the trick though to Thomas's great dismay. It was the rattler that had crawled into the sleeping bag, because Thomas didn't zip it up when he was done. "Better you than me," he mumbled. The memory stirred his anger again. "Eileen!" he yelled. "I'm hungry! God almighty, woman, do I have to go out and kill something in order to get fed? Get your lazy butt moving! You've got a man out here!" He laughed out loud. "As if you would know what a man was." Eileen wiped her nose with her hand and then cleaned her hand off with one of the slices of fresh baked bread soon to be served to Thomas. "Always the best for you my dear Thomas," she murmured.

Eileen was putting the finishing touches on his dinner tray. She spit in his tea glass and poured the tea slowly over the ice. Next, she carefully crumbled up a dead bug and mashed it into the mushroom sauce on his meatloaf. She had intended on cooking steaks, but they would be put back in the refrigerator for a later time. Meat loaf was so much better to hide special treats in. "Almost done," she replied with tenderness. Thomas liked his gravy a little of the salty side. Eileen was pleased with his taste buds. It made her addition to the recipe so much easier to serve with delight.

Thomas's voice interrupted her scheming. "I think I might replace the deer head with one of the camper's noggins!" he said with amazing relish. "I have had a long day pulling pranks on the trespassers. It's very tiring work. Do you think you might be able to split some firewood after dinner, Eileen?" There was no answer. "Are you listening, dear?"

He heard a childish giggle. Thinking it was Jennifer, he ignored it. He shouldn't have.

"What do you think sweetie?" He scratched the back of his neck. Trying to get a rise out of his wife he added, "I just might go for a walk with you. Would you like that? We could go up to Shallow Grave and enjoy the view," he paused, "and if you get tired, well, I could always drag your tail up there."

Eileen fought to keep the bile down. Oh, how she hated this man, more than she hated going anywhere near Shallow Grave. With every bone in her being, she hated what he was; and even more, she hated that she had allowed herself to put up with it. She picked up the butcher knife and held it tightly. "Would I like what? *What,* Thomas, what do you think I think about?" The words were barely audible. "Do you *really* want to know what I think after all these years, Thomas? Do you *really* want to know how much I hate you? How much I despise *every* thing about you? Do you want arsenic with your tea, Thomas? No, I think not..maybe you'd like more bugs in your food! No...o...o, I have it, squirrel droppings right on top of your apple pie." She sighed. Eileen kept a special jar underneath the cabinet. It was pulverized squirrel droppings kept especially for him. She grinned. 'My how he has enjoyed these,' she thought.

Unexpectedly, the radio interrupted Eileen's raging thoughts. *"Breaking news folks,"* the announcer said. *"A sad note for a North Carolina family, Wilford Breems was admitted to Mountain Side Hospital with an apparent heart attack that some say was due to a prankster's cruel sense of humor. It happened near Elk Ridge, five miles north of what the locals call Shallow Grave. Folks, what would you think if this happened to your loved one?"*

Thomas laughed and slapped his knee. "I would mess my pants!" he answered.

Eileen had come into the room, the knife still in her hand, and stared at the radio. "That's close to our property," she said with disbelief in her voice. "Isn't that the ridge a couple miles down the road?" The reality of the situation suddenly came to her. "Oh, God, were you there with Jennifer? Did you actually take her to that place?" Her voice began to reflect the panic she was feeling.

He pondered for a moment. "...Yes, it could be," Thomas answered slyly, "but there are a lot of woods. What's your point? It's not like you are ever going to do anything about what I do." His stomach growled. "Hand me an apple, Eileen. I really must eat more apples. I have been stopped up lately from your cooking. You know what's strange?"

"What?" Eileen responded.

"Your cooking has gone down the toilet!" Thomas laughed at his own joke. I thought if I bought you a few cook books my appetite would increase, but lately," he paused to pat his stomach, "...your cooking ... something is just not right." Eileen thought she was going to vomit right in front of him, but the thought of laughing right after she vomited would be somewhat strange.

The announcer continued with the news of Wilford Breems. *"At that spot, folks, is where Wilford Breems was terrorized by what some say was a 'scare tactic.' Now, folks, that's a big city word to describe how someone attached a fake bear head to a fishing line and then dropped it right into the middle of the campsite. It seems Mr. Breems had a weak heart, and the terror of having a bear come straight at him was enough to cause him to collapse. Mr. Breems, who shared his love of the outdoors with his young daughter, was camping with her and his wife when the scandalous prank occurred. The hospital reports that the daughter was traumatized by the event. Mr. Breems is being watched carefully by the good doctors and nurses at Mountain Side Hospital...just a minute, folks."* The radio went silent. Eileen realized she had just stopped breathing. *"We have just been informed that Mr. Breems passed away less than thirty minutes ago."* The announcer paused again. *"Folks, I don't know about you, but anyone who has that kind of humor needs to go to a head doctor! Folks, if you come across any kids who look to be full of themselves or looks to be out of place, call the sheriff's office immediately. We don't need this kind of fooling around in our back yard! It's time to take a break and go to our sponsor."*

Thomas grinned. "...my property, my campground, poor man," he said sarcastically. "He should have stayed at home." Eileen was glaring at him. "How was I to know he didn't like bear heads, Eileen? Trespassers, vagabonds, what's the world coming to? This guy must think he is Orson Wells!" Eileen said nothing. "Ain't it just awful how those people on the radio can make up such nonsense and expect us to believe it?"

The news continued. *"Mr. Breems' wife says her husband stepped out of the tent and the bear head fell on him."* Eileen swallowed hard, and responded to the announcer's words, "Did you pull the string or did you make Jennifer do it?" Thomas ignored her question as Eileen stared at the radio. The news continued, *"He immediately collapsed. Mrs. Breems and her daughter ran for help, but it took an hour before Mountain Rescue could arrive. Mrs. Breems says her seven year old daughter is still not talking. Again, folks, if anyone has any information as to why someone would do this, please come by and talk to me at the radio station or contact the sheriff."* Eileen turned the volume down.

"Turn it off, Eileen," he said loudly. "It's obvious he doesn't have a funny bone!"

Eileen stared at the radio and asked, "Tell me the truth, Thomas. Was it you? Did you do it? Was Jennifer there with you? Has it come to this?"

He stood and yelled at her. "I said, turn it OFF, Eileen!!! I was nowhere near that area! Now, hand me an apple and a knife before I starve to death! What's a man got to do to get some dinner around here?" His tone became menacing. "You've been sitting around here all day, and I see nothing on the table! I don't see any firewood! I still see the clothes hanging out on the line! And by the way, while I'm at it, if you gain any more weight, it will take a tank to pull you out of here!"

He laughed. "Just fooling around, darlin'! You are not fat at all! You could slide down a crack in the floor if your head wasn't attached to your shoulders!" He cleared his throat, "Honestly sweetie, I don't know how you manage to keep your girlish figure," he paused, "...what with all that food you have stashed in the woods!"

Eileen's face had become stone. "You promised me you would not do any more pranks that involved hurting people!" Her voice was becoming louder. "And by the way, while *I'm* at it," she mocked, "dinner will be on the table very soon. Will you be joining us, dear? Please, Thomas, *I have a surprise for you!*"

Thomas turned back to her. He began to admire a trophy from his childhood --- a turtle shell with the dried up head of a snake sticking out where the turtle head should have been. He reached and picked it up. "Now this is something to be proud of!" he said. "Actually, at the time I felt kind of sorry for this little fellow...who'd of thought that that idiot would have stomped on it? What kind of an idiot thinks a snake would want to masquerade as a turtle?"

Eileen felt her stomach turn again. She walked back to the kitchen and spit in the sink. "...you, that is who."

Thomas began to mimic her with a whiny voice. "You promised, you promised," he said. "I will do what I damn well please, woman! It was not my fault he was scared of bears! What idiot goes camping out in the wilderness and does not expect to see some wildlife? Besides, it was just a prank!" His voice was once again a roar. "Hell, it's getting so that nobody can take a joke!" He began to laugh again. It was a laugh she had heard so many times, a maniacal laugh that could still send a shiver down her spine. The laughter abruptly stopped, and he yelled, "I smell macaroni and cheese!"

Eileen's stature stiffened and again she looked down the hallway.

She gripped the knife one last time and walked slowly into the living room. "This has got to stop, Thomas. It is going to affect our daughter. Why must you do these things? One of these days you will get caught, and then what?"

Thomas was once again eyeing the deer head closely. "I just might do some adjustments on this and take it with me the next time Jennifer and I go camping. Want to come?" Eileen stopped behind him. If he realized how close she was, he didn't let on. He had never hit her. His words hurt enough throughout their years of marriage. "Don't you know by now that money takes care of everything, my dear? Wasn't it I who took care of you when you had that mental breakdown? Didn't I see to it that you were not left alone when all the other wives' husbands went off to war? Yes, I know, it was my hand that kept me from going, but if I had known you would have been such a lousy cook, well, I would have winged it!" Thomas laughed, still not turning around to look at her. "Winged it! Get it?"

Eileen took a deep breath. "…I have cooked your meals for over thirteen years, tended to you when you were sick, washed your clothes and ironed your socks and my culinary handiwork has not killed you … yet, and I have put up with your cruel jokes and my mama took care of everything that made her life uneasy," Eileen said proudly. "Money does not take care of everything, but I will admit that a good sense of humor goes a long way," she paused, "I married you."

She stepped back thinking that today just might be the day that he raised a hand to her, but he did nothing. For a moment she thought God might have struck him deaf while she was saying those last words of courage.

"What's that you say?" Thomas said still admiring the deer head. "Well, I took care of the *electricity*, didn't I? You should have seen me! I marched right up to the head of the REA and *demanded* they get a line up here so my precious wife could have electricity. It is amazing how some green backs will entice an underpaid employee to do a job no one else would! You were the only housewife within *fifty miles* who had electricity! You have nothing to complain about," he warned, "Just look at what a grand home I've given you!"

He still did not turn around.

Eileen moved a step closer. "Over nine hundred other people also got electricity," she corrected. "But you were right about the money part. It did take money to get that line up here, but it wasn't *your* money that enticed them."

He ignored her and kept his back to her. He shouldn't have. "My sweet, you don't recognize all the niceties you have. You are cooking on the finest of stoves. You have all the things a woman from the city would beg for! You are a country ham sitting right in the middle of Fifth Avenue." He finished his sentence slowly and deliberately, "and…you… don't even…appreciate…it!"

"I never asked, much less begged, for *any* of this! You are the one who doesn't seem comfortable with it! You forget, Thomas, it wasn't your money that got you on this land." Eileen saw his back tense. "Would you please turn around when I am talking to you?" No movement. "Thomas, you are a jackass and today my life will begin anew."

The back of his neck twitched. She had hit a nerve.

She stepped back and calmly asked him, "Do you care at all that I hate you." She looked down and saw that his fists were clenched. She *had* hit a *raw* nerve, and it was not something she had intended to do so soon, but her brain was telling her to not speak yet her mouth was still moving and strange new words were coming out of her mouth, all directed towards him. "Are you deaf? Have you stuffed some of your own bullshit in your ears? Is it possible for a man's virility to be affected by what his wife puts in his food? Do you miss him at all?"

Thomas blinked. "Do I miss *who* at all? What are you on woman? Where do you get off talking to me like that?"

He turned his head to one side and whispered; almost like it was something he did not want anyone to hear. "Eileen, if it's the last thing I ever do, it will be to out live you; now, get my dinner ready as fast as your little hooves can walk and bring it to me in my chair," he paused, "You sound as if you are catching a cold," he paused again, "if *I* were *you* I would not want to be sick with me as your nursemaid."

Chapter five

Eileen didn't move. "I don't suppose you might want to apologize for all the hurt you have caused me?"

Thomas didn't move. Instead, he fingered the muzzle of the deer head mounted over the fireplace mantel. "This needs to be dusted," he muttered, and then he looked down. He looked closer and bent down, fingering the edge of what he thought was a tarp. It was. He turned to Eileen very slowly to see why her voice had changed so quickly and mouthed the words, "...apologize? Shut your stupid mouth, and get in the kitchen and do what you were born to do."

He pondered for a moment, stepping back to the mantel, and crossed his arms. "Why is there a tarp under this rug? Did you spill something on it? Jesus, Eileen. This rug was hand picked...by me!"

Eileen flinched. "...no, I did not," she murmured. He straightened up and continued staring at the tarp's edge. "Did you hear me, stupid? You may serve my dinner in the living room, and make sure it's not cold like our love life. Later, I'll show you the difference between a jackass and a bull," he nudged the edge of the tarp. "...and then you will tell me what got spilled on the rug, and then you can scrub it with your toothbrush until the stain is out...got it?"

There was no answer. Thomas mimicked her again, "This has got to stop. Are you going to hand me that apple or do I have to...?"

"Dinner is served, funny man," a voice interrupted from behind him. Suddenly he realized it was not Eileen's voice at all, and for one split second he had the realization that he should have been nicer to his wife, much nicer.

It sounded somewhat quirky. Eileen dropped the apple, and then a knife plunged dead center into his spinal cord. Without remorse, the

27

handler of the knife twisted it, cutting his throat. "You are a cruel man, Thomas Martin. I hope they tell jokes where the Devil lays his head."

Eileen cried out to him. "I would have my baby right now if you hadn't pulled one of your stunts. *Here* is your dinner! May the steel fill your cold, cold heart!"

He fell backwards; the knife was dropped. His last point of vision was Eileen standing in the kitchen. She was standing there, motionless, and for another split second he wondered just how she managed to stick him and get to the kitchen without any blood on her. He was confused. The pain in his back was unbearable, and he could not breathe. As his eyes rolled back in his head, he tried to reach for the poker near the fireplace, but it was gone, and then he felt a strong hand pulling his head back further. For one brief moment he wondered, "What is worse? The knife wound or the fireplace poker stuck in my neck?" Neither...it was the thought of him being castrated in his own home.

And then the last thing he saw was the poker lying near his leg. His eyes flickered, and he knew why he had smelled macaroni with cheese sauce when he came in. He was not confused anymore about why a tarp was placed under the rug either. His eyes closed, and he tried one more time to kick at his assailant. He managed to look up at the deer head... it was being pulled off the wall.

His assailant's foot was on his chest. The assailant was not sure what his last words were, but it had something to do with a female dog. His assailant chuckled, and with his head pulled back again, the assailant cut his head clear off. It had been difficult to replace the deer head frame above the mantel, but strength in numbers helped.

Now Eileen's apron was smeared in blood. In time she might get used to seeing his head...maybe. It certainly looked handsome above the mantel and she certainly had dreamed of it being there many times. "Some kind of a sick joke, huh? Not so funny now, is it? Would you like to tell one more joke for the road? And to think, you didn't get the chance to take one bite of that special mushroom sauce! What a terrible waste of good crickets!" She pondered for one moment and reflected about the taste of crickets. They weren't so bad with a little salt and a sprinkle of crushed pepper.

Eileen walked to the front door, opened it, and walked into the wilderness, night gown and apron tied neatly around her waist. Jennifer turned to see her mama walk past the large sycamore. "Mama?" Jennifer felt a prick in her backside and slowly fell to the ground; her last thought was how she could fall from the rock ledge so gracefully and land on the moss without hitting her head.

Chapter six

Tuesday, July 23rd, 1940

Thomas Martin was found by the handy man. At least, his head was found neatly hanging from the mantel like a stocking hung with care.

The handy man craned his neck to look into the living room and pulled out a plug of tobacco from a small tin he kept in his back pocket. "I come 'round this time 'bout once a week. I never had seen a dead head before, much less, one hangin' over a mantel. It was a dreadful sight, but I got to tell you…he probably deserved it. Is the girl going to be alright? I never did see the wife or the girl and I looked, too. Who is goin' to give me my money? I knew somethin' was horribly wrong when I saw his head hangin' from the mantel. Can I go now?" The first officer on the scene nodded to the truck that had just pulled up into the driveway. "Better check with the boss before you run off into the woods."

Charlie Holtz opened the door to his truck very slowly and turned to glance at his associate Danny Storm, aka, 'Chaser.' "Do what you do best, lay your good eye on this mess and get back with me. I'm going to interrogate the gardener." Danny grinned and rolled down the window. "…I have to take a leak, and do me a favor will ya?"

Charlie moaned as he stepped down onto the gravel. "I know, I know…don't scare the shit out of the gardener." Danny nodded towards the direction of the side of the house, "…and don't let him go scaring you off." Charlie watched Danny walk around to the other side of the Martin's home and take out his notebook.

At times Charlie had no tact at all questioning people. Danny kept him from getting into trouble most of the time. Charlie loved Danny like a son. It was a friendship with no boundaries.

~

Charlie Holtz almost choked on his chewing gum when he saw the gardener coming around the corner. He was wearing a coonskin hat and bib overalls. His beard came down to his waist and he smelled of smoked meat. "Were you peeking in the window, sir?"

The handy man took offense. "...*just then* or when I saw the dead head?"

Charlie held his laughter in. "Both times. Are you the gardener or the keeper of the still?"

"...no still and my name ain't Tom. It's William Lee. No sir, I did no such thing! I just thought it strange that the girl was not around, and the curtains were pulled all the way open. They are usually closed that time of day. That sweet girl always liked to talk when I was takin' care of the place," he paused to spit. "Sweet thing she was, *is*, oh dear, do you think anythin' has happened to her? Her mama was always so nice to me, but him, he was a real ass. Are you goin' to pay me for last week's work? Now, I ain't no one to talk poorly about the dearly departed, but Mr. Martin was a son of a gun, if you know what I mean. I can't recall ever seein' him doing anythin' outside of the house, but he sure did like to run off into the woods, and he took that girl with him most of the time. The whole family seemed to do a lot of hiking and watching people, but the last time I checked there ain't no law against hiking and watching people. I don't think he was right in the head, know what I mean?"

Charlie spit his gum out onto the gravel. "No, not really, and there is no law against hiking but there are a few laws about how people watch people. Can you shine more light on this mess?"

The handy man took off his hat and wiped his brow. "The missus was very kind. I'm goin' to miss the extra money, too," he paused to adjust his overhauls, "she always had fresh baked cookies for me when I was done with the list she would give me," he paused and scratched his chin, "funny though, she always baked a separate batch of cookies, some for me and some for him. He really loved his cookies, especially the oatmeal ones with raisins," he cocked his head, and pondered for a moment, "I never did eat any of those. She told me she baked oatmeal cookies for him all the time and she would giggle about it."

Charlie shrugged his shoulders. "Why would that be *funny?*"

31

"Well, she baked me some cookies one day. I think the girl told her it was my birthday coming up, it was and I asked her if she was going to give him any of them. He might of gotten jealous, ya know with me being so darn good lookin' and all." Charlie chuckled, and responded, "...yes, I know what you mean." William Lee continued, "She laughed and told me that she baked him some special cookies that only he could eat. You'd of thought that she put bugs in the ones she baked for him. The missus got hysterical," he paused, "ya know, like ha-ha hysterical, but *he* was another story. I would catch him lookin' at me at times. It was like he was jealous of me, and the relationship I had with his wife."

Charlie looked past the handy man to a path that led to deeper forest. "Do tell, and just what was your relationship with the wife? Do you mind telling me?"

The handy man glared at Charlie. "...just a minute,"

he snipped, "there weren't anythin' going on between us. I have been married to the same woman for forty years," he paused, "thirty-two of them good years." Charlie chuckled again. William Lee sat down on a stump, and continued, "I got the impression she just really liked talkin' to me. There was somethin' real sweet about her. But I don't mind if I do tell you what I know. The missus was pure lady and she was a real looker, too. Most women wear a little bit of all that makeup, but her, naw...www, she didn't need any of that. She was just plain pretty. He was a hateful man, but even at that, no man should have his head hangin' from his own mantel," he paused, "shucks though, I don't mind telling you I was thinkin' he deserved it. When I looked in the window, it was an awful sight. I've worked for her for some time now, and I never heard her say one cross word to him. To tell the truth, if I had been his wife, I might have just killed him myself, but that is another story, too."

Charlie continued to stare at the forest. "Hm---mmm, do you think *she* could have done this William Lee?" William Lee grinned at Charlie. "You can call me W.L."

The handy man shook his head. "No, I don't think the missus could have hurt a flea much less the dog it came in on. She was always nervous when he was around, but the girlie was not afraid of him. That youngin' was never outright disrespectful to him or her, but she stood her ground when it came to her mama." Charlie looked off into the woods, "...tell me more W. L." William Lee continued, "She talked to him straight up and defended her mama," he paused to spit again, "Oh, lordy be, you ain't thinkin' the girl did somethin' to her own papa?"

Charlie looked away and replied, "I don't want to think about it but I have to ask you these questions."

The handy man continued. "Now one thing about the missus was that she looked pretty darn skinny but she was a fire cracker when she split wood. She wouldn't let me touch the fire wood. I watched her one day just as I was leaving, and she was a sight wheelin' that axe," he paused again. "Guess I shouldn't be tellin' you that, huh?" He looked over his shoulder. "And one thing that was really strange was her spellin' out his name when she split the wood," he paused, "T-H-O-M-A-S! Dang, you'd of thought his head was on the block. I ain't never seen any woman split fire wood like she did that day."

Charlie's eyebrows raised and he turned to the man. "I would think you'd tell me all that you know so we can catch the person who did this." Charlie moved into the shade. "Did you ever see him hit his wife?"

"…no… How come you ain't taking any of this down? I thought detectives wrote everythin' in one of those little books. Say, where is your badge?"

Charlie chuckled. "My partner takes the notes and I don't need no stinking badge, because I have a mind like a steel trap. Please continue W.L."

"You asked me if I ever saw him hit her, right?"

"And you said, no."

The handyman turned his head to one side. "I saw him hit the girl one time."

Now the handy man had Charlie's full attention. "You saw him with your own eyes, hit the girl?"

"Yes, I was just leaving one day and heard a commotion. He didn't use his fist. It was more of a quick 'pop.' Still it brought tears to the girl's eyes."

Charlie folded his arms. "I'm listening."

"Well, the missus liked to garden. She had a real green thumb. She would come out once in a while when he was not home and we would talk. She had a real sweetness about her. We would chat about gardenin' and the mountains. I don't talk to many people about much, but her, well; she talked about these mountains like they was her soul. I felt a kinship with her, and somewhere down the line, I think her kin and my kin knew each other at one point in time. Oh, how she loved these mountains. He liked to eavesdrop, real nosey-like when he was around. I made it a point to speak real low so's he couldn't hear what I said to her. I think it pissed him off. Do I look like I cared?"

Charlie chuckled again. "No, please go on."

"She told me once that she was thinkin' about goin' on a trip. She was so excited. He was just around the corner and heard it. You'd of thought someone lit him on fire! He came at her like he was going to push her down, but the girlie stepped up and held a pitch fork right in his face! Shucks, I really thought she came pretty close to pokin' his eyes out!"

"And is that when he hit his daughter?"

"No. She is a pistol alright! I thought I would fall over myself and I was real sure he peed his pants right that very minute," he slapped his knee and laughed loudly, then returned to being very serious, "he looked like some hungry bear wantin' to pull her down like a deer," he took a deep breath, "he popped her upside the head but I sure wouldn't have let him hurt her real bad. I ain't never raised a hand to my wife. She never gave me no reason to want to."

Charlie pulled a notebook out. W.L. looked at him strangely. "…what happened to the steel trap?"

Charlie smiled. "…it needs oiling. What happened next?"

"The blame fool laughed! Can you believe it? He actually laughed, and when he walked away, he said the most peculiar thing."

"And that would be what?" Charlie asked, pulling out a piece of gum from its wrapper.

"Well, he saw me coming up the path and you'd of thought he saw a ghost! Cowards are like that. Mr. Martin, and I use the name lightly, well, he was more of a bastard. He looked straight at me and asked if I knew of anyone that could shrink heads. Ain't that peculiar?" W.L. scratched his beard, "Now, I know how to cure skins, but heads on a stick, well, that is not my idea of fun."

Charlie did not look surprised, and replied, "As in a taxidermist?"

W.L. laughed and slapped his knee, then smirked, "Heck no man, as in head hunter. I wouldn't have thought anythin' about it, but the missus smiled at me and said somethin' parculiar, too. But the last time

34

I heard there weren't no laws against asking questions or speakin' poorly to anyone."

Charlie did not smile. "...what did she say to you?"

"She wanted to know if I knew how long it took for a bear to find fresh meat. I would think someone that had been raised on this mountain would know that. And do you want to know what else she asked me?"

"Yes," answered Charlie.

"She asked me if I had ever put animal fat in my compost."

"What did you tell her?" Charlie asked.

"Shoot, anyone that knows anythin' about gardening and growing food knows that you don't never put animal fat in good compost."

"Well, enlighten me. I am not a compost kind of guy."

"It will draw varmints like bees on honey! Heck, the flies move in and before you know it...a maggot carnival!"

Charlie continued to stare out past the trees. He took his wallet out and handed the man two Abe Lincoln's and thanked him. "Anything else before I set you free?" W.L. shook his head. "Okay, then," Charlie's voice drifted off as he turned to leave, and then he stopped. "Leave your name and address with the other badge leaning against the truck." W.L. looked at him parculiar, "I ain't got no address to give you and you already know my name." The handy man paused for a moment. "Ain't you the least bit curious as to what the missus said when he popped the girl upside her head?"

"I was getting to that," Charlie responded.

"She watched him walk away, real slow like, and whispered in my direction, "Do you think it's possible for a headless man to see his attacker?"

Charlie had to sit down.

W.L. kept talking. "One time I was raking leaves and almost had a heart attack."

"Why?" Charlie asked. "Did you see a bear in the tool shed?"

"A bear wouldn't have scared me as much. That damn fool had set up some kind of trap that had a hair trigger on it. My rake hit the wire and a stinkin' dead squirrel came flying up at me. It was full of maggots! He heard me yell and came to see what happened, as if he didn't know, but he was more surprised to see that it was *me*. I knew the minute he laid eyes on me that it weren't me he wanted to have a heart attack."

Charlie's eyebrows moved. "And…"

The handyman leaned towards Charlie. "…and I looked at that squirrel real close a few minutes later and…the maggots were gone. It was as if someone had picked them out. Ain't that peculiar?"

Charlie folded his arms and nodded, "…very peculiar indeed Watson." W.L. cocked his head, "…my name ain't Watson Lee, it's William Lee, and the blame fool apologized and said it was intended for his wife. I didn't think it was a darn bit funny. And to think, she was expectin' at the time! What man would do that to his pregnant wife? If you'd ask me, well, the man was a few rocks short of a ledge."

"Some kind of real nut job I would imagine," replied Charlie as he started towards the back door to the kitchen.

"Can I get on down the road now?" asked the handyman. I got chickens to still…I mean to cook."

"Yes, I know what you mean. You can go now, and I won't be looking for you. Thank you for a most interesting exchange of words, but if you come across something else peculiar give me a holler."

Charlie walked inside and looked at the mantel of the Martin home. Danny poked his head around the corner of the kitchen. Charlie placed his five and dime sun glasses back in his pocket, and said, "How the hell did she get it up there? Talk about being cuckoo. One day you're relaxing in your rocker and then, 'Bingo!' you've replaced an elk on the mantel." He paused," …I suppose if one can cut three to four cords of firewood…"

Danny replied, "It's a buck, Charlie, not an elk. See the antlers?"

Charlie scratched his head and replied, "Better yet, where is the wife?"

Charlie offered a piece of gum to Danny. "I never was one to shoot four-legged creatures. I shot a two-legged one a year ago."

Danny looked at him strangely. "…come on Charlie, when did you shoot a kangaroo?"

Charlie looked back at him and grinned. "…why would I shoot a kangaroo?"

Danny laughed. "Oh, I get it now. Sorry."

Charlie continued. "…this man might have deserved to be hung up, but what woman hangs the head of her dead hubby on the mantel?"

Danny looked around the room. "Oh …the girl. A relative came and got her. Man, he must have really ticked the little wife off."

Charlie folded one arm across his chest and with the other hand he supported his chin. "You'd think that cutting his head off would have been enough but to put his head up on a mantel where the elk was…is," he paused, "kind of funny, huh? It is almost like the perp was saying, 'Look what I can do.' I've seen some crime scenes, but this one takes the cake," he paused, "well, actually…it takes the head." He looked at the floor, and paused, "Where the hell is the body? What kind of person disposes of the body and keeps the head for display? I'm getting one of those headaches."

Danny looked at the floor also. "Not much blood for such a gruesome murder." Danny scribbled on his pad as he walked around the room. "She definitely cracked, that's for sure. What did the gardener have to say?"

Charlie sat down in the big over-stuffed chair and looked up at Thomas Martin's head covered with a plastic sack. "Now, I could take some serious naps in this thing." He smirked, "Real leather, too. Do you think there are any ties to this and the hikers last month? Maybe we've got a maniac running around out there and don't know it. If it was the wife, I wonder why she didn't just put his head on a stick and place it in her garden, ya know like a scarecrow. And where is the rest of the body? One thing for sure," he closed his eyes, "once the rest of him starts to smell, well, all we have to do is follow the stench."

Danny shook his head and looked out the large, bay window, "…somewhere, out there, is a bear having a good meal. I asked you what the gardener had to say. Charlie, are you feeling alright?" Danny peered at the family photos hung on the wall and mantel. "All these pictures would lead anyone to believe that they were the happiest of families. Heck, anything is possible." He shook his head in disbelief. "Nothing is out of place. It looks like they were getting ready to sit down to a nice meal." He ran his finger across the mantel. "This place is spotless. It's almost like it was dusted right before the murder," he looked closely at the mantel, "…and after, clean as a whistle, no smuges, and no smears. Do you smell lavender?"

Charlie closed his eyes and remained in the rocker. "…or after, and about the gardener, Mr. Crockett, aka William Lee, W.L. He thought the missus was a real nice lady, but the hubby had some issues, and he called him a bastard, too. It seems the girl stood up for her mama from time to time," he paused to sniff the air, "…yes, it is lavender and just a hint of lemon." He snapped his fingers and got up. "Hey, where was that family camping? You know the guy who was scared to death. Or was it his wife? I heard the news about the bear head scaring the husband to death, eventually. Wasn't it up near this place?"

Danny looked around again. "...seriously Charlie, was his name really W.L. Crockett?"

Charlie winked at him.

"Yeah, it's just down the road, but what does that have to do with this case? The bear head prank was probably just some kids fooling around. It wasn't even real."

"Thank God for that or the whole darn family would be dead. Hell, it's not even Halloween."

"Bears get a bum rap," Danny said solemnly. "Everywhere campers go they see the signs, 'Don't feed the bears,' and what do they do? They feed the bears! They throw them candy bars and yell at them."

"So you've never been tempted to throw a Baby Ruth at one?" Charlie asked.

"I'm a city boy; but I don't throw candy bars at anything."

"What do you throw then?"

"I don't throw anything. I'm a cop. I flash my badge."

Charlie Holtz smirked again and replied, "...could be kids, could have been her? Maybe it was the gardener. Maybe it was a random killing, but one thing for sure, it was connected to this. I have one of those gut feelings again. The hiker last month, I'm sure, had no intention of being hung upside down in a fake, giant spider web. You saw the pictures, right?"

"Yes, I saw them, but I still don't see the connection. That was definitely freaky though. I still say it's kids. It was probably the *same* kids. This mess here is totally out of character for this family. Look around. It's neat and tidy. They even have electricity! It's a very modest home, but these furnishings are very expensive. The wife had all the newest house wares. I don't see any evidence of family discontent but *something* was just not right. We need to focus on the locals around town. Maybe the guy ticked somebody off. Come on, Charlie, look at these pictures! Happy as clams, wouldn't you say?"

Charlie sat down. "We'll see, Chaser. This was too devious and calculated for any kids to put together, now that I think of it. I can't imagine a kid getting that deer head down and replacing it with the deceased's head. It took planning. I feel a little sick. Man, I wish I had grabbed a donut when I had the chance," he looked down, "…someone put a tarp under the rug that was here," he paused and pointed to the carpet as he slowly turns around, "…see the slight discoloration, there was a rug here and someone did not want any mess getting on the carpet that was under it. Tidy… and neatly done, but it took team work."

Danny watched Charlie walk over to the big picture window. "You're putting a picture together, aren't you?"

"Yeah, give me a minute. I am definitely getting a picture." Danny looked at him briefly, and then spoke, "You're not putting a picture together about the crime scene at all are you?" Charlie grinned, and continued to stare at the scenery, "Chaser, you know me too well. I was putting a picture together of a hot-tub, a six-pack, a full-moon and …"

Danny smiled at his friend, "…your next line had better be 'Callie holding grapes to my lips.'" Charlie tapped on the window and breathed in deeply. "…*it was*, but a hiker is alone, comes across something really weird. He figures himself some kind of sleuth in his expensive camping gear and continues hiking. He starts to get little curious, hikes further up the mountain, and comes across something weirder. Real animal skins wrapped up in what he thinks are spider webs. So now it's late--- too late to look for clues---and goes night-night in his itsie-bitsie tent."

"There was no tent. He had a hammock. Actually, it was a home-made sling," Danny replied solemnly. "I don't see where you're going with this."

Charlie glanced at him and shrugged his shoulders. "He hears something strange in the middle of the night. He comes out of his tent and Bingo…! There's a huge spider sitting right in front of him. He is scared crapless at first, and then realizes it's a joke, and he gets ticked off, really ticked off. So he takes his bow and arrow and his little pecker of a gun that he couldn't shoot straight if his life depended on it and starts out on his hunt. Now, this is where the tide turns, or shall I say where the 'leaf' turns 'cause it is the wilderness out there, right? Elliot Ness wants his man."

"Right, go on," his partner said, "But Ness wouldn't have let anyone sneak up on him, and he wasn't a hiker or a camper …was he?"

Charlie snickered. "You know, sometimes you just have to have an imagination. He tracks the nut job who tried to scare him to death, and now he is very sorry that he ever tried to become a boy scout with an arrow, much less be a mountain- man wannabe."

Danny continued taking notes. "This wouldn't have happened to a boy scout. I was a boy scout, and I would have been prepared."

"I thought you said you were a city boy. It doesn't matter. From what I ascertain whoever this person was knew a lot about this countryside and the goings on of all the little critters that like to camp in it or crap in it, whatever their tastes were. Say, did you ever pull pranks on people?"

"Sometimes I did but not to hurt anyone. My mama would've tanned my hide." Danny paused and then walked toward the kitchen. "So, do you mean big city critters, like bear heads and things that have fur?"

"Well, I think it's simple. Look around. What do you see?" Charlie asked.

"A great view from this window, and a hell of a lot of money wasted on gardening," said the young detective.

"Yeah," Charlie said in a slow deliberate drawl. "Why touch it if it doesn't need fixing. On the other hand, have you ever eaten a fresh tomato right off the vine? This is a very modest home, but it is well made. There are nice things all around, clean and tidy that's for sure, but something is just not right here. I'm not the best of housekeepers that is for sure." He let the next sentence trail off. "No checkers, no kids games of any kind, no woman's books…no slippers, no Africans, or home-made comfy stuff." Danny shook his head, "…no Africans? Don't you mean no afghans?" Charlie smiled, "That is precisely what I meant, but it sounds funnier."

Charlie pondered as he looked out the window. He looked around the living room again, taking his time before he responded. "This place reminds me of a hospital room. It even smells too clean. "It's like," he paused. "…well, it's like one of those model homes. Everything seems to be too tidy. There are no fingerprints on anything! With the exception of the lovely perfume permeating off his head and starting to draw flies," he paused again, "…that lemony-lavender maggoty kind of smell, well, I'd bet money somebody took the time to pick up and dust. Are you listening Danny?"

Danny came back from the kitchen and looked at the curio cabinet. "Perpetrators most likely cleaned up. This place looks like it has been cleaned with a fine tooth comb with the exception of the dearly departed's head hanging over the mantel."

For one moment Danny reminded him of himself when he was much younger. Danny's mannerisms had mimicked Charlie's many times. At times he really did think of Danny as the son he never had. "No, that's not what I mean. *Nothing* is disturbed. *Nothing!* I get the feeling that this was real personal. Other than the mantel having a few drops of blood on it, well, it's like this place was never lived in. No magazines lying around, no ashtrays, no slippers by the fire place, no cob webs. The wife must have been a cleaning freak."

"…maybe," Danny said. He could have been the one that made her that way. He could have been the one that had to have everything just so, but what gives you that idea?"

Charlie thought for a moment. "It's just not homey enough. I got one of those feelings, Danny. Give me a minute." He took a deep breath, exhaled slowly and breathed deeply again. "There are no girly things! Everything is…well, for lack of a better word…tight-assed. I see no visions of sugar plums floating through the air at Christmas time, no Easter baskets being hidden behind the couch either, and I sure as hell don't see popcorn being passed around."

"That's a two-worder, *tight-assed,*" Danny humored.

Charlie walked over to the cupboard and opened it. "See these? These are door mats. Who the hell keeps door mats in a cupboard? There are six of them. Someone was wrapped a little too tight in regards to wiping their feet. She must have had to replace them everyday. And who labels their canned goods with the day they were actually bought? The floor is clean enough to eat off of, and the windows are so clean they squeak. Hell, I might have killed him myself if he made me keep the house this spotless. Something went on in the house, something not right." He opened another cabinet door, "Look…three of everything, three plates, three bowls, three cups, three saucers." He looked up to the next shelf, "…and here we have one plate, one bowl, one cup, and one saucer." He paused for a brief moment. "Goldie Locks had her own shelf," he looked at Danny, "The porridge thickens."

Danny sat down on a stool and looked at his watch. He nodded to his good friend and pointed. "They found the girl just sitting on the ledge out there. She was ca-ta-phonic."

"Is that one of those city words? I think you meant ca-ta-tonic," Charlie said snidely, shaking his head. "You really need to get out more." Danny giggled, "...no, I just need to meet a ca-ta-tonic African."

Charlie looked in the direction of where his partner was pointing and replied, "...good one Chaser, man, what a view! It's to die for, huh? You could lose you head over all this."

"You are a sick bastard at times, Charlie." Danny shook his head and turned around. "I prefer a view with skyscrapers and night lights. I've gotten used to the city lights and the sounds, you know? I'll take a balcony overlooking a city street any day."

"You're not a visionary, are you Danny? Can't you just see the sun going down past those mountains? I, on the other hand, love the flowers and the birds and those busy little bees. And I also wonder why anyone would kill the hubby and take the wife, but not the kid? They, he, or she wanted to make a statement. They wanted to hang him up for display. This is a humiliation killing. Somebody really did not like the guy this head was attached to and from what Crockett told me, well; I might have stuffed the deer head up the south end of this northern-faced head's ass myself."

Charlie looked around and saw the bookcase. He glanced at his young partner and grinned, the grin that told him he had figured out something that would help make the case. He eyes a most interesting picture.

Danny's eyes narrowed. "No way, man, *it was* him. You honestly think he was the prankster!!? Where's the evidence?"

Charlie picked up the picture and handed it to Danny. "Good likeness, don't you think?"

"Well, I'll be a son of a bitch!" Danny whispered. It's the old man holding the bear head and the girl must be his daughter!" He paused and looked at the picture more closely, "She doesn't look too happy." Danny sat the picture back on the mantel. "He took his daughter with him? Damn, do you think she was there when he strung up that poor kid? And what about those campers they found tied up and covered in honey? Who the heck ties up campers and pours honey all over them?"

"It must have been un*bear*able," he paused, "now *bear* with me. I think you know the answer to that Danny. It was the same sick bastard who played around with giant home-made spiders, and it was the same sick bastard who made bear noises in their direction when they smelled like Granny's cinnamon rolls. And it was the same sick bastard who buried a dead squirrel and rigged it so it would scare the living shit out of his wife."

"Sometimes you give me the impression that scenes like this don't bother you, Charlie."

"…*bear* with me. If I were to let any of them bother me, I couldn't do my job. I can take almost anything, but there is one thing I cannot stomach."

"…doing laundry?" Danny asked.

"Funny…just the thought of having to change a baby's diaper, ya know… number two, makes me nauseous, and you should know that by now. I can look at blood and guts all day long, but force me to change number two diapers and I'll lose my lunch every time!"

Charlie saw the radio and turned it on. "Hmmmm, they were not a fan of The Great Gildersleeve."

It was tuned to the local news station. "I wonder if Mama Bear ever got upset when Baby Bear went with him."

"I don't listen to the radio much at all. I read a lot." Danny shrugged his shoulders. "From what I can ascermain, she didn't have much to say about anything."

"It's *ascertain*, and I'm going to buy you a dictionary." Charlie looked out the window and crossed his arms. "They haven't found the wife, yet, and they most likely will not. She is most likely dead. How the heck can a young girl just sit for a whole day on a ledge and not have been a part of it? Besides, the gardener said nothing about seeing her while he was here." He rubbed his temple, "I'm going to lose some sleep on this case. Was she really catatonic?"

"Yes, they said it was like she was in a stupor. She doesn't know anything. At any rate, the mother must be long gone. There have been too many bear sightings. Then again, maybe she will show up." He hesitated. "Why would you think the wife is dead? She probably got her head on straight for one minute and then panicked, ran out, and is eating pine nuts somewhere. Maybe she ran from the killer or killers." Danny stared out the window, his eyes narrowed, "Could be she's scared shitless to come home, could be she is watching us right now and just waiting for us to leave so she can come back and pack a few things."

He paused, and then added, "A mama bear would not leave her cub for too long. Would she?"

"There are many caves through this region. She is probably hold up in one of them. I am not a bear expert, but I know one thing for sure. Maybe she diverted the killer's attention away from the kid. Maybe they or he or she decided that this was not a good place to play hide and seek. Maybe they were city bad guys and realized that the great outdoors was not their cup of tea. I have a headache. I always get a headache when I go up a mountain."

Danny pulled out a drawer from a small dresser near the kitchen door. "'To Jennifer, Love, Daddy.' Looks like the poor kid won't get her present. Should I open it?" Charlie shook his head, "No, the kid is most likely looking forward to getting a present on her birthday and I am going to see that she gets this one," he paused, "...is there anything else on the note?"

Danny unfolded the note, "...yes, it says, 'I'll be watching you.'"

"Well, that is enough to make *me* sleep with one eye open." Charlie pointed in the direction of the Smokey Mountains. "Mama is probably out there somewhere in the belly of the bear. She's a goner, maybe not. But one thing for sure, she needs to be found. And another thing..."

"What's that boss?"

"*This was very personal,* and I don't think for one minute that it was an outsider that did this. If it wasn't the wife, it was someone who knew the family."

"Look at *this* picture," Danny said. It sat on the opposite end of the mantel. He handed it to Charlie. "Now, I ask you, don't this look like a happy family outing? Does that lady look like a lady who might have difficulty getting lost out here? She is dressed like Davy Crockett's stand-in."

Charlie stared at the picture. "...she actually asked the gardener if he knew how long it would take a bear to find fresh meat. She looks like a man with this get up, huh? She is a looker for sure. The daughter looks a lot like her mama. I wonder why she is smiling like he is. The girl doesn't look too happy." He squints and gives the picture a closer look. This was taken around Shallow Grave, not too far from here."

"Have you done any climbing?" Danny asked.

Charlie chuckled. "I have climbed into my bed many a night after I said goodnight to Jack Daniels." He looked back at the picture. "Shallow

Grave is before your time. It's a local name. They call it Shallow Grave because it's where they found some honey-moaners. It was before your time, Chaser."

Danny chuckled. "Don't you mean honey-mooners?"

Charlie did not crack a smile. "No, I meant honey-moaners. Anyway, couples used to go up there to make out. I thought it was always too creepy. These honey-moaners got a little too rambunctious and waltzed to their deaths. There are two shear rock cliffs that butt up against each other, and you have to be a magician to get over it without falling in! Once you fall, you're dead. The Mountain Rescue stuffed wire in it at one time so no once else ended up in a shallow grave, but it really isn't shallow at all, just looks that way 'cause it's pitch black all the way down. The rangers have a heck of a time keeping the hikers out, too. The view is just too beautiful to resist. I think it's on private property now. Hikers have been known to have some very close calls up there. It's like one of those things in the desert, a massage."

Danny chuckled and slapped his knee. "You mean a *mirage*? I think you're the one that needs a dictionary."

"Maybe we can share one."

"So, why is it called Shallow Grave again?"

"It's only shallow for about ten feet down and then it widens to a wall of nothingness. If you don't focus on something, you could walk right off the edge. These mountains can play tricks on you if you don't pay attention to where you're feet step. Come to think about it, it might be private land by now. It *is* a very dangerous place, but, man, the view is spectacular this time of year. It has to be one of the prettiest places on earth."

"You've been up there with a sweet heart?"

"One or two, maybe three, but who's counting?" Charlie smiled and sat down. "Yeah, way back when there were cave women up there. The honey-moaners were never found. Some people think little green men got them," he paused to rub his temples, "...little green men with coon skin hats. It was like they just dropped off the face of the earth into thin air. There have been a few locals from time to time who have fallen in, too. At least, it was assumed that is what happened to them. They were never found either, but their spouses said that's where they had been headed."

"How'd they know the honey-moaners were even up there?"

Charlie frowned. "Well, the local sheriff at the time found a night gown---real silk---and a hiker's pack with some items that one might bring on a honeymoon, ya know…a six pack, a few cigars, and a back scratcher. Excuse me; I gotta take a leak in the great outdoors."

"Is that your idea of what a honey-moaner's pack ought to have in it? Were you part of the team that investigated their disappearances?"

"No, I worked alone back then, did private P.I. jobs. The government called my name and I had to go elsewhere. Anyway, the case was closed. They did find their car parked not too far from here, and it seems they were going camping. Weirdest thing about it all was the radio. They found a radio close to where the edge dropped off, and yes, that is my idea of what a honey moaner's pack should have in it. A six pack goes a long way, and if the cigars are Coo-ban, well, it brings back some fond memories of having my back scratched by a young lady with the longest legs of any woman I ever had the pleasure of …."

"How the heck did electricity get up there?" Danny asked quickly.

"Didn't need electric. They found a radio kit with a valve receiver. Apparently somebody was playing the radio and then," he snapped his fingers, "they were sucked up into the atmosphere. The little green men must have had a hay-day."

"What's a couple of campers doing with a radio kit?"

Charlie chuckled. "I thought it was kind of funny, too, and I voiced my opinion. They thought I was nuts. That's when I decided to become a city cop. Too many tight asses telling me how I could or should not have run my investigation after I made it quite clear when they hired me that I don't answer questions, I ask them." He looked off into nothingness. "That part of my life seems like it was a lifetime ago. There was a time when I had a real sweetheart of a girl, but I screwed that up. She and I would go up to Shallow Grave when I took the week end off from the city lights, oh well, too much beer has passed over these lips since then."

Danny chuckled. "So, it is possible that Cupid hit you with an arrow?"

"It wasn't an arrow. It was a smooth-flowing bottle of cheap wine mixed with moonlight and wild roses. Don't you remember what I told you last year?"

Danny grinned and nodded, "…let the lady pay for the beer, light your own Coo-bans, and when all else fails let the back scratcher do the talking." Danny shook his head. "You should go strictly private again. There is more money in it."

"Yeah, I am thinking about it. Going private would sure be a good way to retire. The only people who can afford the good stuff are the well-doers," Charlie replied. "This guy, Thomas Martin, could have been one of those well-doers. This is a nice home, great view, lots of hobbies...like..."

They both pointed at one particular picture on the wall.

"It's the dearly departed, and he's holding an award for..." Danny started.

"...son of a bitch', Radio hobbyist," Charlie finished soberly. "Bingo! Ain't it grand when a puzzle piece falls into place? We need to talk to the daughter. She may be able to shed some light on all this, poor kid. I hope Baby Bear didn't see Mama Bear kill Papa Bear." Charlie paused and fingered another picture on the wall. "He sure was full of himself. He is grinning like a chesser cat in this one." Danny stepped forward and took a closer look. There stood Thomas Martin all decked out in what looked like a Davy Crockett costume. Danny smirked. "What an idiot. Say...do you really think the mother could have killed him?" They both took a closer look at the picture. Danny looked at Charlie with a straight face and replied, "He has a tie on."

Charlie kept looking at the rest of the pictures. "Hmmm...*do I* think the mother could have killed *this* idiot? Let's not be thinking along those lines right now. We don't know who killed him, but she is a good suspect."

"Well, one thing for sure, the daughter sure ain't going to have to worry about money problems," Danny said. She'll inherit a lot of dough once her mama's remains are found. That is, if she's found at all."

Charlie cocked his head and looked at Danny. "And where did you find out that bit of information, Chaser?"

Danny chuckled. "I think I may have finally got one up on you, Charlie," the young partner replied.

"How you figure that?"

"*Thomas Martin and Eileen Martin*, don't these names ring a bell with you? Or are you going senile on me?

You really need to read more! The missus' maiden name was Thorpe."

Charlie turned to look at his young partner and drummed the counter top with his fingers. "I'll be dipped in manure, and rolled in oatmeal," he said straight faced. "Damn, was *he* the other half of Thorpe Properties?"

"Yeap. The one and only dead Thomas Martin who married Eileen Thorpe, the one and only daughter of Therford Thorpe, entrepreneur and millionaire philanthropist and founder of Thorpe Properties. The name got changed somewhere down the line. Thorpe liked to hike, too. How odd is that? And you know what else is weird?"

"Jennifer is the granddaughter of Therford Thorpe, and if Mama Bear *is* dead, Baby Bear is a very, very rich young lady."

Chapter seven

Charlie stared straight ahead through the large plate glass window and replied, "Yes, it is very weird that one can have all this and not have peace within oneself. It took a cool penny to put up this piece of glass. How could anyone be contrary when they got up in the morning and saw this view?"

"Are you going soft on me?" Danny asked. Thorpe disappeared into the wilderness, too. The Thorpes were right in the middle of a nasty divorce when he disappeared. They couldn't make up their minds about who got the kids. The wife..." Danny paused, "I think her name was Clara, ran off to the Orient and never came home."

Charlie looked at his partner with amazement. "How do you know all this stuff?"

"I read a lot; ya know the news in *print*."

Charlie looked a little perplexed at his partner. "Didn't you just say there was only one daughter? Wasn't Eileen the only kid? I thought you said there was just one kid?"

"Ah-ha! You are paying attention. There were two daughters, but Eileen was the biological one. The other one kind of fell off the map when his will was made public, but the paper did not elaborate about her at all," he paused, "seems she was a bit of a wall flower. It was assumed she left with the wife. Eileen changed the title of Thorpe Properties to Caleen Properties after the father was officially pronounced dead. The half-sister never turned up to get her share and left Eileen with the piggy bank. It seems the authorities thought they found what was left of his body, so it was cut and dry as to the decision of the will. It also seemed that Clara signed everything over to Eileen long before *she* fell off the face of the earth."

Charlie unwrapped one more piece of gum and put it in his mouth. "Now that has opened up a whole new can of worms." Charlie pulled out one of the loose-leaf notebooks on the shelf titled *The Joke's on You* and started reading it. "These are very interesting. I read a lot, too."

"I wonder how much a place like this costs," the young detective replied. "I certainly could never afford it. I barely make it from payday to payday."

"A man's gotta have a dream," Charlie paused and looked at his partner. "*I wonder why she just didn't wait for him to die.*" It was more of a question to himself than to Danny.

"What do you mean? How could she know he was going to die this way?"

Charlie handed the loose-leaf notebook to Danny. "He could have died real soon according to this," Charlie said pointing to the hand written letter which was now in Danny's hands.

Danny read the letter outloud. "*Dearest Eileen, It seems I have a cancer. Ain't it funny how things work out?*

You should be laughing yourself to death by now; sorry I was not the one to make it happen for you. Personally, I don't find it a damn bit funny that it was me that went first. If you are reading this letter, well, you know I have already kicked the bucket. Heck, I didn't even get to say goodbye my way. I hope you gave me a good send off. Was it me, or was I a real jackass to you? I must apologize this one time and tell you I wish I had scared you with the bear head. Tell Jennifer she can cry now, and I was never in love with you. You made all that money so inviting. You were always so pitiful. Look out the window. Do you see me? If you see my hairy ass, kiss it. Fond Regards, Thomas." Danny handed the letter to Charlie. "...what a jackass."

"...yeah, one with a hairy ass," Charlie mused. He was using it for a bookmark. Look at the titles of all these notebooks, 'You Can Make It in Comedy,' 'Laugh and the World Wants More,' 'Fun with Tricks,' 'Pranksters at Large,' 'So You Want to Be a Comedian,' 'Make 'Em Laugh and Walk Away,' he continued, "These are not *even books*. They are hand written! How weird is that? The guy was in love with himself."

Danny thumbed through one of the notebooks. "I'm not so sure this was something that any of them suddenly came up with over a period of weeks. He seems to have written all of them himself. It's definitely not a woman's handwriting."

Danny pulled another one from the shelf and started reading. "It's definitely a man's handwriting. What a weirdo! Heck, Charlie, listen to this. 'Went to town, took Eileen with me, and left her on the side of the road after she told me she had to pee. It was raining, but what the hell. I hadn't let her bathe in two weeks.'"

Charlie's eyes narrowed. "Please continue."

Danny shook his head. "He was a real piece of work. Listen to this. 'Locked her in the shed with some wasps...she yelled for an hour and then busted out the window. She looked like she had marbles under her scrawny little neck. Jennifer got really mad with me.' His eyes widened, "Oh, hell no, listen to this, 'I tied her to a tree for a whole day. I told Jennifer she had the day off. Eileen never cried, not once. I am not a heartless man. I brought her water and day old biscuits. The same day old biscuits she tried to serve me for supper.'" Danny paused. "And the list goes on and on. What kind of sicko are we dealing with?"

They both looked at the head hanging from the mantel. Charlie whispered to his partner. "Someone dealt with the sicko." Danny looked down. "Someone swept the carpet, too," he paused, "...you can still see the marks that the broom left. Hmmm...I think he got what he deserved if all he wrote is the truth," he paused again and stared intensely at the carpet, "...Good Housekeeping right down to the last minute."

Danny sat down. "I think we have our prankster. He went out in a bang at the expense of those hikers, though."

Charlie went into the kitchen and found a paper sack. "Bag these, all of them; I have some reading to do."

"Aren't they considered evidence?"

"They will be, but who's to know about them but you and I? The dearly departed liked to write about his gallivanting through the wilderness and I love a good read."

Danny pulled out another one. "This is a child's handwriting. Oh, do you suppose? No, please tell me the girl had nothing to do with it?"

"Okay, I won't. Let me see it."

Charlie thumbed through the pages. "This is a child's handwriting, and there are pictures of the great outdoors drawn in pencil. She is a very talented young lady. Some of these are quite good. Oh, Jeez, Danny, look---here is a drawing of a big spider and a stick man hanging from a tree, but it looks like she drew Daddy Bear hanging from the noose."

Charlie looked around the living room again. "Where the hell do you suppose the rest of his body is? How far is the place they took her to? Did you find any drag marks outside?"

"Nothing to indicate anyone dragged a body part out of this house and the place is not too far," Danny replied. I believe its north of the main highway, turn left on Hickory Hammock, go five miles or more, turn right again and follow the white fence. Want me to go with you?"

Charlie shook his head. "No, but do me a favor, will ya? Stick around here for another hour," he paused, "and make sure you keep an eye out for bears."

"No problem," Danny replied. "But wouldn't it be better if I kept both eyes in my head?"

Charlie couldn't help but grin at Danny's comment. He knew as long as the two of them had a sense of humor working together, the case would not get long and drawn out. "Go get that present for the girl. I may need a peace offering and I'll just follow the bread crumbs," he paused to chuckle, "the badge in the car told me how to get there, too. I'll check it out myself. See you tomorrow."

Danny smiled and walked towards the patrol car. He turned to look at Charlie and said, "Yeah, we will see each other tomorrow but I will stick around for a while just to make sure 'Goldie Locks' and the other two bears don't return."

The main highway was not the main highway at all, but it was used so much by the locals it was called 'the Main Highway.' Five miles seemed like twenty as Charlie turned into the road that would lead him to Mountain View Hospital.

It was paved well to be a rural drive. He was impressed with the parking lot and landscaping. For a mountain hospital, it looked more like a hidden retreat. He wondered who kept it up, certainly not the locals.

Charlie pulled into the parking lot and looked around. It was a private hospital that was for sure. With a guard at the gate and one at the main entrance, he knew immediately this place had some backing. He found it very interesting that the guard let him in without any questions. "Go on in, sir. I have your name on my sheet. If you give me your keys, I will park your vehicle out of the sun."

Charlie smiled and tipped his hat at the ancient guard. "If I go nuts, I hope I win the numbers and get to bunk here," he replied.

Charlie walked in and was greeted by a stout but very strong-armed woman. "You must be Mr. Holtz. I am Nurse Williamson, but you can call me Hilda. I'll take you in to see Jennifer, but if she starts to get upset by any of your questions, I will toss your white-tail out of here faster than I can throw Saturday's wash water out the window." Her demeanor changed quickly. "She is a sweet child, and I take the doctor's orders very seriously. I have a third eye right in the back of my head," she paused to look at the wrapped gift in his hands. "How nice of you to bring her a gift."

Charlie shook his head and replied, "...I believe it is intended for her but it is not from me. Would you see that she gets it? I have two granddaughters of my own, and I promise you I will not upset her. How'd you know I was coming?" Hilda winked at him. "Pay no attention, sweetheart. I said I have a third eye in the back of my head."

"If I upset her, well, pull my hairy white tail out of there, but I really need to speak with her concerning her father's death and her mother's disappearance. I won't be long."

Hilda put her finger to her lips and looked down the long corridor. "...take your time. Keep it down. I have taken care of everything. Last door on the right at the end of the hall and if anyone asks, tell them you're family, but just to be sure...," she reached for a white jacket hanging on a hook on the wall, "just say you are the new doc on the block. No one will know any different. He is not expected to be here until next week. I have no problems with making schedules work for my benefit."

Charlie peeked into the room through the small glass viewing area. "She appears to be fine. Why is she locked up in there?"

"Her doctor has not been able to crack her for now. She absolutely will not talk to anyone but her aunt and me. It's like she is a grown woman in a child's body. You will see what I mean when you speak with her." Charlie leaned up against the wall. "I hate this part of the job."

Hilda looked at him strangely. "You are the detective, not me. I just have a feeling she will warm up to you. Give it a try. Today is her birthday. Be nice."

Charlie straightened the collar on the jacket. "Do I look like an ogre?"

Hilda smiled pleasantly and replied, "I'm just doing what I'm paid for and trust me, it ain't enough, sugar."

Charlie folded his arms. "Yeah, well, from the looks of this place somebody gets paid enough money to find out what her problem is."

Hilda frowned as she took the key out that would open the door to Jennifer's room and whispered, "They wanted to put straps on her, but her aunt wouldn't have any part of that. Her aunt, bless her heart, has not left the hospital since Jennifer came. She is just down the hall, but will be leaving soon."

"Could I talk to the aunt?"

"I don't see why not. She's in the arboretum, but if you tick her off, too, you're on your own. When Jennifer gets better, her aunt already has the papers started to take her out of here. Oh, and just between me and you," Hilda looked down the corridor, "Jennifer loves the arboretum, too."

"What's her aunt's name?"

Hilda winked at him. "Now, you are asking the right questions. Her name is Callie McDermott."

Charlie's eyes widened. "Callie McDermott of the McDermont dairy?" he asked.

"Yes, so you know her then?"

Charlie couldn't help but smile. "You can never be sure. I might have known her briefly one particular time in my youth. We might have been in separate canoes passing in the night, with the exception of my canoe going over the waterfall!"

Hilda smiled pleasantly again. "That twinkle in your right eye tells me you two have a history, and maybe you ought to go say hello. She needs a shoulder to cry on."

"Why would you think my shoulder is the one she needs to cry on?"

"Hmmmm, my third eye tells me so. Goodness, when Ms. Callie goes in there," Hilda pointed to a sign that said *'ARBORETUM.'* She rocks back and forth in the rocker and names all the plants for Jennifer, one at a time. She can tell you the name of every tree on this mountain. Are you sure you don't know her?"

"I've known many women. Why *do you* think I would know her?"

Hilda smiled. "She said you'd say that. This lady knows a little about the great outdoors and you, too."

"An outdoor kind of girl, huh?" he asked. "Do you care about all the patients in this place like you do Jennifer?"

Hilda became huffy for a moment and took her hand from the door knob. "I care about all my patients, but Jennifer is different from any child I have ever seen. There is a strange sweetness about her; I just can't explain." Her tone changed again, "...I see someone else in those eyes when I look at her."

"Why is that?"

"She has a sense of humor that is very odd for a child her age. With all that has happened, well, it's like..." she paused, "It's like she is a puppet on a string."

"Hmmmm..." Charlie replied.

"I shouldn't be telling you this, but I'm going to retire next week, rather early, too. Ms. Callie has offered me a job I cannot refuse. This is my one chance to do something really good for one of my patients before I leave. You seem like a decent man, so I will tell you what she told me, but not now," Hilda checked the corridor again, "You go on in, and I will watch the hallway."

"Can we talk somewhere else? I feel like I might be hauled out of here if I get caught. Are you sure it is okay to go in here?"

Hilda unlocked the door. "Yes. She wouldn't hurt a fly."

"I'm not a fly. I bleed blood," he paused, "...what do you think? Freud or Hyde? Ya know the jacket?"

Hilda looked through the small window. "...Elmer Fudd. Oh, she's smiling. It's alright to go in, but I'm going to keep a lookout for her aunt. Wouldn't want her to leave and you not have a chance to say hello." Hilda pushed the door open. Charlie glanced at her and replied, "...please stay for just a moment."

Hilda nodded and replied, "If you raise your voice to her, I will pop your white tail off your feet."

"I do not yell at children," he whispered. He turned to Hilda and asked, "Will you do the introductions?"

Jennifer sat on the edge of the bed. She had long auburn braids that hung just below her chest line. Her eyes were so brown they almost looked black. She was quite pale but did not look malnourished at all. Jennifer was a beautiful young girl. Charlie looked around. It reminded him of what a military academy room might look like. Nothing was out of place. He tried not to gawk. Her room was more than tidy; it was immaculate. No dust anywhere that he could see. Nothing left unattended. The extra blanket was squared off and lying on the corner of the bed. Her shoes neatly placed under the bed. Each toiletry had its place. Even her pajamas looked like they had been pressed with starch.

Charlie cleared his throat as Hilda stepped forward and placed her hand on Jennifer's left shoulder. "Good morning again, Jennifer, this is Detective Holtz. He would like to ask you a few questions. Would that be alright? Do you feel like answering some questions or should I ask him to leave?"

Jennifer turned her head slowly almost like it was on a pivot. Hilda removed her hand and replied, "If you do not want him here, I will toss him out."

Jennifer looked straight at Charlie as if she was looking right through him and replied, "Have you ever been tossed out prior to a meeting with a nut case? And why are you wearing that ridiculous doctor's coat? *You don't fool me.* I know a detective when I see one. Hey, you're old. Did you bring me a present? Today is my birthday. Daddy promised me a pair of binoculars, and I still don't have them. Do you by any chance have some gum? That idiot doctor said I couldn't have it. Do they actually think I will hang myself with *gum?*"

Charlie cleared his throat and glanced at Hilda, and then he smiled at Jennifer. "I'm an honest man, most of the time. Certainly for you I'll be honest and yes, I have been tossed once or twice, and I have some gum. In all my years of being a detective I do not recall anyone hanging themselves with a stick of gum," he winked at Hilda, "...maybe those idiot doctors might think you will use it for an escape."

Jennifer grinned and showed off her perfectly straight teeth.

Charlie continued. "And for your information, I'm not old at all. My mama tried to iron me when I was born, and well, as you can see I did not take to it at all."

"Are you trying to make me laugh? You have to make me laugh first, alrightie-ditie? Humor at times when used incorrectly has a tendency to get people killed. And for your information, '*one must be so very careful as to what comes out of their mouth, for it may cause them to lose their head.*'"

Charlie suddenly got a chill and looked at Hilda.

Jennifer turned away from them and stared out the window. "If I had a pair of binoculars, I could see up in the trees. I could make eye contact with a squirrel and he might be able to help me get out of this outhouse! It smells like the inside of a pine tree," she paused, "…not that there is anything wrong with that, but why can't they just let everything go back to nature?"

Charlie wasn't sure how to respond to her outburst but he gave it a try. "If you could smell my laundry basket you would think this place smelled like roses."

Hilda tugged at his jacket and whispered, "It's a thing with her. You have to tell a joke and make her laugh at something."

He whispered back, "I'm not a comedian. Can't I just make a face?" He looked at Jennifer carefully. "What happened to her nose? Did she fall?"

Jennifer stood up and walked to the window. "…there is nothing wrong with my hearing and I know you're not a comedian. She just told me you are a detective. I am a lot smarter than they think. One doesn't get to be the Woodsman's daughter with acting stupid. Make me laugh or she will toss you out, alrightie-ditie? And I know you're curious about my nose. It's nothing serious. I did fall. I fell from the fan." She reacted as though she saw the look Charlie gave Hilda. "For your information, I was dusting the fan. This place needs a good cleaning. You'd think with what my aunt pays them they could dust the top of the fan blades, or am I just a nut waiting to crack?"

"Oh, tough guy, are you? Have you ever seen anyone tossed around?" Charlie teased.

She did not smile, saying, "…tough *girl*. Giggles do not count. You have to make me laugh like one of those characters on the radio, you know, hardy-har-har---and a slap on the knee. But no, I have not seen anyone tossed around. If you are referring to my papa mistreating my mama, you're wrong. They never raised a hand to one another. Think of something to make me laugh or get out of here. I have a schedule to keep, places to go to, and people to piss off."

He smiled at her and nodded. "…okay…there once was a man from --- Maine that didn't like standing in the rain, so he put on a ---cat he thought was his hat and ended up with a head full of --- how's that?"

"That's not funny," Jennifer replied with a straight face. "That didn't even squeeze a giggle out of me. Try again."

"I apologize," he said earnestly. "I never finished my degree at Laugh College."

Jennifer turned around quickly. "I wasn't aware there was any such college. Is there? One more try---and this time if I don't laugh, you're out of here. No cake for you, either."

Charlie glanced at Hilda who was just about to leave. She nudged Charlie. "She's serious."

He cleared his throat, "Okay. There once was a girl from the Smokey's who liked to say 'okey-dokeys', but one day she fell and brokie her nokie and started to say 'all-rightie-dities.'"

Hilda shrugged her shoulders. Charlie folded his arms and replied, "Well, that obviously did not tickle her funny bone. Maybe I should go, but I hate to miss free cake."

Jennifer turned around and looked at him. Her shoulders started to shake. Charlie looked at Hilda perplexed. "Is she going to start crying? Oh, crap I've upset her. I will leave."

Jennifer folder her arms and stared at Charlie. She began grinning from ear to ear and then fell over laughing. "That was a good one! You may ask me your questions. A deal is a deal. Have you ever thought of quitting your day job and becoming a comedian?"

"No," replied Charlie, "they pay me far too much money," he rolled his eyes at Jennifer, "...now, that's funny."

Jennifer grinned. "That would be a wise decision."

"Thank you," he said. "I like my job for the moment. I wish somebody would give me a raise though."

"Have one of the doctors shove some yeast up your butt. That will give you a 'rise.' Do you like to hike?" Jennifer asked.

Charlie cleared his throat again, "No, I'm a fat old man; it would give me a heart attack. I hiked around here when I was much younger, though. It sure is pretty."

Jennifer leaned into the window and pressed her face against the metal grid covering the window glass. "Yes, isn't it though? I think it is the most beautiful place on earth." She turned back to Charlie, "You should eat more veggies. You're not a fat old man. You're just over the hill, well, in your case, over the mountains. Your face reminds me of a road map. Have you ever been to New York City?"

Charlie grinned. "You shouldn't quit your day job either, but that was a good one, too. Yes, I have been there, but I did not like it."

"Well, why the heck not?"

"The pigeons kept pooping on my head."

She looked at him straight faced. "*Funny.* Hiking can be fun. I always had fun with my father, but sometimes he did things that weren't very nice. Really mean things. I shouldn't tell on him."

"Can't you tell me about some of them?"

"I can, but you have to promise not to tell the doctor about them, okay? If he finds out, he might not let me go to the arboretum, and then I might have to pull a prank on him, like filling his stethoscope with pee."

Charlie chuckled. "...okay...now that would make me laugh. I don't like doctors, either, but I am sure if you did that, it wouldn't be in your best interest. They're trying to help you. Don't you want to get better and leave this place? I understand you love the outdoors."

"I do, but if I have to, I will live in the arboretum for the rest of my life. I'm not a --- what is it you guys call someone who tells on people? I seem to remember it has something to do with a bird sitting on a pole."

"I think what you want to say is stool pigeon. Will your aunt let you do the things that you did with your father, like hiking and camping out?"

"Aunt Callie is cool, and, yes, she will let me do what I want as long as it's safe. I think she is what you old coots like to call a 'stick in the mud' but, then, she's an old coot, too. Just how old are you Charlie?"

"Hmmmm, I guess that is a fair question. I'm young enough to drink too much and too old to care, but whose counting."

"Aunt Callie is forty-six, but she looks a lot younger. I do so like her cooking, and she braids my hair and puts feathers in them, see? Her favorite dish is pasta. I think it is perfectly yucky, and so did my papa. Mama absolutely hated it. Am I filthy rich?"

Charlie cleared his throat again. "I'm not sure I can answer that, Jennifer. Are you worried about not having any money? It seems someone has taken very good care of you so far."

Jennifer layed back on her bed and looked up at the ceiling. "No, I am not worried about money at all. My mother is the one who had all the money. I think she rubbed it in Papa's face a lot. Maybe that's why he was so mean to her and the others." She sat up and looked at Charlie directly in the eye, "…Detective, I'm not as nutty as you may have been told. Do I look crazy to you?"

"No, not at all, the world is crazy, that's all." He remembered the notebook at the house. "Do you like to draw?"

Chapter eight

Jennifer suddenly seemed agitated. "Yes, but you know that already, so why are you wasting my time with things you already know?" Playing on the word, she continued, "Did you know that today is my birthday?"

"I seem to remember Hilda telling me something like that. What kind of cake will it be? I'm sorry I don't have a present for you, but happy birthday, okay?"

"The cake is chocolate with strawberry icing. Strawberries are my favorite treat. Mama loved them, too, but Papa would not let her have them in the house. He made her eat them outside like she was some kind of monkey." Jennifer quickly changed subjects. "My aunt told me we will celebrate as soon as all the papers are signed."

"What papers?" Charlie asked.

"Hey, did you find a pair of binoculars at my house?" She paused briefly and started to undo her braids. "…papers, you know… *papers* that will get me out of here."

Charlie smiled at her. "We may have found a pair. I will see that you get them if they cross my path, okay? Jennifer, let's get serious for a moment. I'd like to ask you a few more questions about your parents. Why did your papa make your mama eat strawberries outside? Did you have to eat them outside also?"

"Well, isn't it obvious? She dropped one on the rug, and the stain would not come out. Papa made her scrub it for an hour until her fingers bled. I ate them wherever I pleased. I was always very careful, but I think he liked me being defiant at times."

"Why so?"

"He always told me I was the best side-kick he could ever ask for. Say, isn't there supposed to be a lawyer here?"

Charlie chuckled. "You are not on trial, and you will not be in any trouble with answering my questions. I hope when I leave here you will be able to make some sense of what happened."

She looked at him innocently. "No one will ever make sense of what happened to him, but it makes a lot of sense that my mama decided to go into the mountains like she did. He's dead now, and he never had any c-e-n-t-s, get it?"

Charlie got it. "I think I do get it. Did you happen to do anything to him after he made your mama scrub for an hour?"

"Gosh, funny you should ask that question. As a matter of fact, I did."

"Would you mind telling me what you did?"

She stared straight ahead not making eye contact with him. "I put hot sauce in his coffee and then I sprinkled ants on his sandwich, dead ones, of course. Mama thought it was very funny." She grinned. "Sorry, it's the comedian in me. Do you always carry a gun? Why don't you just carry a rifle?"

"Do I look like Davy Crockett?" Charlie responded. He attempted to pull the conversation back. "Did you see your mama hurt your papa?"

Jennifer appeared not to hear his second question. "That was funny! Hey, do you have one of those Davy Crockett hats? The gardener always wore one. I liked him a lot. Papa scared the poop out of him once," she paused, "with a dead squirrel."

"No, but I do have a real raccoon tail hanging from my rear-view mirror. Does that count?"

"No, but if you somehow can glue it to the top of your bald head, it would be very funny."

Charlie couldn't help but laugh again. "That would be funny!" He became serious. "Did your mama ever tell you that she was planning on hurting your papa?"

"Good grief! Not that I can recall, and I asked her if she ever though of it. Why would she tell me anything like that? She put boogers in his eggs most of the time."

"She did what?"

"Is there something wrong with your hearing?" She got louder. "*I* said she put *boogers* in his food most of the time. They are handy, don't you think?" Settling back down, she stated in a normal tone, "She never told me when she did it, but I saw her do it on many occasions. I wish I had thought of it. You'd think that a man who loved food like he did would have known his wife put boogers in his food. He was very picky about what was served to him. He was always bragging about his taste buds being more important than his bowel movements but *there was* one thing he did that," she paused, "I found rather revolting."

"Do you mind telling me what it was?"

"No, I do not mind. He is dead," she paused, "One time he told her to get his bath ready. She did. She peed in the water, and I thought I would pee my pants thinking about it."

Charlie tried not to laugh, instead he smiled. "I used to put frogs in my granny's toilet when she was mean to me."

Jennifer laughed out loud. "Did it scare her or did she really laugh when you did it?"

"Oh, she laughed. She liked it. We were always pulling pranks on each other. I would have never hurt her. She used to tell me if I smiled, the world smiled with me. She would have tanned my hide if I did pranks that hurt anyone." He paused. "Would you agree?"

Again Jennifer ignored his question. "I don't like the doctors here. They don't have a sense of humor. Mama would say that they look like they have a corn cob stuck up their butts. I think they are what someone your age would call 'straight laced.' She seemed to be in her own little world, and continued, "Wouldn't life be boring if we could not have a sense of humor on our worst of days?"

Charlie grinned. "...hmm, I will have to think about that. My boss is 'straight laced.' He asked the question again. "Do you think your mama hurt your papa?"

"That depends on what your definition of hurt means," Jennifer finally replied. "Did it hurt him when she put weird stuff in his food? No. Did it hurt him when she spit in his coffee? No. Did it hurt him when she mashed up a spider and put it in his meat loaf? No, but it sure was a knee slapper! I'm not really sure what she did to him. Mama was always telling me that Papa was dumber than the dirt he ate for supper. Mama was very afraid of him most of the time, but she wouldn't have hurt a flea, and papa never hit her...that I know of, and I would know because I watched her bath in the creek many times when he refused to let her bath in the tub. She liked it, really. She sang to me."

Charlie cocked his head and stepped forward. "Jennifer," he paused, "you do know that your papa is dead, right?"

"Of course, I do," she said with a perky tone. "I *will* miss him. Do you think Mama will turn up? There are a lot of bears on this mountain. If you let me out of here right now, I could probably find her. Papa taught me how to look for animal tracks," she paused and shrugged her shoulders, "I never did hear him yell or scream. He told me never to cry when I hurt myself. He said the Woodsman's daughter should never cry. It was a sign of weakness, *but when I saw him*, I cried a teensy-weensy bit. Mama loved Papa. People should not hurt the ones they love, wouldn't you agree?"

Charlie spoke to her in a low tone and continued the questioning. "…so you did see your papa and what happened to him at the house?"

Jennifer put her hands on the metal grid and pressed her face into it. "I just don't recall, but if she didn't love him, she wouldn't have put squirrel guts in his eggs, and why waste good boogers?"

Charlie the kidder tried not to laugh, but Charlie the grandfather said with great seriousness, "Sometimes we can hurt the ones we love, *wouldn't you agree?*"

Jennifer tried not to cry. "Sometimes we kill the ones we love. Believe me, I know that. Mama always used to say to me, 'if you're going to say bad things to the people you love," she took a deep breath, "you had better be prepared for what comes your way, but the one thing that was surely engraved in my brain was this, 'One must be so very careful as to what comes out of their mouth for it may cause them to lose their head.'

"Can you explain what she might have meant by that?"

"…I will try," she paused, "Well, Mama was expecting, and I was very excited about it, but Papa was not," she smirked, "as if he had nothing to do with it, right? He kept on trying, he kept on trying…"

"What do you mean by, 'he kept on trying?" Charlie asked.

"He kept on trying to scare her, and finally it worked. I think that's when I really started to hate him. He was very mean to her. I should have done something to him about it when he was so mean to her. I did *some* things. Would you like to hear what I did, or are you just here for the cake?"

Charlie smiled and teasingly replied, "…the cake."

Jennifer smiled back and glanced at Hilda. "You have already heard this, so you can leave now. Do you mind?"

Charlie was a bit shocked at Jennifer's remark but Hilda got up and winked at him, closing the door quietly behind her. Jennifer continued. "He liked scaring her, and one day, she fell down the stone steps. Papa laughed, but I got even for Mama, and I must say, I did enjoy it."

"He laughed?"

"I don't like it when you reply with a question, alrightie-ditie?"

"Okie-dokie," he answered. "So what did you do to him to get even for your mama?"

Jennifer sat on the bed and leaned up against the head board. "I mashed up some maggots and put them in his oatmeal. You would be amazed at how well they blend in with oatmeal and I really think there must have been something terribly wrong with his taste buds." She paused. "Mama lost the baby a few days later. Papa told me to go for a walk right after it happened. I didn't want to go." Another subject change. "Did you know if you sprinkle dead ants on meatloaf they look just like pepper?"

"No, I didn't, but then again…I don't like meatloaf. Did you go for the walk?"

"Yes, and you're doing it again," she replied. "I started getting headaches. I don't like it when people yell. Say, would you mind getting me a soda?"

"Sure," he replied. Don't you go anywhere, ya here?"

Jennifer stared straight ahead, as if he was not even there in the room with her and whispered, "…one must be so very careful as to what…." Then as if someone had pinched her, she looked at Charlie and asked him, "Are you going or do I have to get the soda?"

"I'm going. You can be very bossy, ya know?"

Jennifer grinned. "Yes, I know."

Chapter nine

Charlie came back in the room and handed Jennifer the soda. "I hope you like rootbeer. It seems they frown on giving chips to kids in here. You're right. They are tight- asses."

"You're amazing, Detective! How did you know I love root beer?"

"I saw the empty bottle in the trash by your bed." He looked at her and asked, "Jennifer, did you see the baby?"

"Yes," she responded simply.

"Was it wrapped up in something?"

"Yes."

"Can you tell me what it was wrapped up in? What did you do with it?"

"I didn't do anything with it. Funny you should ask, though. It was wrapped up in the funny papers. Some kind of sick joke, huh? I'm not real sure about anything. 'Some kind of sick joke, huh?' I think that's what she said." She sighed deeply. "And I didn't do anything with the baby. Everything seemed to get blurry after it happened, but Mama took me to get ice cream and everything was alright. Mama served up something real special for him the next night. Want to know what it was?"

Charlie was not sure what his answer should be. "When did she take you to get ice cream? I thought you said she stabbed him."

"You wouldn't be trying to trick me, would you? I didn't say that. You're not very observant for a detective man. I said I wasn't sure what she did to him, and Mama lost the baby long before she ran off into the woods."

"What did she serve up the next night?"

"She baked a crow for him and told him it was a pigeon. For city folks, it would be a squab."

"Actually, if one is a good cook and can do many things with spices, I would think he couldn't tell the difference. Did she happen to stuff it with something special, too?"

Jennifer giggled. "Now you're catching on. She stuffed it with her special recipe...wild mushrooms and maggots marinated in white wine, well, it was actually apple cider with some sugar mixed in but I pretended to have a stomach ache. He got to eat it all, and mama told me I was a very thoughtful daughter."

Charlie swallowed, clearing his throat. "How could he eat it? It had to have smelled something awful."

"Papa drank from time to time. This particular night he had a snoot full. I sat at the end of the hallway and listened to their conversation. Papa was always so nice to her when he was drinking. I think it was the only time she actually wanted to sit with him. If you look to the south of my house and down the ravine, you will see where he threw all the bottles. It always made Mama so mad. I never understood how Papa could be so particular about the housekeeping and do that. What do you think?"

"I think he did it just to be mean to your mama. Jennifer, did you have anything to do with your papa's death?"

"No, and Mama did not kill Papa, either."

"That isn't what I asked you. Did you have anything to do with it?"

"I will have to plead the fifty on that one," she said cheerfully. "Isn't it time for cake yet?"

Charlie chuckled, "It's the fifth, Jennifer. You don't have to answer any of these questions. I will leave if you want me to."

She stood up and reached for him. "NO! Please don't go! He may come back and make me go out in the rain! And besides," her tone turned almost flirtations, "Who will help me at the cake?"

"Jennifer, honey, did you see who killed your papa?"

Before he knew it, Jennifer wrapped her arms around his neck and began to sob. "Well, of course I did, but it was a joke! I did it to humor Mama. She was always telling me she wondered what his head would look like hanging over the mantel. Funny, don't you think? My mama wouldn't hurt a flea, and how the heck could I possibly put his head on the mantel? So Detective Boltz...have you come to a decision about who caused the loss of my father's head?"

Tears fell like giant oval diamonds from her eyes and Charlie became the grandfather, not the detective. "No, honey, I have not, and I am sorry for the loss of your father, and I truly, truly hope that your mama is found and you will be reunited with her very soon."

~

For a few seconds he was in the past. His precious granddaughters had just been brought to him at two o'clock in the morning. He opened the door and almost cursed at the young officer. "Who the hell wants a busted lip? It's two o'clock in the morning!" It was Officer Daniel Storm, and there in front of him were Laura and Emily. "Hey, Granddaddy! Mama ran off again." Laura said joyfully. "Can we stay with you? Can we have waffles in the morning and listen to the radio all night long? Can I sleep on the sofa? Will you promise not to have gas?"

Charlie held in the laughter. "Yes, you two can stay with me forever, and you can have waffles and listen to the radio, but not all night long. I will sleep on the sofa, and, no, I can't promise you that I won't have gas."

Emily giggled. "Goodie! It makes me laugh!" Laura groaned, "It makes my nose hurt!"

The young officer handed him one small suitcase. "This is all I could round up for now. The boss said you knew the particulars and told me to bring them to you. Sorry to disrupt your sleep. You sure have some special grandkids."

The young officer motioned for the female officer to step forward. She escorted the young girls into his home and then the young officer whispered something to Charlie. "Step out here for a sec, Detective, sir…please."

Charlie's heart started to pound. He whispered, "God, what now! Is she dead?"

The young officer answered, "No, sir, but the boyfriend is. Angie, your daughter, is in the hospital. I'm so sorry to have to tell you this… she most likely will not make it. He messed her up pretty bad. I understand that it's been a real struggle with your daughter. Here's the number for the nurses' station. It seems she and her boyfriend left the poor kids for two days. The older girl fended for the both of them until she finally got up the nerve to make a break to the neighbor's house. She's a very brave girl."

Charlie stared blankly at the officer. "…I should have been there. Do you know any of the particulars?"

"Well, apparently the boyfriend needed a fix and threatened to hurt the kids if she didn't go with him, and, well, I think he forced it on her afterwards. Laura, is she the older one?"

"Yes."

"Well, apparently she kept the little one hidden while it was going on. She is one brave young lady. The doc didn't seem to think your daughter took the drugs on her own. She was tied up to a radiator, both hands behind her back. I'm so sorry, sir. I wish I could have been there to stop it."

Charlie cleared his throat and started to walk away as he replied, "Thank you. I will take it from here. I knew it was only a matter of time. There will be no red tape on this mess. I tried 'til I was blue in the face to get custody of them, and this time I will. God help the bureaucrats if they mess with me this time or I'll shove their red tape up their collective asses."

"Yes, sir, I understand."

The young officer reached for Charlie's arm and said to him, "Hey, I'm not married, but I can go get something for them if you need me to. Just let me know, and I'll be on it."

Charlie smiled and said, "What's your first name, Officer?"

"You, sir, can call me Chaser."

~

Charlie blinked and was still cradling Jennifer's head on his chest. "Are you trying to tell me that you were the one that hurt your papa?"

She sniffled. "I'm not sure. I think I was there, but as I look back it could have been Mama that did it. Mama used to tell me when you're busy doing several things at once, things tend to run together. Do you think I'm nutty as a fruit cake?" The word cake reminded her and she straightened up, "When do I get my birthday cake?" She returned to her bed. "Hey, is it true that when people are under a lot of stress that something called adrelolum makes them have the strength of an elephant?"

Charlie realized Hilda was hovering over him. She whispered to Jennifer. "Yes, honey, there have been stories about it. And the word is 'adrenalin'."

Hilda smiled and pointed to the door.

Charlie nodded. "Let me just get my coat. I don't know what to think about all of this. I want to thank you for answering my questions, Jennifer, and if you don't get your cake, let me know. I'll take care of it." Hilda handed Jennifer the present Charlie had brought with him, "I think this is what you wanted." Jennifer took it, unwrapped it, and with great joy she yelled, "Finally...he came through...finally!"

Jennifer glared at Charlie. "Well, if you're going to flash your badge around, then make it happen, at least get some presents, too! Okay?"

He grinned. "I'll see what I can do, but I can't promise you anything. One more question, okie-dokie? What happened to the baby?"

Hilda sat down and nodded to Jennifer.

"What baby?" Jennifer asked.

He stared at her blankly, and then asked, "You don't remember the baby?"

"Are you done asking your questions? I have to use the toilet, and it's almost dinner time. I swear, if they serve me mac and cheese, I will surely throw up right on this floor!"

"By all means, use the toilet," he said. "I'll wait right here." When Jennifer left the room, he turned and asked her protective nurse. "Hilda, is she going to get a cake? The kid needs a cake."

He stood there for a moment and then heard Jennifer humming. "The kid is humming. What kid hums after what she's been through?"

Hilda put her hand on his shoulder. "The cake is on the way. Want to stay and have a piece? And there will be presents. Besides, I thought you wanted to speak with her aunt."

Jennifer came out and sat on the bed. "I don't recall anything else." Without warning she looked at him as though she had never seen him. "Who are you mister, and where is that fat lady who takes care of me? I want my aunt! Where's my cake? What does a fruit cake have to do to get some damn cake around here?" Her head turned in a manner that looked somewhat mechanical. "Hey, you look familiar. Are you the guy who is going to look for my mama? Are they going to serve that yucky macaroni and cheese again? I won't eat it. None of us will eat it. We hate it. I'll throw it right out the window. Excuse me, but do you think I could get room service? You have to go now. Sorry, but I really must get ready for the party."

Charlie headed for the door. Hilda went first and waited. Charlie spoke quietly. "I think I may have caused more problems, Hilda. She doesn't know who I am, and she wants her aunt. Is she on any drugs?"

"The aunt or Jennifer?" Hilda asked.

He gave her a stare and replied, "…Jennifer."

"Jennifer is not on any kind of medications—yet. If you want to see her aunt, she just left the arboretum. You can probably catch her. Could be she might want to talk, too. I have the feeling the two of you have some reminiscing to do."

"Do you have psychic abilities?" Charlie asked as he quickly went down the corridor as he saw the aunt go out the clinic door.

"Excuse me, m'am?" he said slowly.

Callie turned around. "You used to call me 'Flower Bird.' What's up, Doc?"

Charlie looked her up and down. He was dumbfounded. "Flower Bird, is that you, Callie? I had no idea you were the aunt! What's going on around here? Do you run this place?"

"I am on the Board of Trustees, and I do have some pull. My last name is McDermott now," she looked him up and down, "Nice get-up, Moonstone. The coat is too small for you, though," she said politely. "How have you been?"

Charlie realized he had walked out with the doctor's coat on. He looked around for a security guard. "Do you have a few minutes to spare for an old man who really is dumbfounded by seeing you after all these years?"

She smiled again. "It hasn't been that long, Charlie. You look pretty good for an 'old man.' It must be the mountain air."

"If pushing fifty some years is over the hill, well, I guess I had better put a down payment on a plot."

They sat down on a wooden bench overlooking a small flower garden. Charlie shook his head and smiled pleasantly at Callie. "What happened to you? What happened to us? I left for the war, and you left this mountain."

"Do you mean what happened to me in the sense that I look like an old bag, or do you mean what happened to me after our torrid love affair?"

Charlie pulled out a stick of gum. "Want a piece?" She took one. "First, you look really good, so forget the 'old bag' talk. Next, I thought you ran off to the Orient the second time around and I never thought our love affair was torrid. It was the best thing that ever happened to me." There was a pause. "So, what happened to you? Got any kids? Break any more hearts? Is there a hubby at home waiting for you to make him pancakes? There must be, because your last name used to be Swenson or was it always Thorpe?"

"It was Swenson for a while. I never did like the idea of taking the Thorpe name." She rested her hand on his. "Oh, Charlie, people pass in the night—you know their canoes go bump and sometimes they end up on the wrong river, but I was one of the lucky ones."

"Yeah, you were smart enough to leave this hole in this mountain."

She looked at him lovingly. "And then I came back. I was lucky enough to find you among all those guys who never gave a hoot about me, and you were the one who made me realize it wasn't all about having wild sex and drinking cheap beer."

He grinned. "It wasn't? I kind of liked the cheap sex and drinking wild beer."

She giggled. "Always the funny man. And you can still screw up a sentence! Now, answer the rest of *my* questions."

"I would never have expected you to marry a cattle man."

"Life happened to me, Charlie. To make a long story short, I only broke your heart that I know of, I got lost in a dairy, there's no husband to speak of for now, and there aren't any kids." She sensed his discomfort. "You're the reason I'm the person I am today. Now, don't get me wrong! I still braid my hair and put feathers in it, but you helped me grow up and find my dream."

He chuckled. "Your dream was to be a dairy maid? I sure didn't know that! Is it true what they say about dairy maids?"

"Are you referring to a roll in the hay or the ability to milk two cows at once?" They both laughed. "No, silly. Family ended up being what it was all about. I thought this mountain was my enemy. I thought that beyond all those big hills there was gold at the end of the rainbow. Then one day I ran into…"

"Me! And you broke my heart," he finished. "Why the heck didn't you answer my letters? I must have written you a thousand."

"Nine hundred and eighty-eight," she said. "I was in love with the era, Charlie, but I did love you, too. You had to know that! But our sight was clouded by one night stands and too many jugs of the local moonshine. A lot changed."

"Yeah, no kidding. You have a niece suspected of killing her father, and her mother is nowhere to be found. I didn't even know you had a sister! What's going on, Callie?"

"It's a long story."

"I'm still on the clock unless you want to tell me over a bottle of chardonnay."

"Well, your tastes have changed over the years. Don't you like cheap beer anymore?"

He ignored her question about the cheap beer and said nothing.

Callie stared off into the wilderness. "How is Linda?"

He turned his head. "Linda passed…"

"Oh, I didn't know! I would have come to the funeral. I don't recall reading anything about her dying. I'm so sorry."

Charlie grinned at her. It was that same old grin he would throw her way over twenty years ago when he was pulling her leg. Callie put her hands on her hips. "She's not dead, is she? God will get you for that! Are you divorced? Any kids?"

Charlie ran his hand across his thinning hair. "Sorry, couldn't resist. There was a daughter but she died sometime ago. Linda is not dead, but our life together is. I caught her dancing in the moonlight with our neighbor of ten years. She passed by the house last month and waved. Oh, she's a good old girl. I hope she's happy, and I have two lovely granddaughters. She sees the girls regularly. To be honest, I wasn't a very good husband."

"Did you step out on her?"

"Heck no! I thought the world would come to an end when you and I parted our separate ways. I almost became celibate and ran off from everything that resembled these mountains. I found myself in a very dark place. I loved you. You broke my heart. Linda was my hand up out of Shallow Grave. We had a daughter who gave us two beautiful grandkids—both in college. One is still trying to find Mr. Right, and the older one wants to conquer Mount Everest."

"No chance of reconciliation with Linda?" Callie asked.

"No chance. I was always faithful to her, and if it hadn't been that she let the bastard use my mower, I would have let her come back. But I loved that mower. A wife shouldn't try to separate a man from his mower."

"Didn't he give it back?"

"Yep, and I burned it."

Callie slapped her knee. "You haven't changed a bit!"

They shared a good laugh, and then Charlie settled back into detective mode. "I'm more than curious how your niece ended up here. How'd you end up with being connected to this place?"

She stared again into the wilderness. "It has been one of Thorpe's properties for a long time. I even worked here for a while. Yes, I have connections." She looked back at him. "So, how did you end up on this case?"

"I was hoping you could tell me." Callie maintained eye contact but didn't respond. "I thought it got passed down to the last man on the totem pole. Maybe somebody in the office thought I needed it for a good send off. It's my job. I need to put a few more years under my belt before I can get a pension. That extra dollar ninety-nine in my pension check will pay for fishing lures! Take your pick." Callie smiled; Charlie relaxed. "Back to the question at hand, Callie. What's going on with that niece of yours? The poor child doesn't know what happened in that house from a hole in the ground."

"Oh, she'll come around. I don't have to explain anything to you, do I? I had to pull her down off the ceiling when I arrived. I'm taking her out of here tomorrow. I'll not let them make a guinea pig out of her. Her bump will heal, but I'm not so sure about what's inside. She was literally hanging off the ceiling fan! Where the hell were the doctors? If I hadn't come in, she could have been killed! The toilet had overflowed, and it seemed she didn't like getting her feet wet. She gets absolutely terrified of the rain at times. I can get it all straightened out. She doesn't belong in here. I'm sure Jennifer had nothing to do with her father's death. She was in a terrible state when she was found. Want to know what she was doing up there?"

"Oh, I don't know…dusting the fan blades maybe." Callie shot him a dirty look. "Who found her?"

"Didn't they tell you?"

"No, I didn't ask, and 'they' wouldn't like me and what I have to say about a child being in a place like this. Now I'm asking you. First, how can you be so sure she didn't have anything to do with it? From what I saw at the home, her papa was a real prize. How did they get along?"

"Charlie, if there was one thing that you could say about me when I die, what would it be?

"You can make a pretty mean lasagna."

"Seriously, Charlie."

"Okay, you *never* lied to me, ever."

"I know she didn't have anything to do with Thomas' death because *I know her.* She's definitely affected, but she's not at fault. I've got her away from there, and I'll get her out of here, too. Thomas was so mean to Eileen most of the time, and the rest of the time he was just plain cruel. I hated him and he knew it; now, you know it, so does that make me a suspect? Did I want him dead? Yes, many times. Did I ever consider hiring someone to kill him? Yes, but I did not. Did I have anything to do with his death? No, I did not."

Charlie decided not to pursue any farther. "Where was Hilda when she was hanging off the fan?"

"Don't start on Hilda! Hilda has been a God-send. She's coming with Jennifer when she's released."

"So, that's what she meant by her comment about retiring. I would love to retire." He concluded wistfully.

"Can you believe it? A pile of red tape to deal with and the woman hasn't had a raise in five years! I can pay her what she's worth. I can't take care of Jennifer and the dairy, too. You'd think with all the money that has been poured into this place, they could give that woman a raise."

"No hubby at home to help, right? What's going on with him?"

"He passed, too," she said and turned her head.

"Sorry, I didn't hear…"

Callie turned her head back and grinned at Charlie. "Gotcha!"

Charlie rolled his eyes. "Seriously, Callie, where is he?"

"He ran off with the milk maid four years ago," she said with glee. "I didn't burn the cow, though, but I sure as hell burned our past."

"So, you're running the dairy all by yourself?"

"Heck, no! I do the books, and I get a hefty check every month from my inheritance. I don't intend on marrying again, so don't get any ideas, Charlie 'Moonstone' Holtz."

"How come you never told me you were part of the Thorpe family? Are you Eileen's sister or are you Thomas Martin's aunt?"

"Now you are getting serious," she said with a straight face. "I would have hung myself if I had to be part of his family tree! What an idiot! He had more kinks in his brain than any psycho could ever dream of. He should have been put in here a long time ago. When you have time, I'll tell you about some of the things he did. And just for your information, I was adopted, but I never took the Thorpe name, not on paper. Eileen carried all the pain with having the Thorpe name. Being adopted was entirely Mama's idea. Papa never had anything to do with me. I was not attached to his family tree. I was adopted by her, not him. Eileen was always good to me, and that's why I intend doing right by Jennifer. Eileen had a good heart, and she was smart, too. She read all the time and loved to hike. He deserved to die for the things he did to her."

"If I didn't know you better I might say you would make a good suspect. Jennifer tells me her mama used to put boogers in his food."

"Me? Suspect? Do what you must, Charlie, but if he had done those things to me, I would have put something more substantial than boogers in his food. He'd be dead from arsenic!" she paused, "I knew she put stuff in his food. It was her way of keeping her sanity. She did not kill her husband. She was terrified of him. She used to tell me from time to time as long as she was able to stir up a few good bugs in his food without him knowing it, well, laughter kept her going."

Charlie shrugged his shoulders. "I have to be serious right now. It's my job. I need to find out what happened in that house. Jennifer tells me she thinks she may have killed him, and then she tells me she doesn't know me, and then…"

Callie quickly put her finger to his lips. "Oh, that I can't explain. But I *am* her mama's sister, and before you ask, I ain't hurting for money, either, so Jennifer's money is safe. I don't get a dime of Eileen's money. I don't need it, nor do I want it. But let it be known, I will not let them make a pin-cushion out of that child! I'll answer any of your questions. This place needs a lot of fixing up, and a fat check goes a long way to accommodate an empty bed."

"Oh, I wasn't inferring that you were up to something! Jeez! Did I imply that?"

"It's been a long time, hon. You don't owe me anything. I don't owe you anything. Eileen had a fancy document written up if anything was to happen to her. She sure as hell wouldn't have left Jennifer in his care. I had sole custody if anything happened to Eileen. He didn't love that child at all. Jennifer will be taken care of. I'm her legal guardian. There is one thing that really bothers me, though."

"What's that?"

"Eileen is still out there, and I don't think anyone will ever know what happened to her. What if…"

"How could you know that?"

"Eileen told me if she ever cracked, she would never come back to that house. Oh, I tried to get her to leave him, and I almost had her convinced, but she got pregnant again. She was mistreated by him, but he never laid a hand on her. Isn't that the most peculiar thing about it all? He was just a sicko who liked to scare her with practical jokes."

Chapter ten

"So, do you want a cup of coffee?" Charlie asked.

"No," she said firmly and then grinned." I do have time for one of your famous rootbeer floats, and I could probably rustle up some burgers. My cottage is a couple of hours away from here though."

"You have a cottage? Don't you live near the dairy? Oh, please tell me you have some of that lasagna in the oven! Are you still following your rigid schedule about always having Italian on Fridays, or was it burger night I remember?"

She smiled that wonderful smile he remembered from so long ago. There were a few more lines around the eyes, and, of course, the laugh lines were more enhanced, but Callie still had that zip.

"Tell me where you live," he quipped. "I'll bring the dessert. But I gotta tell you, I don't drink and drive so if you have a spare room…"

"Goodness, here it comes," she paused, "how many years and you *still* try to wiggle your way into my bedroom!" she teased.

Charlie blushed. "I'll sleep on the couch. I'm a very restless old salt. It's just that I don't want to go back into the city for the weekend. I promise I'll be good."

~

Hilda had peeked out the window and saw them walking away in deep conversation. She turned to Jennifer. "Everything will be alright, honey. Your aunt is talking to him now. I can usually spot somebody who has a kind heart, and that man has one." Jennifer tugged on Hilda's arm and asked, "When are you coming to live with us?"

"Real soon, honey, real soon," she replied as she hugged Jennifer. "Nobody is going to hurt you as long as I'm alive. You just do what your auntie tells you and things will be alright."

"Am I still leaving the day after tomorrow? Can Mama come, too?" Jennifer asked.

"Oh, honey, your mama is around somewhere. Up on those mountains—somewhere. She'll show up eventually. Sometimes when bad things happen like it did, well; the people who know about those things have to lay low."

"And sometimes people like us don't have a clue as to what you're talking about," Jennifer replied.

Hilda kissed Jennifer on the top of her head. "I have a few people I need to tend to. Save some cake for me."

~

Callie reached for him. He did not expect her to hug him so tightly. "What no kiss good night?" he said.

She nodded and told him where she lived. She was smart and cunning. She had him investigated in her own way. She knew Charlie Holtz was ready to retire, but he needed to work a couple of more years to get that much needed extra on his pension, but she would work on that situation, too. He had no idea how lasagna night at Callie McDermott's was going to change his life, and Callie had no idea how he was going to change her life, too. They both needed each other desperately. Two old canoers were about to set off on a most interesting journey over a slightly rough course.

No more lonely nights for Callie; no more sitting on the back stoop crying over being sorry she never answered his letters. Now he waltzed right back into her life when a crisis put everything on the line for her only niece.

Jennifer stood up and watched through the window as Charlie walked to his car. He turned and looked in the direction of Jennifer's window. Jennifer waved and threw a kiss to him. For some reason her window fogged up. He wasn't quite sure but he could swear she drew a face with her finger. It was smiling. "What kid draws a smiling face after she witnessed her father being killed?" he thought.

~

Charlie decided to go back to the Martin residence. Danny was sitting on the ledge where Jennifer had sat before she had fallen into unconsciousness. Charlie stepped down the path slowly. "I was hoping you'd still be hanging around."

"So, what did you think about the girl?" Danny asked. "Hey, did she lead you to believe that she had anything to do with it? Maybe we'll come across something this time. Got your notepad? Want a donut?"

Charlie put his hands in his pockets and to his surprise found a note in his right side jacket pocket. He pulled it out. "What do we have here?"

"…looks like a note to me," Danny replied.

"…oh, this is interesting. She gave me a note."

"Who?"

"The aunt put a note in my pocket."

"What does it say?"

Charlie read it to himself and paused before he answered, "I'm going to retire early, I think. There are too many sick people in this world, and, thank God, some of them end up on mantels."

"…is it love at first sight? So…you think the wife did it?"

Charlie paused again, "…it's the aunt's address. She has invited me for tea at her cottage but yes and no to your question. Maybe one of the victim's kin retaliated, but it's not up to me. Maybe there was a witness to his shenanigans, and the witness was very patient until he knew the asshole was home. The wife certainly could have done it. She was strong enough. Say, did you ever look around in the storage shed?"

"Yes, I did. I saw nothing suspicious," Danny looked at him strangely, "…hey, since when do you drink tea?" Charlie grinned sheepishly and replied, "Since it comes served while taking a dip in a bubble bath."

Danny shook his head. "…yeah, right, and I saw nothing that would lead me to believe the rest of his body could have been buried anywhere near the house. All the tools were in place, too, and I took a long walk around the perimeter, no undisturbed dirt, no rocks moved or dug up. No foot prints with the exception of Mr. Crockett's." Charlie motioned for Danny to follow him inside the house. He stuck the note back into his pocket and then thumbed through some papers sitting on a desk near the mantel. He glanced at the photos on the wall leading to the master bedroom. "It seems they all liked to hike, and the wife was really into it at one time. She even had her own hiking clothes initialed. Who needs their initials on hiking clothes?" He turned around and saw a chart taped to the opposite wall. "This is interesting. It's a chart that clearly dictates who was responsible for all the house whole chores." He fingered it. Danny stepped forward. "The kid's name is not on any of these chores. They are all marked as her mama's responsibility. Why would anyone insist that their, house be swept and the floors cleaned twice a day?" Charlie walked off into the dining area, "The more I find out about this 'dead head' the more I dislike him."

"Me, too and that's for sure! But who would kill the 'dead head' because he ran a tight ship? What does that have to do with his death?"

"Sometimes we miss things that have everything to do with a murder. He could have been part of it all, too, you know—the missing campers and the man who had the heart attack. The missus could have been in on it all, well, at least some of the time. Now, don't get me wrong. I think he deserved to die for what he did to her mentally, but maybe this was part of one of those husband and wife teams, you know? Comedy on tour through the Smokies and something went terribly wrong. Still—there is something I'm not seeing," he folded his arms across his chest, "I think someone cracked under the presser of seeing the wife living like a neurotic house wife." Danny smirked. "Yeah. She lost her sense of humor, and he lost his head."

Charlie grinned at Danny. "Ya know the younger I get, the older you get like me," he paused. "Well, she may have done it. I just can't see the girl having anything to do with it. Her papa had a wicked sense of humor, but little girls love their daddies no matter what. She loved her papa; yet, she told me some things that very well may incriminate him as being the prankster."

Danny looked at him pensively. "That's not your call, partner. What makes you say that unless the girl told you something? Are you holding out on me?"

Charlie shook his head. "No." he said firmly. Then he continued. "I'm retiring as soon as I can. I've had it up to here," he motioned just under his eyes, "with red tape and all the crap we have to go through to get a decent pension. It's not worth it. I'm going to enjoy my retirement with a clear conscience while I can. You got a problem with that?"

"Hey, this is Danny looking at you, old man. No need for an attitude, okay? Is the girl going to have to stay in that place?"

"No. At least, I hope not. After I saw to the girl, I spoke to her aunt. It seems the auntie and I have a past. She will see to it that the girl is well taken care of. I guarantee Jennifer Martin will not do without."

His partner gave him a hard stare. "She *will* do without her mama, it seems. Maybe she did just pick up and leave, never to return. You can identify with that, right? She has the ways and means to do anything she wants. I think she's out there somewhere. She'll show up. She has to. Mamas always come home to tend to their babies, eventually. Mama bears never leave their babies unattended for too long."

Danny put his hand on Charlie's shoulder. "Sorry, man, I didn't mean to bring up the past."

"No problem. Did I ever thank you for what you did for my grandkids?"

"Yes, many times, but it wasn't necessary. You did what you had to. Sometimes rotten things happen to good people, and all we can do is just be thankful that we were able to help out. Do the kids ever ask about her?"

"No. You do know that I trust you with my life, right?" Charlie asked.

"Sure, and the same goes from me to you, old man."

"Well, off the record, this kid's aunt is an old girlfriend of mine. It seems this old world is awful darn small. Anyway, the aunt, Callie, was the one who found her. She was the one who put the girl in the hospital, and she's the one who will take her out. Aunt Callie McDermont is rolling in dairy farm—the McDermont Dairy Farm."

"No kidding? So, Jennifer is going to live with her at the dairy farm?" Danny asked.

"I'm not real sure about any of this, but I have a dinner date with her, and I'll let you know. I am sure there is more she wants to share."

"...like her bubble bath salts? Keep me posted," Danny replied. I am going for some supper, want to come?"

Charlie shook his head. "I'll keep you posted. I have plans for dinner."

Danny waved and got in his car.

Charlie on the other hand sat in his truck for a few moments. He pulled out the note again and read it aloud.

'My dear Charlie, It seems fate has put us together again, not on a river, but on this mountain. I have thought of you often, I have dreamed of you a

lot, we have met under these circumstances for a reason. Do you believe in fate? I have never stopped loving you. Can you ever forgive me for marrying someone else? Before you ask, yes, I made sure it was you that investigated my sister's death,' he looked up and spoke out loud, *"...your sister's death?"*

He did not finish the rest of the note but drove off wishing what he was thinking was not true.

Chapter eleven

Five miles north of the Martin home someone lurched in the shadows. It was Eileen Martin. She was disoriented and desperately needed to find shelter and water. She was trying to remember which hollow tree she had put the jug of water in, and somewhere close by were canned goods tucked away in an old barrel.

From the far end of the slope she eyed a tent and started heading in the direction of the two campers who were now eyeing her. "Is that a woman?" replied the female. Is that an apron she has on? Oh, Lordy be! She's covered in blood! Quick, get the first aid kit!"

Her male companion stood up and adjusted his pajama bottoms. "…she needs a doctor! Yes, it *is* a woman. Yes, she's coming *this* way. And, yes, it *is* an apron! Forgive me for being sarcastic, but since when do they give cooking lessons in the wilderness?" His girlfriend pushed him. "Damn. She's not bad looking at all!"

"Go help her!" shouted the young woman, pushing him a second time.

"She has a knife in her hand! You go help her, and I'll get the shovel!"

"Who do you plan on burying?"

"Nobody! I *plan* on defending myself! She looks a little crazy, don't you think? Damn. It's Betty Crocker gone wild!"

"Help me! Help me!" Eileen wailed as she staggered towards them with the knife.

"Lady! Put the knife down now!" the young woman shouted.

"Are you the police?" Eileen asked as she swayed towards the young woman's direction. "Have you come to arrest me? Do you know where my daughter is? Can you please tell me where the highway is? What have you done with my daughter?"

"No, lady, we are not the police, but they are on their way!" His tent companion looked at him as *if he* was the one who was nuts, and replied, "...they are?" He glared at her.

"Sit down here. What are you doing out here? Where's your family? Are you and your children camping around here? Is someone chasing you?" He paused and looked around, "...have you seen any bears?"

Eileen blinked and then lunged at the young man. "I want my baby!! What have you done with my baby?!"

"Get away from us!" the young woman yelled. Then she whispered in the direction of her boyfriend. "How could you know the police are on their way?"

Fran stepped closer to her companion and whispered, "Ask her where she lives."

Again Eileen waved the knife around and yelled, "It's not funny that you did this to me! Why are you so cruel? Where is Jennifer?"

"Who's Jennifer?" the young man asked. Where did you come from lady?"

Eileen turned around and started crying. "I need my Jenny. What have you done with her? Thomas! I know you are out there somewhere!"

"Lady, just sit down, and we'll get you some help. Get her some water, Fran. I'll stay here, and you go get help."

Fran whispered again. "You cannot stay here with a woman wearing a blood-drenched apron. Besides where would she go?"

"Sometimes, Fran, you amaze me."

"Why?"

"Here we are with a woman who might have killed somebody and you think where can *she* go? Now, call me stupid, but she had to have come from somewhere! Look for a camper because that nightgown she has on did not come from the local thrift shop. This lady comes from money. Look at the pearls around her neck! You go look for a camper or a house. Someone will be looking for her. Somebody didn't get their coffee this morning. That's for sure!"

"You amaze me, too," Fran said calmly.

He stared at her. "Why is that?"

"She obviously killed her mate, you idiot! Nobody is looking for her! I am really sorry I came with you. I hate camping!"

"Oh, yeah!?! You're right on that point, but one of us needs to go find out where she came from!"

"We're out in the wilderness!" Fran shouted. "I'm not going to look for a dead person! There are bears on this mountain."

Fran watched Eileen step in the tent. "She's in our tent! *She's in our tent!*"

He stuck his head in very slowly and gripped their camping shovel in a defensive manner. "And now she's passed out in our tent! Let's go."

"We can't just leave her here!" Fran shouted.

"We can, and we will! Are you going to stay here with her and wait until someone comes looking for her? We can go find help. I'll wave down the first person we see."

Fran almost laughed. "...the first person you see might be the one that is trying to kill her! I think we should just go and let her family find her or the authorities. Let's grab our stuff and get out of here now! We aren't even supposed to be out here. Don't you remember the signs we saw down the road? 'Keep out,' 'Private Property,' 'Beware of the Bears,' or can't you read English?"

Fran stuck her head into the tent and looked at Eileen. "Do you suppose she will miss those pearls?"

Her boyfriend jerked his head around and stared past a huge hickory and whispered, "Hush, I think I hear a bear."

"I would rather you *hear* a bear than *see* one. At least we would know where it is."

"Sometimes, Fran, you are the dumbest female on the face of the earth."

Fran shoved the pearls in her jacket pocket, and they both ran in the direction of their vehicle. They did not look back.

Eileen Martin did not move on her own accord for eight hours. She had one puncture mark on her left buttock. The campers would not return. They were thieves, and with Eileen's pearl necklace firmly packed away in their glove compartment, they would not return to the crime scene at all.

Chapter twelve

September 19, 1955

The setting was perfect. The backdrop of the North Carolina Mountains enveloped the Woodsman's vision. Breathing in the early morning aromas of fresh baked croissants and coffee made from hand-ground beans the Woodsman sighed and stretched. "Never underestimate the usefulness of anyone who knows their way around the kitchen," the Woodsman whispered. "I am such a lucky person. This, and lunch, too! It's perfect."

The trespassers were being watched. They were oblivious to their surroundings and who was doing the watching as the female pulled up her skirt to use the woodland "facilities."

It was obvious the female was pregnant. The husband was not attentive at all to the mother-to-be as he fumbled through the back end of the pickup truck. "Where are the tent sticks? Where's the hammer? I thought I made myself clear that you were to put all the things we needed in a sack."

The Woodsman sighed. "Oh, please, do not make that her responsibility. It will be unfortunate for you if you do something unacceptable in my line of sight," the camouflaged silhouette whispered.

A hand with manicured fingernails pulled back the string on the bow. A gold bracelet shimmered in the sunlight. The quiver lay on the ground. The Woodsman pondered the next move.

The Woodsman popped another piece of Juicy Fruit gum and crouched down. It would have been so easy to drop Paulie right where he stood, but then the mother-to-be would have to be consoled. It would be very inconvenient at this time and place, and the Woodsman was not prepared for a grief seminar. Besides, the Woodsman hated whiners.

The discreet figure fumbled around for a few seconds before pulling out the binoculars. "Please be nice to the little lady. I don't want to be late for dinner. Leftovers are not my cup of tea."

Molly Driggers had never been terribly excited about camping, but, unfortunately, it was their way of life. Although the place he chose was only a mere fifty yards from their pop-up camper, the scenery was breathtaking, and if it was just him, Paulie Driggers would live right where he was, forever.

The camper had to make do for now. It was all they could afford. It was Molly's second trimester, and she was still having bouts of morning sickness, but her husband, Paulie, had convinced her that the only choice she had was his decision. The mornings had already begun to feel 'crisp' and Molly wondered if she would ever see the light at the end of her tunnel. She loved Paulie more than anything. He loved her, too, but the one and only reason they were there was to hide from Frankie Fuller, Molly's father—a backward, loud-mouthed, abusive, tobacco chewing, Saturday night bather and prankster, all wrapped up into one big pile of body odor and a stained tee-shirt and a sweaty crotch.

The Woodsman stood up and stretched. The camouflage worked well with the backdrop of the North Carolina woods. The Woodsman's stature blended in with the surroundings. "Crap! Now *I* have to pee." The urine soaked the camouflage pants of the silhouetted figure, and the "want-to-be" parent tried to wipe the tears away. "Pathetic bladder. If I hadn't lifted all those losers. Oh, well, some people just don't deserve to be parents."

A little voice whispered in the Woodsman's ear, "Give the guy a chance. There are not all idiots and losers."

The Woodsman's stomach growled. Putting down the bow, the Woodsman set the quiver of arrows up against the tree. Opening the lunch box again was a mistake. The aroma of the tuna salad drifted through the Woodsman nostrils. "What a wonderful chef," the Woodsman replied. "...always packs more than enough." The Woodsman's saliva glands went into full overdrive at the thought of the home baked bread that encompassed the tuna. The Woodsman's better half had made an extra effort this particular morning while preparing lunch, the "optimal snack" as it was called. Not only was it tuna salad, but it had almonds and plump raisins mixed in. Yum, a favorite. Oh, how the Woodsman loved the attention to detail.

The coffee was great, but as the Woodsman swallowed the last bite of tuna salad, a thought came to mind… 'Trying harder not to give the cook such a hard time might be something worth while.' After all, being a gourmet cook and replacing that expertise would be difficult if the chef really got ticked off. "Silly," the Woodsman thought. "My chef would simply die if there were no one to cook for, literally."

Then the Woodsman's body jerked a little. "Sure, right." The tiny white pill started to dissolve slowly under the Woodsman's tongue. The Woodsman had gotten use to the bitter after taste, but as always there was a home made sugary treat, a sugar cookie dipped in Belgian chocolate. "Yummy," the Woodsman whispered.

~

Paulie sighed. "This will be the third time you had to pee in the last thirty minutes. Maybe you have one of those infections. I don't have the money to take you to the doctor again."

"Maybe I just have to pee because I'm pregnant," Molly snipped at him. "Do we have enough money to buy a used foam pad?"

He looked at her with his "look" and then frowned and replied, "Well, no, right now it seems that we only have enough money for food and water."

He looked like he was about to make a gesture that the Woodsman was so familiar with, and thought, "Oh, please do not do what I think you are about to do. It would be unhealthy for any future Driggers."

The Woodsman raised the bow and waited. The Woodsman did not say or do anything. The Woodsman's blood pressure dropped to normal.

Molly sighed and rubbed her stomach. "You know my back hurts. Maybe we can slip by Mama's and borrow one," she paused, "he won't be there."

Molly hoped he would give in to her this one time. She missed her mama's wisdom, but she did not miss her hateful papa.

His head shook slowly as he said sternly, "You know that's not possible, so please, Molly. Don't mention it again. Maybe I can get some overtime, but that would mean you're here at night by yourself, and you know I don't like to do that. The thought of some maniac finding you is something I couldn't live with. Remember the stories we heard about? Somewhere out here is a lunatic!" She pointed towards the pop-up camper. "I got my pistol and you know I can shoot real straight, besides, I ain't afraid when you're not here."

He reached into the back of his beat up truck and pulled out the rolled up foam pad and threw it on the ground. "Thought you had me, huh? I bought it at the thrift shop. Two bucks! Ain't that a deal? Oh, I swear, Molly, I will make it up to you!"

"You're the best, Paulie!" Molly answered obviously elated.

He smiled and reached for her.

The Woodsman smiled and adjusted the quiver. "Good man. Good answer. Today you will not die."

Paulie pushed aside the rumpled sleeping bag. "Did you remember to put the ice in the chest and chill down my beer?"

The Woodsman smiled and pulled out an arrow again. "Too good to be true and here it comes! Maybe this morning won't be a waste of time after all. Here the two of them are, in the wilderness and not a pot to piss in nor one to throw it out of, and *he* has to have his *beer*."

Molly looked at him with her "look" and frowned, saying, "No, I didn't. I thought we would make do with water and lemonade, but I did make biscuits. And I didn't forget the homemade jam!"

"Molly, honey, what are we going to do with biscuits and honey?"

The Woodsman frowned. "*Eat them* you idiot. Here it comes."

He stared at her blankly and said, "You're kidding right? It's the one day I don't work, and you forgot to ice down my beer. Do you think biscuits are going to make up for it?" he paused and looked at her strangely. "When did you find time to make biscuits and how did you cook them? I thought we were out of flour, well, I suppose I can make a fire."

Molly hated lying to him. "…I think there are some matches in the …"

It was more of a question than a statement.

"Molly, I asked you a question. Where did you get the biscuits? Was your mama here?"

The Woodsman spit towards the family picnic and sighed. "You don't need any stinking matches, mister."

Molly giggled. "I put them in the glove compartment. Did you get me some ginger ale?"

Paulie put his hand on her shoulder. "Where did you get the biscuits?" She rubbed her lower back. "...someone left them for me, *us*. I forgot to tell you. Sorry. I was going to tell you."

He started digging through the chest. "You can't be serious, Molly! You really expect me to believe a stranger left us some biscuits," he pondered for a moment, "it's alright if your mama left them, but it is best we move on. I cannot take a chance that your papa will find us! I know I can take him on if he shows up but what if he shows up at night? And I ain't here?"

Molly started to whimper. "Please, don't yell at me again."

"I ain't yelling."

He walked over to her in a robot-like fashion and hugged her tenderly. "Sorry, I wanted to cut back anyway. Shall I get the tablecloth?"

"No table, you idiot," thought the Woodsman. "But attitude speaks volumes. Please do not push your luck, Paulie."

Again the Woodsman crouched behind the large cypress and whispered. "Yes, please do not yell at her again. I have a dinner engagement later, and I really don't have the time to skin you alive."

Chapter thirteen

The Woodsman was not a man at all.

Jennifer had taken up the hobby of hiking long ago with her father, but for the past fifteen years it had been her "silent" passion. She paid particular attention to her skin. She never let herself get sunburned. Her better half loved her flawless skin and she loved how 'it' teased him. He was obsessed with her beauty but she was not, still she had always taken great pride in how she looked to others.

Thick black eyelashes surrounded her beautiful eyes, and the natural beauty of her hair accentuated her oval shaped face. Her hair was pulled back in a tight bun surrounded by a few feathers, a trait that her mama had passed down to her. From time to time she did have her nails done, but they were never painted 'harlot red.' She kept all things simple when it came to the care of her skin, and she always smelled like lavender or mint somewhere on her body.

There were times that she was gone for days and no one knew or cared. She liked it that way. She liked the solitude and the quiet beauty of her private domain. She liked the fact that she didn't have to cook or clean. Her husband did it all. She paused for a moment and remembered the times when she lived in the house near the dairy. Things were simple then. She gladly did her share of the chores.

With the help of Hilda, Callie had made her childhood dreams come true. Childhood dreams in the form of ongoing nightmares calmed by drugs allocated through illegal channels, yet made tolerable. Home schooling had started at eleven years of age, then college breezed through her life and she excelled, graduating at twenty, and then she decided that city life was not her forte. She landed a job at a psychiatric hospital which is where she met her husband, and life was good, so she thought.

She smiled when she pictured Hilda in the kitchen whipping up her famous waffles. Life was so very simple then, but now, well, life was good, not simple, but just the way she wanted it. She did as she pleased. She had never had to work at all, but she did. Her inheritance was tucked away and she only used it when she deemed necessary. She would be the first to tell anyone that she enjoyed the better things in life, but the simplicity of the mountains was more than she needed.

It had been almost fifteen years since the death of Thomas Martin, her father, and not much had changed as far as the landscape of the Thorpe/Martin property. Of course, the trees were taller. The new and improved "NO TRESPASSING" signs should have taken care of any nosey two-legged varmints, but Paulie Driggers and his young wife had been living in an abandoned cabin not too far from Shallow Grave, and their second home, a pop-up camper was more than they needed. It was the one place Paulie knew Molly's father would not find them. At least he hoped so. He had been going from town to town for over six months hoping that his father-in-law would tire of looking for them, but so far, he had not. Frankie Fuller had made it known if he found Paulie and Molly together, he would castrate him and bring Molly home where she belonged.

Paulie and Molly were in love, and Molly was very pregnant. They collected their water from a nearby creek and had stockpiled supplies for six months in anticipation of the baby. Right now, all they needed was each other. Paulie had one true friend who helped him once in a while. Molly's family would have helped, but they had decided not to tell her family where they were, at least for now. Frankie Fuller had made Molly's life a living hell. He truly believed that Molly was his property and anything coming out of her was his property, too.

Unknown to them, however, someone had been watching them for some time. They were still being watched. An occasional basket of treats were left from time to time. Molly was always the one who found them, it was planned that way. She especially liked the honey comb and the muffins drizzled in caramel and there was always a jug of milk sitting in a nearby bucket with ice. She believed in angels.

The Woodsman had been keeping vigil over the young couple for more than four months. The Woodsman had even left Molly little treats and, up to now, Molly had not told her husband about it. The last "treat" was a box of baby formula with a note attached and of course, the wonderful biscuits. Molly had made Paulie believe that she stretched every penny she could. The Woodsman had told the cook they were for the ladies auxiliary's annual fund raiser. It displeased her to have to lie, but it pleased him to be doing something for a good cause.

Molly looked at the note again, *'You'll need a lot of this. I could baby-sit once in a while.'*

When Molly showed the note to her husband he was obviously distressed. "How long has this been going on, Molly?" he asked, with obvious agitation.

"For about two, maybe three months," she replied shyly. "What's the harm?"

"The harm is that it could be someone hired by your papa to find us! Did you ever think of that? The harm is that it could be the lunatic trying to get on your good side! What does he look like?"

"I never saw him. I believe it is an angel sent here to look after the baby. I think it's somebody who is just being nice and wants to help. You know, like a guardian angel."

"Honey, there are no guardian angels out here in this wilderness. Please, don't take anything else. Now we have to leave because of this."

She started crying. "No! I like it here! We have shelter, and it's never too hot or too cold. I love the flowers and the creek. I want to stay because it is not that far from my Mama if I need her when the baby comes!"

"Molly, it's going to get very cold once winter hits this mountain. Up to now, we have been fine, but I've got to tell you I'm a little nervous about the baby coming. What if you have problems? What if the baby decides to come early?"

"Everything will be alright," she said softly. "Maybe Papa will change his mind about you and we can go home."

"No!" Paulie almost shouted in reply. "I will never put one foot in his house again after the way he treated you and your mama. Jesus! Have you forgotten the things he did to your Mama," he paused, "if not her, how can you forget him making you eat rotten eggs, or how about the time he refused to let you in the house when it was colder than a well-diggers butt! You almost died! I should have killed him myself!"

"…please don't yell. I forgive him! He didn't mean any of it." Molly shot back. "And besides, we don't have to worry about anything when the baby comes. I have all the diapers we could possibly need. The guardian angel has taken care of all those things. If this person was evil, don't you think he would have done something by now? I ain't afraid to stay here by myself, and I know things will get better for us. I have faith in you Paulie."

He looked away and began speaking to her very softly. *"He meant it Molly.* You forgive him and I cannot, but for you, I will try." Paulie started to open the door to the truck. "He meant it. He's a hateful, vindictive man, and if I never see Frankie Fuller's face again, it will be too soon! If he ever puts his ugly face within one foot of you, I will skin him alive! Why does your mama put up with his antics? His practical jokes cause nothing but harm. He is and always will be a son-of-a-bitch. You cannot be so stupid as to think he did not mean all those things he did to your mama!"

"Stop it! Please!" she cried.

"Aw, Molly, honey, don't cry. I hate it when you cry. I tell you what—I'll call Maggie and see if everything is alright with your mama. Would you like that? And maybe you, and them can meet up somewhere. Okay? We'll have one of those out-of-the-way picnics. Maybe if you leave a note for the guardian angel he can bring some fried chicken and home-made ice-cream." Molly did not smile. "Now, you're making fun." He reached for her, "…I was serious about the picnic though, and you got to admit having some fried chicken and all the fixings would be wonderful!"

Jennifer Martin Carter stepped back into the shadows and took a deep breath. "Interesting," she thought. I will have to give Mr. Frankie Fuller some of my time."

~

Frankie Fuller owned the local concrete company. He had his hand in everybody's business that needed a handout. Only, he didn't hand out anything for free. Everything came with a price. For as long as he and his wife had been married, Frankie Fuller had beaten his wife and verbally abused his daughters. Molly always got the worst of it. He knew he could get away with it because he had done favors for the people that counted—the sheriff.

Margery Fuller was his faithful wife of forty years, but Frankie was never faithful to her. He lived comfortably, and yet she still had nothing to make her life better. He would say to her, "You owe me, little lady, for pulling you out of that heap your papa called a home," and then he would slap her around. He also liked pulling practical jokes on her, really cruel jokes that caused great pain and tears for Margery. He had gotten away with it for too long.

Jennifer sat back and closed her eyes. She hoped Paulie would continue on about Frankie Fuller's rants. He did. "Molly, honey, I am sorry I didn't get you out of that hell hole sooner," he rubbed her back tenderly, "but I am thankful you stayed for your mama. To the day I die," he paused, "to the day I die, I will never understand how a man can treat a woman like your mama so poorly."

Molly wiped away the tears. "...I just wish I had been strong enough to stop him from doing some of the cruel tricks he played on her. I should have done something...I feel like I let her down."

Jennifer's ears perked up. "...tricks? Tell me more."

Paulie continued. "Have you forgotten about the time he tied your mama to a tree 'cause she burned his supper?"

Molly sniffled out only three words. "I tried...too."

He threw his arms up in the air. "And, oh, how about the time he held her hand down on the burner 'cause she forgot to pay his fine for..." he paused, "...what was the fine for?"

She sniffled out two words. "...drunken disorderness."

Jennifer picked up a twig and snapped it in half. "...bingo."

Frankie Fuller's life as he knew it was about to come to a halt, but first she would have to put in an order for fried chicken, home made ice cream and all the fixings.

~

Jennifer found her way back to her vehicle and changed out of her 'woodsman's' outfit. She decided to take a short cut that would bring her right past the quaint little office of the local 'fortune teller and town gossip.'

Jennifer couldn't help pause to look at the sign posted to the left of the door, 'Maggie tells no lies, cash only.'

Jennifer opened the door slowly and quickly adjusted her wig. Maggie Fuller Jones had her feet propped up on her desk eating a bag of potato chips. She quickly sat back up and put on her glasses. "... mornin', may I help you?"

In a very southern accent Jennifer answered, "Yes. My name is Rosemary Goodman, and I was wondering if you could point me in the direction of Fuller's Concrete? Is that an Avon scent you have on? It is wonderful, and I simply *adore* what you've done with the angels! Do you do your own hair?"

Maggie spun around and looked at her collection of angels on the wall. "Oh, thank you, honey. It's just something my husband picks up for me on my birthdays, holidays, special occasions—you know! Are you an angel lover?" She paused and looked at Jennifer carefully. "Are you sure you want directions to his place, honey?"

Jennifer tried not to scratch her wig. "Yes, my husband and I want to repair our driveway. We've just moved here, and I hear he is reputable."

Maggie leaned over the counter. "Honey, his employees do a good job, but you don't want to go over there. Why don't I just give you the number, and you can have your husband take care of it, alright?"

Jennifer was intrigued. "Is he some kind of nut case? I was thinking of driving over there and taking a look-see at some of his pictures. Do you know if he has an album of any jobs he has done for the locals?"

Maggie pulled a slip of paper out from her desk drawer and looked outside for a moment. "Just a minute and I will make you a little map, okay? I'll be right back."

Jennifer smiled as she adjusted her wig while Maggie slipped into the other room. Maggie was stout but great attention had been given to her appearance. The color of her shoes matched the blue of the flowers on her dress. One small bow was affixed to the top of her head; it too, was the same color blue. Her skin was flawless and if she hadn't been a little too plump, she could have passed for a younger Lucille Ball. Jennifer sniffed. The scent of lemon filled her nostrils. "Is everything alright with you?" Jennifer asked.

Maggie returned and looked past Jennifer's shoulder. "It's just down the road, honey. You can't miss it unless of course you accidentally drive off the road or hit him with your car," Maggie said with a smirk. "Make sure you read these directions real good, honey. You look like a city girl. Are you familiar with brass knuckles? I have some I could let you use," she paused and reached for Jennifer's hand, "honey, please, don't go there by yourself."

Now Jennifer was really intrigued. "Why would I need brass knuckles?"

"Honey, I'm not saying you will definitely have to use them, but I'll pay you twenty dollars just to smack him upside his head. I couldn't sleep tonight thinking you didn't take them. You look like a real sweet lady, and he is not a nice man to any lady. I left his home the first chance I got," she paused, "but you don't want to hear about my problems, sorry."

Jennifer nodded and stuck the paper in her pocket. "Just between you and me, I have my own set of brass knuckles. We city girls can't be too careful. Thank you, though. I can take care of myself quite well. It is so nice of you to be concerned about my welfare. This is a nice little town you have here. Maybe you and I could have lunch some time and you could fill me in about the locals," she paused to sniff again, "Where is the scent of lemon coming from? It smells so fresh in here." Maggie smiled. "Oh, I use fresh squeezed lemon juice on the floor. It keeps the ants from coming into the office. Would you like your fortune told? It's on the house."

Jennifer wasn't sure if she should be having some overly-nice townie holding her hands but she decided to take the chance. There had been three child psychologists who hadn't been able to figure her out, so why not give Maggie a chance? "Sure," she quipped and sat down.

Maggie adjusted her glasses and smiled. "Thank God, this is my last day. If I never see Fuller's Concrete again, --- it will be too soon. He's my father, and I hate the ground he walks on. You be *real* careful now when you go over there, okay? I have a cute little hand gun if you'd like to use it on him. It can't be traced. Are you interested?"

Jennifer smiled pleasantly at her, and thought, "...*she's actually serious.*" "I'll pass on the brass knuckles and the cute little gun—for now. I have my own little gun. Thanks." She reached across the desk and put her hands out.

Maggie touched them gently and closed her eyes; she hesitated at first but continued in a quiet voice, "I feel a sense of apprehension in your soul." She paused, "I sense anxiety over a childhood lost, but you have a good soul. You enjoy the outdoors a great deal, and you are always for the under dog." She continued to keep her eyes closed, "...you love chocolate," Maggie giggled, "I do, too," she continued, "Your past has been brought into the future but you manage your life quite well. You are organized and hate liars." She opened her eyes and looked straight at Jennifer, "…are you about ready to cry?" Jennifer wiped one tear away, "…no, not at all, and I cannot allow this one to be on the house." Maggie withdrew her hand, "Oh, I have insulted you. I get carried away sometimes. Pay no mind to what I told you."

Jennifer stood up, "…no indeed, you have managed to put everything in a nut shell and make it all so plain and simple. I do think about my past a lot, but I enjoy the memories, and I do so love chocolate." She reached in her purse and pulled out a ten, "Here, go buy yourself some Whitman's." Maggie grinned. "Well…thank you." Jennifer started to leave but turned to Maggie and asked her one question, "What is your favorite kind of ice cream?"

~

Jennifer turned on the engine of her newly upholstered truck and took the piece of paper out of her pocket. She then paused a moment to look at Maggie who was staring at her through the window. Jennifer read the note.

'He's a creep. He's my father, and he doesn't treat women kindly. He might tell you he will let his dogs loose, but there are no dogs, just hogs. I hate him. If you have a mind to, throw the bastard in his burn hole and kill him dead. Please do me a favor and get rid of this note.'

"My, my," Jennifer thought, "It just keeps getting more interesting."

Jennifer waved at Maggie and smiled again as she looked down at the sack lying on the floorboard. "Have a nice day, Maggie," she thought. "I don't need any stinking brass knuckles, and I sure as hell don't need a gun to take care of you, Frankie Fuller," she paused, and in a child-like manner she finished her thought, "…well, maybe just this once."

Chapter fourteen

Carter residence

Jennifer dialed the number for Fuller's Concrete after she swallowed the last of the note. It excited her to think of what was she was about to do.

"Fuller's Concrete. We pour it, you adore it. Talk. It's your dime," a gruff voice said.

Jennifer stared straight ahead through her bathroom window and admired the wooden sculpture she had made with an unusual piece of wood. "Hello. My name is Rosemary Goodman. My husband and I were thinking about hiring you to fix our road. Could I drop by and explain to you what he would like done? He's out of town for a couple of days and, well, I want to surprise him before he comes home. He's a good man, and I thought it would please him."

There was the sound of a man spitting and a "ping" as it hit a can. "Is he really a good man?"

Jennifer was caught off guard. "Excuse me, sir."

"Sorry, honey. I like to kid sometimes with the customers. Are you new to the area?"

She hesitated for a moment. "...Yes. We're buying the place just off of Plentytree, and my husband thinks the road might need some repair. Goodness, is it called a road around these parts? I don't know anything about this kind of stuff. I get all confused with these manly business deals. Do you have an album you might be able to show me?"

The man on the other end chuckled. "Honey, the only album I have is my wedding album, and that ain't something you would want to see!" He chuckled again. The "ping" sounded a second time. "I don't recall

Plentytree needing any repairs," he continued. "But I'll go take a look-see. I can meet you in a half hour. Will your husband be with you?"

Jennifer wasn't expecting the offer. "Well, no, I said he is out of town. I'd rather meet at your office. Will you be there for the rest of the afternoon? Maybe I could just slip by."

"Shucks, honey, I ain't going to bite you. I ain't going nowhere. What time can I expect you?" he asked as he scratched a festering sore on his neck.

Jennifer pulled off her wig. "Well, I need to go shopping, but if you don't mind, I really would like to speak with you in person. I could leave you a down payment. Do you think I could just take a peek at some of your pictures? I'm one of those city girls that likes to look at pictures."

"I ain't got no pictures, but we could take a drive, and I could show you a few things." Jennifer didn't care for the tone in his voice on this last comment. He cleared his throat. "I don't take no checks, cash in hand only, lady. And if you want proof of my business, just go look at the Carter's driveway. I did the whole thing."

She felt her pulse pick up. "Carter's? I'm not familiar with the roads around here. Is it far from where I am?"

He snorted. "Lady, it ain't a road. It's a last name. I don't know where you are. I ain't no mind reader, ya' know what I mean?" Fuller scratched at his crotch.

Jennifer thought about what was in the sack on the floor board of her truck and she smiled again. It was tied tightly with wire but undulated on its own. "Goodness, what am I thinking about?" she replied in her too-thick Southern drawl. "I'm calling from town. Let's see…if I get on Wind Road, will I be headed in the right direction? There's an old barn with a big blue flower painted on it just down the road."

It sounded like he blew his nose on his shirt. "You'd be headed in the opposite direction of my place. Turn around and go back the way you came into town. Go through town and stay on Main. My place is five miles on the left. Carter's is just before my place on the right. You can't see it from the road, and there is a big iron fence…"

"Oh, goodness! I've seen it! I just can't get the hang of all these silly roads."

Fuller belched into the phone.

She held back the bile and took a deep breath. "Now I seem to recall their place. They must have spent a fortune on it. It looks real nice. I do have cash; that's not a problem. I was wondering, though, do you have any dogs on your property?"

"No, m'am. Ain't got no dogs, just hogs. They don't like the taste of pretty city-fied legs anyway." Jennifer could hear the leer in his voice. "Come on over."

"This was going to be an adventure," she mused to herself. "Thank you so much. It's not that I don't like dogs, but I have to get your word that they are secure. They just scare me somewhat. Silly, don't you think? I'm not used to this mountain life. My daddy loved..."

Fuller interrupted and replied, "Are you coming over or not? I don't have any dogs, so don't worry about it. I was thinking about doing some fishing, and I'm the only one here. Take your time 'cause I got one more thing I need to take care of. If I am not back just sit your pretty self down on the step and wait, okay?"

She gripped the phone tighter. "How convenient," she thought. Then she smiled again at the thought of what was in the sack. "I'll do my best," she said into the phone. "I may get lost, so you take your time, too, but still...pretty please, stay open for just a few more minutes."

She heard him spit but didn't hear the "ping" of the can. He must have spit on the floor. "Barbarian," she thought. "I understand," she heard him say. "Come on over when you have the time. But don't waste *my* time and not show up at all!! Ain't nobody here but me, and I close early on Fridays. Don't be surprised if the sign says 'OPEN' whether I'm here or not. Did you say you were in town right now?"

"Yes. I'm right across from the little market."

"Well, then, would you mind picking me up a couple of beers?"

Jennifer smiled at his audacity. "That wouldn't be a problem. Do you need anything else?"

She was positive he put the phone to his chest and made a rude comment about his needs. She ignored it. He put the phone back to his ear. "How'd you hear of Fuller's Concrete, lady?"

"Oh, a very nice young woman who works in that quaint little office right next to the market told me about you."

"...too plump for her own good, yeah, that would be Maggie. What did she have to say about me?"

"My goodness, she had nothing but good things to say about you. Why do you ask?"

"She's my daughter. And she must've been drunk 'cause her and me don't see eye-to-eye," he snorted again, "not that anyone could meet her eye-to-eye. She is part troll!"

If he knew what she was thinking, her whole day would have been for nothing. "*The only thing that would want to see Frankie Fuller eye to eye was a dead goat.*" "Well, goodbye for now, Mr. Fuller."

Click…and the sound of the dial tone in her ear.

~

Jennifer drove right past the entrance to his business and almost laughed as she eyed the gate of his property. "Why, yes, some nice young woman gave me directions," she said aloud in her exaggerated Southern accent. "Her name is Maggie. Do you know her? She gave me directions alright, and she had some nice things to say about you, like how she hated your guts."

Then her mannerism changed from country lingo to gruff redneck as she mimicked his words. "Oh, Maggie, yeah, me and her go back a long ways. Heck, she's my daughter. Did she actually get up off her fat ass and walk you to the door?" She glanced at the sack on the floor board again. "Be patient my little friends." Her face twitched unexpectedly.

~

Jennifer drove her truck one-tenth of a mile out of the way. She had already determined earlier that his property was accessible on foot. As though she would have any problems with cross country! She loved the thought of what was about to happen as she threw her overnight bag over her shoulders and hand carried the sack at a safe distance from her side. Fuller's property was about four acres and it etched up against the most southern part of the Martin property.

She checked the hand-written note and made sure it was secure on the windshield. Leaving a note for the village idiot, better known as the sheriff, was something she had always done to let him know not to bother her. She was busy. He would pull the note off the windshield and dismiss it like he had before, never bothering to call it in. It was an agreement the two of them made a long time ago. After all, he was on her payroll.

It took Jennifer a good thirty minutes to make her way through the deep woods. She was used to it. Finally she spotted the fence line to his business and made sure he was not outside. She crept over to the front gate and turned the sign over. She waited in the shadows. She continued on with her plan.

Suddenly the door to his office opened. She stopped in her tracks and hid behind an old clunker. Fuller walked slowly to the metal shed and belched. He pulled out a set of keys and yelled, "Come on, girls! It's party time! Time to play, 'Mess with Margery'! We got to make it quick 'cause Daddy has got a lady coming over! I got to slick my hair back and turn my t-shirt around backwards so's I look more respectable." He snorted, and coughed loudly.

Jennifer thought she would puke. She watched from a safe distance, wondered if she misunderstood the note Maggie had written. She was far enough away that she didn't think he would spot her, but a good hound would know she was there. She opened the side pocket of her vest and looked at the note again. "...no dogs. What an idiot!" she thought and felt for the doggy treats she kept in her side pocket. Oh, how she hated liars.

She froze at her post when he opened the shed door. She felt as though a ghost had stuck a thousand pins in here spine. Scratching to get out were two over-sized hogs! Not dogs at all, but two slobbering, smelly, nasty looking pigs. She looked to see if she could tell if they were male or female. She couldn't tell. They were bigger than any hogs she had ever imagined. Rolls of festering fat hung down their sides as they waddled to get past him and strapped to their backs were leather-bound saddles with spikes protruding upward. Fuller practically slobbered over *them*. "There are my big girls! Are you ready for some fun?" Jennifer felt sick to her stomach.

The hogs waddled out and started snorting at the ground. "This is going to be interesting," Jennifer said under her breath. She was taken by surprise when Fuller opened the door wider and revealed one deer carcass with a red poncho draped over it. "You've got to be kidding me!" she thought. Jennifer was mesmerized by the absurdity of the scene, but then she smiled, narrowed her eyes, and said to no one in particular, "So, you want to play a game." Her face twitched again, and slowly slipped her right hand into a side pocket. The peppermint would take care of her queasiness.

Fuller stopped briefly and pulled a cool one out of a dilapidated ice chest. "Come on, come on. Let's go see what the old lady is up to," Fuller said nonchalantly. "Get along, little hog-doggies!" Fuller belched loudly and prodded the hogs with a long stick.

He should have taken the time to see if the "CLOSED" sign was facing in the direction of the office. But he was stupid and never suspected anything could be different from the way he left it. He was stupid. But Jennifer was not. She had even taken the time to put an old lock on it; everything was secure for the upcoming party.

Jennifer was a little nervous as she looked around. No dogs, just hogs—really, really big hogs, and Jennifer knew a hog could do as much damage as a dog given the right set of circumstance. True, these two did not look friendly, but they weren't acting like they might be a threat to anyone, either. The larger one slobbered at Fuller's heel and snorted.

Fuller pulled out one treat for each of them, and they flopped to the ground. "That's my good girls!" he cooed. "Let's go see the old lady, shall we?"

Jennifer was more than curious now so she decided not to change into her girlie clothes just yet. She began to follow Fuller from a discrete distance being ever so careful not to upset her friends in the sack she carried. "You'll get your turn, sweeties," she whispered, sounding frighteningly like Fuller talking to his "girls." "Be patient."

Fuller walked towards the back of the property. He fumbled for more keys and opened the large metal gate that led to what Jennifer assumed was the outside of the property that might lead to a corral of some kind. She couldn't be more wrong. Hiding behind an abandoned truck, she whispered, "What are you up to, old man? Please don't waste my time by relieving yourself in the woods." Then she spit on the ground. Her hand started to tremble and she realized she had not taken her special pill. She took it.

To her surprise a bend in the road revealed a simple home landscaped with attractive plants. Fuller walked to the front door, but then he did something very peculiar. He *locked* the door! "Why are you locking the door? So no one can get out?" she thought.

Then it all became clear to her. From around the corner came a woman carrying a bucket. It must have been Margery, the unfortunate wife but she was holding one thing that might be in her favor, an axe.

She was very frail with thinning hair and a complexion as pale as a ghost. Fuller had locked the door so she could not get *in*. His wife knew immediately what he had done. She froze and dropped the bucket but not the axe. "Please," she pleaded. "Not today, please. You know I'm sick. Not today. You promised!"

The childlike quality to her voice reverberated inside Jennifer, causing her to flinch. Margery was very frail. Her skin was pale as was her dress, faded from wear. Surprisingly her hair was put up in a perfect bun. She, too, seemed to have lovely skin just like Maggie. The resemblance was uncanny.

The hogs seemed to slobber when they saw Margery. A wicked smile played across Frankie's face. "There she is, girls. Go get her!" he said and began to sing. *"Lick her up and down. Lick her all around. Then she can go to town!"* He laughed menacingly. "Ain't that right, Margery?"

"You have got to be kidding me," Jennifer whispered. "He sings to his pigs? Oh, this is going to be fun!" Jennifer suddenly felt sick to her stomach again, and she knew a peppermint would not take care of the problem. She had taken her special pill but she took it on an empty stomach. Stupid! She knew better. "Crap…" she whispered and fumbled for the side pocket of her pants. Quickly she pulled out three dried figs and popped them in her mouth.

Chapter fifteen

Jennifer pulled out her handgun that been her grandfather's and took the safety off, whispering, "You have got to be kidding me."

Margery Fuller started to back up. She pleaded with Frankie again, "Please," she said softly. "Dinner is on the table. Donny is coming over," she paused. "I thought you said you were done with all of this. I thought you said you would behave just this one time before I leave." She dropped the axe.

Jennifer was surprised at how she said, "Please." It sounded almost like a question.

"Run, lady. What's your problem?" she thought. *"Pick up the bucket, do something... pick up the axe and cut his damn head off or knock him upside the head with the bucket! Get some backbone!"*

Fuller started laughing. "Come on, now! Just scream for me one time, and then I'll take them back. You know they've always liked the smell of that cheap perfume."

"I'm not wearing any perfume. Please! Take them back now," she begged.

"Jeez, you have one little womanly operation and you deny me of my one thing that makes me happy. You-u-u stupid women get all the fun! They ain't going to eat you! They just like the way you smell! Get over here!" His voice had moved from low and sarcastic to loud and demanding. Frankie was in no mood to be denied his entertainment.

"Don't you move, lady," Jennifer worded silently as she saw Margery start to back away like an animal trying to get out of a corner. She bent down to pick up the axe. *"That's it Margery...that's it, take your time, aim low, and make it smooth."*

"...don't even think about using that axe on me woman! You can run, but you can't hide, Margery!" Frankie said soberly. "Goodness, did you leave your keys lying on the dresser again?" he baited her. Then, almost viciously, he said, "You never learn."

Jennifer put the sack down and breathed in slowly. "Just give me a reason, sleaze bag. One reason, and…"

Suddenly she heard an engine. Someone was coming down the road from behind the house. "Crap," she thought and ducked down. "I hate interruptions."

A young man stepped out of the truck holding a hand gun in one hand. "Fuller, put the hogs away, or I swear I will shoot them. Margery is not well! You know that! We have all had enough of your meanness."

Fuller snickered and spit in his son-in-law, Donny's, direction. "Take her inside and make sure all her stuff is gone. She's no good to me now—and you never had the balls to kill a squirrel! So put that piss-ant gun back in your purse!"

Fuller threw the keys at him and now Jennifer was really confused. She waited.

Margery picked up the keys while the hogs focused their attention on a flower bed in the front yard. Donny went into the house just as Fuller sat down on the stoop.

Fifteen minutes passed, and then Donny came out of the house. "I have it all. God, almighty, Fuller! I hope you realize how lucky you are that the law didn't come and get you this time."

"Hell, she's my *wife*! I didn't mean to lock her up in the shed! If she'd stopped nagging me about picking up my drawers, I might have left her alone," he paused to spit, "always with the nagging! Damn, I married her, didn't I? What's a man got to do around here to get some respect?"

Maggie was in the truck, too. She rolled down the window and yelled at him, "You are a pig, Daddy! Heck, Donny! Go ahead and shoot him in the balls!" Jennifer giggled.

Fuller grinned. "Have you forgotten? The law is on my side, remember? It was an unfortunate accident, or at least that is the way Simms wrote it up. The sheriff and I have an agreement, or don't you remember what I taught you?"

"Oh, I remember," Donny replied. "Maybe your memory won't fail you when you're sitting on the side of the road wondering where your money went."

Fuller laughed again and nearly fell over. Then he looked at Donny soberly and replied, "What did you say?" No one answered him. He was quiet for a moment and stared hard at his wife. "What's he talking about, Margery? What have you been up to?" He started to get up and made the mistake of picking up a rock. Margery raised the axe and threw it at him. Fuller's scream riveted through the tree tops as he grabbed his left foot. "You stupid two-legged cow! You have killed my foot!" The axe had hit him on the outside of his left foot and was partially embedded in the stump he sat on.

Margery's facial expression did not change at all. Fuller pulled his foot free. The axe remained embedded in the stump along with two of his toes. Maggie giggled and held her side as if it hurt her and then she rolled the window back up. Her giggle slowly matured into a cackle. Jennifer read her lips. "…and those little piggies did not get to go to town!"

Jennifer sat quietly. In her mind she was applauding Margery's vengeance. "Good aim, Mama…" Her face went blank and she remembered something Fuller had just said, '…or at least that is the way Simms wrote it up.' Jennifer blinked, "…that son-of-a bitch."

Margery ignored Fuller and got in the truck where she sat quietly by her daughter who had scooted over to the middle of the bench seat. Finally, she rolled the window down again and spoke to her husband. "Your daughter is not as dumb as you think she is. It seemed that mail-order class in accounting paid off big time." She stared straight at her husband as her next few words spat like venom from her mouth. "Tell me, you sack of shit. When was the last time you looked at your savings account balance?"

Fuller's eyes narrowed. "What savings account? If you think that worthless daughter of mine has figured out some big secret, you can tell her to kiss my royal ass. She's still pissed because I fired her for tellin' tales!"

"That's not what she meant," Margery said as she waved a piece of paper out the window.

Maggie leaned over, craning her neck to look at Fuller. "I may be a fat ass but when it comes to numbers, I'm a whiz! And if I were you Daddy, I would tend to those little piggies that left your foot!" Maggie cackled so hard she started choking. Fuller struggled to get up as blood oozed out of his boot.

Fuller had made an attempt to stop the bleeding by taking his sock off and wrapping it around his foot. He limped towards the gate he had come out of and prodded the hogs back toward the gate. "...this little mishap won't keep me from taking care of you later on," he paused to moan, "Oh, so now you're a whiz kid!" he snarled. "You wouldn't know a savings account if it bit you on your ass!" He leered at Margery. "Get while the gettin's good, woman. And don't even think of coming back and gettin' anymore of your precious mementos."

She motioned to the back of the truck. "I have been getting my mementos out for quite a while, Frankie. Or haven't you noticed?" Margery actually began to tear up, but she held them back and smiled. "I have everything I need and more. I sure as hell don't need you anymore! Didn't you ever wonder why you itched so much? Didn't you ever wonder why you always had stomach cramps and crapped yourself? I got my revenge every time you put food in your toothless mouth. You made my day the day you said you loved oatmeal," she giggled, "...didn't you ever wonder why all that oatmeal went down so smooth?"

Fuller stopped in his tracks. "...what do you mean?"

Jennifer's eyes lit up.

Maggie rested her head on Margery's shoulder. Margery cocked her head to one side and yelled out the window at him. "...maggots. Lovely little maggots soaked in honey and sweet cream. Bone-a-pe-teat!"

Fuller grabbed his stomach and screamed again. "...you fed me maggots?"

Margery smiled and answered him one last time. "Yes, dear, and roasted rat balls, goat droppings and those pigs of yours, well, you would be surprised at what comes out of their snouts," she paused to gain her composure, "those sweet little piggies of yours donated all the condiments that you loved to drizzle on your stew."

Fuller bent over and vomited. Jennifer thought she might, but instead she smiled pleasantly and whispered, "My kind of a woman! I had a feeling about you, Margery."

Fuller picked up an overturned bucket and threw it at the truck. "Wait a minute. *What do you mean?* Hell, did you put something in my food? What was it again?" He seemed a little confused about the recent exchange of conversation.

Maggie leaned over her mother and yelled out the open window. "Daddy, you can kiss her ass and mine! We have had it with you! We're all packed up—and guess what, Daddy?"

"What?" Fuller roared.

"You should have taken Mama's name off the checking account. Seems she ain't as dumb as you told everybody. Your concrete company is going belly up in about a week, and all you're going to have is your hogs. If they're as smart as you think they are, they'll leave, too!"

Margery cackled.

Jennifer was enjoying the conversation a little too much and almost cackled herself. Her stomach hurt and she wasn't sure if the reason was due to her having to hold in the laughter or just maybe her period was coming early. She had begged Richard to perform a hysterectomy on her, but he declined.

Fuller shrugged his shoulders. "I got my trucks, and I still have my coin collection. You can't take those away from me," Fuller said nonchalantly as he pointed in the direction of a locked garage door. "And I got money put away that none of you know about. I can live pretty damn good on what I got hid away!"

Margery wiped the tears of laughter from her eyes and smiled. "You mean the coin collection you hid in those old tires in the shed you *thought* you kept locked? *That* coin collection? The coin collection that is earning me money right about now—oh, let's say three percent interest." She looked at her daughter. "Ain't that right, Maggie?" She turned back to her husband, whose situation was slowly starting to sink in. "I found your darn hiding place, you tub of lard. What kind of moron hides his money in old tires?" That set her off on another gale of tear-producing laughter. Maggie threw her head back and laughed, "…I got to pee!"

In frustration, Fuller turned on the only other person available. "Are you finally going to become a man, Donny? Are you finally going to take off your apron?"

Donny climbed in the truck. "Let's go," he said to the two women. "We're done here." He opened the door and standing on the running board he spoke to his father-in-law. "You never did care anything about the good things in life, Fuller. You had the best woman in the world, kids that loved you, and still you abused every single one. It's your turn to suffer now. Margery ain't all hard-hearted. She left you some bottles. You can get a deposit on them when you walk to town." Maggie, Margery and Donny all giggled in unison. Jennifer did not. She was now on her side holding her stomach.

Those last words got Fuller's full attention though, and Jennifer loved it. "Where is a camera when I need it?" she thought.

Fuller stared at Donny. "What are you talking about?" he asked.

Jennifer almost gave her position away when Donny shot the lock off the garage door. "Oh, this is too good to be true!" she whispered excitedly. "A gun battle right in the middle of the Smokies!"

"What the hell are you doing, boy!?!" Fuller asked defiantly. "Get out of here! Just go!"

"I ain't your _boy_ no more!" Donny shot back. "And she ain't your wife. And these vehicles sure ain't going to be didly-squat after I…"

Four bullets came out of the handgun—one into each windshield and one into each of the grills of Fuller's vehicles.

"You lunatic!" Fuller screamed.

Donny blew on the barrel of the gun and smiled. "I always loved target practice. Now, I have some more bullets. Want me to shoot your hogs? I could end your miserable life and no one would ever know. What's it going to be?"

Jennifer sighed. "…shoot him in the balls but don't hurt the piggies."

Now Jennifer was really enjoying the conversation. The pain in her lower stomach was now just an ache. Donny eased back behind the wheel and put the truck in gear. Margery spoke one last time out the open window. "Go check out your bank statement, Frankie. *You know the one.* You told me it didn't have my name on it. Well, it seems it did after all, and guess what else? Maggie and I are finally going on that trip we've always wanted." She looked at her husband defiantly. "I cooked and cleaned for you for forty years, and you never once appreciated any of it. I wiped your sorry butt when you were sick. I forgave you a thousand times. Still, you just treated me like dirt, and finally I made the decision to get revenge, but there was one thing I just could not understand." Fuller nodded, "…and what's that?"

Maggie nudged her mama, "…tell him Mama."

Margery did just that and replied, "How anyone could eat so many bugs and not choke on one of them."

Fuller snorted and slapped his knee. "You noticed."

Margery held back the tears. "You treated those damn hogs better than you did me," she paused as if a bell had just gone off in her head, "Oh, yeah, what did I put in your food?" She put her finger to her cheek, "…maggots, cockroaches, and snotty boogers," she paused again, "and sometimes pig shit."

Fuller stood up and looked in the direction of where the axe was lying. Donny glared at him. "…go ahead, try it."

Jennifer closed her eyes and whispered, "*Shoot him*, Mama. Just shoot him."

"Didn't I make sure you had water when I locked you in the shed—accidentally, of course," Fuller continued. "Didn't I let you walk home that day I promised to pick you up with all the groceries? And didn't you promise to love, honor, and obey me? What about our wedding vows, woman?"

Margery spit in his direction. "…what about them?" She spit in his direction again. "There's your part of the vows, you sorry excuse for a human being. Maybe I'll send you a post card from our trip!"

Fuller acted dumbfounded. "I let you sit in the boat while I fished. You told me that was a fine trip. I didn't think it was nearly as good as when you 'tripped' down the stairs!" Fuller did the unthinkable. He laughed hardily.

Jennifer checked to see if her knife was in its sleeve. It was. She glanced at the sack again.

Donny looked in Fuller's direction past his wife and her mother. "Well, we're going to love spending the rest of your money, old man. And when I track down Paulie and Molly, they'll have fun with all your money, too. You are going to be a sad, lonely old fart by the time the tax people get done with you. Good-bye, you sack of…"

"Ka-ka, doo-doo, horse shit, and crap," Jennifer finished. "Touchdown—and pass me the ball!"

The truck began to pull away. Margery gestured at her husband. It wasn't at all ladylike, but Jennifer figured Margery was due one little "bird" after forty years of taking care of his sorry, lard butt. She grinned. Maggie flipped him off, too. "Good-bye, Daddy! Kiss my …, too!" her voice trailed off.

"Ass," Jennifer finished again. She never could resist finishing a sentence. "Kiss my ever-loving ass." Turning to look at Fuller she muttered, "Not so funny, now, you sack of cow manure."

Fuller, still oblivious to their presence, dismissed his family with a wave of his hand. As soon as they were out of sight he turned and almost ran back to his office. He was frantic. The blood had started to coagulate but he had never had this kind of pain in his whole life. Jennifer watched as he kicked at the hogs and cursed loudly. They ran off in another direction. He practically tore the office door off the hinges he was so anxious to get inside. Within seconds Jennifer could see him through the office window. He picked up an envelope and studied the contents. He picked up another envelope and did the same. He crushed the paper in his hands and screamed something unintelligible. She giggled as she realized it must be the bank statement. His tantrum continued as he threw the paper on the floor and shrieked obscenities. Jennifer ducked down just before he threw something through the window. Glass shattered everywhere. He was saying some extremely unpleasant things about his wife—mostly referring to her sexual behavior.

"Not nice, mister," Jennifer said aloud. "One bar of soap will not be enough for you!" She looked in a side pocket of her hunting gear and felt two bars of lye soap. She changed into something "more comfortable," red, slinky—something Fuller would not be able to tear his eyes away from.

Chapter sixteen

Jennifer's face went blank for a moment, and her mind drifted back to when she was a small child. Her mother had told her father to stuff an object into one of his body cavities. Jennifer was shocked and couldn't move momentarily when it happened. Her mother's mind had snapped for one second, and at first even she hadn't realized what she had said. "Take your pack and shove it where the sun don't shine. I can only carry one pack at a time."

Her father was dumbfounded. Never-the-less he replied back, "Take your pack and shove it where the sun don't shine? I can only carry one backpack at a time?" he repeated with questionable concern. "Why— Eileen, my dear, have you been growing a new backbone?" They were words she would regret.

When they arrived home he dragged her into the kitchen and shoved soap in her mouth. "Never speak to me in that manner again or I will see to it that you choke on this next time. I will not be disrespected in front of my daughter!"

Jennifer was only seven and stood silently in the hallway and cried. That had been the first time Eileen had spoken to him in that manner. It was also the last. That was when Eileen started putting ground-up, eight-legged creatures in Thomas' food. The only good thing about it was it was the first and last time he ever put his hands on her. The rest of the abuse came with words only. It was more fun to him. He loved it when she whimpered. Eileen hated it when it affected Jennifer. Eileen spent many hours looking for creepy crawlers while she hiked in the early morning quiet. Only the best for him; the juiciest of grubs, the crunchiest of beetles, and Eileen's all time favorite, wasp larvae and deer droppings.

Jennifer snapped back to the present. She checked her clothing and crossed that part of the plan off her mental "To Do" list. Next, she made sure the sign was still in the correct position, facing inward.

A knock on the door made Fuller jump. He yelled, "Go away! We're closed for the season!"

He was very surprised when the door opened and a lovely woman dressed in a rather tight but attractive dress walked in anyway. Her hair was pulled back. It accentuated her neck which in turn showed off her lovely cleavage. He was flabbergasted at the sight of her, especially after what had just happened. "Oh, you must be the lady about the job, right?" He attempted to smooth back his hair and cleared his throat. "Sorry about the mess. Did you hear anything a while ago? It seems someone broke in here while I was taking a leak."

Jennifer's jaw tightened, and then she smiled. "Why, no, sir. I only just arrived. Let me introduce myself. I am Rosemary…" She deliberately paused and looked intently at the trail of blood that led to his foot. "…what happened to your foot?"

He most definitely was in great pain but she could tell he was trying to be manly about the whole ordeal. "…my stupid son-in-law has a bad aim. I'll be fine as soon as I get some whiskey in me." He swiveled around in his chair and opened the door to the small cabinet behind him. "Would you like an afternoon night-cap Rosemary."

"Sir, Mr. Fuller, it looks like you need a tourniquet. Maybe I should call for help, and you should not be drinking with an injury like that."

He looked at her strangely. "What the hell is a turn- ni-kit? And there is no need for last names," he interrupted quietly. "You're here. I just need to sit a spell and prop my foot up. We can leave in a few minutes. I just have to find a receipt book. Did you remember the beer?"

Jennifer ignored his question concerning the beer. "Did someone break in or break out, sir?" She looked around the room. Did the maid die? Should I come back later?" Jennifer asked as she adjusted her bra.

His eyes did not meet hers. "No. No, I had a run-in with some trespassers last week. Do you have the cash with you? We can leave in a minute. Where's your car? You sure didn't get her by foot—not in those heels!" He winced, "You wouldn't happen to have any pain medicine with you?"

Jennifer wouldn't have given up a pain pill if her life depended on it, and shook her head slowly. "Yes, sir, you are quite right. I parked just down the road. Sometimes I like to take off my shoes and feel the coolness of the road. Could you please give me that receipt now?" She reached in her purse and took out her check book. He frowned at her, "...I said no checks." She ignored him and took out a pen. "My husband is a fanatic about receipts. I, on the other hand, can look at someone and know if they are trustworthy."

He smirked. "Is that right?"

She purposely bent down and caused him to look more closely at her curves. "I bet you haven't seen ones like these in a long time, have you?"

He looked rather surprised, then suspicious, and answered slowly, "*Excuse me.*"

She pulled out the handgun and smiled at him. "Get your fat butt up and walk out to the yard now. Crawl if you have to but do it now. I really could care less about your injury. This is not Monopoly so you will not be 'passing go' or 'going to jail' 'cause I hear you and the sheriff have been sharing the same bed."

He kicked back the chair and cursed at her. "I ain't one of those. What the hell do you want? Hey, if this is some kind of robbery you have come to the wrong place! I don't keep any cash lying around." He slammed his hand on the desk. Jennifer jumped but remained in control of the situation.

She looked around, and put the check back into her purse. "That would be the truth, for sure. You're flat broke, according to your bank statement, but I don't care about your money. I just want you to tell your wife you're sorry for how you treated her."

"My wife is gone, lady. Besides, how the hell would you know if I mistreated my wife or how much money I got in the bank? Are you from the IRS?"

Jennifer almost giggled. "No, I'm from the W.D.C."

"What the hell is the 'W.D.C.?"

"The Woodsman's Daughter's Club. You really are stupid mister. Get up now or I will shoot you right between your pathetic stupid eyes."

"Please, lady. I've had a bad day. My wife just left me; my daughters have run off and I swear I don't have any money!"

Jennifer grinned. "Are you deaf, too? I don't want your money," she said slowly and calmly. "I want *you* to get *up* and *go* outside. If you don't do what I say, I can't be responsible for my actions. I'm having one of those 'hormonal changes' due to the late arrival of my curse. Ya' know what I mean? Oh, I forgot. *You do know what I mean.* Isn't Margery still getting over one of those womanly operations? Haven't you treated her badly?"

He got up slowly and moved towards the door. *"Who are you, lady...* the president of the Margery Fuller's Fan Club?"

"Men like you need a lesson in how to treat a lady proper, and I told you my name. If you can't keep up with the conversation, that is your fault, fatty, so move! And don't even try anything like calling your hogs on me. By the way, they like doggie biscuits. What else did you scare her with?" she succeeded in holding back her tears; "...I really do detest men like you. You haven't got a clue as to what it takes to tend to women like Eileen." He cocked his head sideways and winced again, "...who the hell is Eileen? What are you talking about? Scare who with what? How do you know so much about me, lady? Is your name really Rosemary? Did my wife hire you to kill me?"

She grinned at him and motioned for him to step down. "I am a one-woman hit man. You figure it out." Fuller paused. "It was that lard-butt, Maggie, huh? I should have known. I bet she hired you. How much did she pay you? I'll pay you double just to leave me the hell alone!"

Jennifer smiled pleasantly at him. "Why, I never thought of it that way. You have inspired me. How much were you thinking about?"

He snickered. "I could give you another inspiration if you'd let me, lady. I don't need ten toes to please a woman like you."

Jennifer stepped back and slapped her knee. "Mister, you could have ten golden toes and a ruby hanging from your family jewels. I still wouldn't have anything to do with a man like you."

"You didn't come here with the intention of any business deal, not dressed like that." He snickered, and wiped the sweat from his forehead.

She almost puked. She shook her head in dismay. "Lord Almighty, mister! You can't seriously think I came here to flirt with you." Her Southern drawl became less pronounced. "That was a mistake, Frankie. I do not take kindly to lewd comments. I am a lady."

"What was a mistake?" Frankie sputtered.

"You snickering the way you did. I don't like it. My daddy used to snicker at my mama, and she hung his head on the mantel, well, at least I think it was her. We used to live just down the road many, many years ago. You might remember them...Eileen and Thomas Martin?"

He stepped back. "...oh, my God! Damn! Are you that crazy broad's daughter?" He paused for a moment, looking at her up and down, "Dang, girl, you sure grew up to be a looker! I remember reading about your papa's murder. That was a long time ago! Did your mama really kill your papa?" he snickered. "I heard he was a mean son of a gun, and some people still say she was just a little off. She was never found, as I recall. I reckon the bears got her."

"Don't strain your brain, Frankie, on trying to figure that out. Mama is where she should be, and you are not one to be talking about anyone's meanness."

He stepped down from the concrete stoop and looked towards the entrance gate. "God, Almighty, lady! Are you going to kill me? I'll do whatever you want...just let me go."

"Am I going to kill you? No. These are," she said with assurance and lifted the sack up higher for him to look at.

"What's in there?" he asked, unable to take his eyes off the sack that seemed to have a life of its own.

"Your family's idea of a good joke," she replied. "Why'd you have to be so mean to your daughters and your wife? I don't know your wife personally, but your daughter seemed to be very sweet. Molly, that is. I only spoke with Maggie for a brief moment. I would be willing to bet it was your wife that planted all those lovely flowers around the house. My mama loved flowers, too, especially wild ones."

"Do you know the way back to the nut farm, lady?" he asked snidely. "None of the women in my family are sweet. Heck, Molly is dumber than dirt to have married that low-life Paulie, and Maggie never could figure out how to shoot out a kid! What's a woman good for if she can't produce offspring? Donny was a half-wit to have married the broad."

"Broad? Did you just call your daughter a *broad*?"

Jennifer pulled out the rubber band from her hair and frowned at him. "Looks like to me you didn't mind them cooking for you, and I bet your house was always spic and span, right? Looks to me like you haven't missed too many meals, huh? Looks like to me you need to burn some of that fat off, huh? Where is your burn hole? Isn't there always some hole that you men burn stuff in?"

Frankie ignored the last of her diatribe and attempted to gain control of where the conversation was going. "Yeah, a man's gotta have a clean house." He pointed towards Jennifer's hands. "Looks to me you don't do much house work with those nails sister."

"Sister, did you just refer to me as your *sister*?"

He recognized the twitch in her jaw. He thought for a moment that it had to be something that all women were born with. Maggie had that twitch many times when she stood up to him, and Margery had it, too, but Margery's got slapped off her face, still, he knew he had pushed her button this time. "…I apologize. Do you know you have lovely skin?"

Chapter seventeen

"What…?" She smiled. "No, but if you hum a few bars, I might be able to sing it for you."

"I don't see anything funny about this situation," he said nervously. "Why don't you just take your pretty self out of here and leave me be? What's it to you if I pushed my wife around anyway? Why do you care?"

"Don't men like you have some kind of pit they throw stuff in and then burn it?"

"No," he stammered. "You already asked me that. I ain't got nothin' like that."

Her mannerism became girlish. Her deep Southern accent returned. "Now, don't lie to me, Frankie. I know you have one. I was just asking to see if you are a liar, and you have not disappointed me." The Southern drawl disappeared again. "Move it. Or I will have to drag your lardy butt, and frankly, I don't want to ruin my heels. I have a dinner date tonight and I really must get home to take a bath."

He walked in front of her at what he thought was a safe distance. "Please, lady. I ain't done nothin' to you. Let me go."

"You're mistaken, Mr. Fuller. You've done something to every woman who ever wanted to escape from a crap-head husband like yourself. What happened to your vows? What happened to that man who promised to show kindness? What happened to honor?? When did you stop loving your wife?"

He seemed to pant as he slowly turned around and said, "Okay, psycho, shoot me and make it quick. I don't give a flying F*** what you do to me."

Her eyebrows rose, and she responded to his four-letter word. "Oh, my goodness, you have gone and said the only word in the English language that I truly despise."

He said it again…this time ending with "you."

Jennifer dropped her pack and then knelt down to feel for the lye soap. Keeping a safe distance from him she paid special attention to where her gun was pointed as she felt in the sack with one hand. "Now, where is my lye soap so you can wash your mouth out?"

"Go to hell," he said calmly. "A female like you wouldn't know what lye soap is with those pretty hands. I bet you don't even know what a toilet brush is." He laughed. "Stupid bi…!" He did not finish the sentence.

She frowned. "No, no, no. Goodness me, Mr. Fuller, you have really gone and done it this time. You almost called me that naughty name, Mr. Fuller. Get down in the hole, please. My mama has taught me not to say those nasty words. Shame, shame on you."

"But I didn't say it," he pleaded childishly. I'm sorry. I'm a stupid man just like you said."

"I saw it in your eyes, you silly little man." Jennifer reached in her pack and pulled out the bar of soap. "Take a bite out of this and swallow it—and don't be shy."

"No," he stuttered. "I ain't gonna take one bite out of that soap and I sure as hell ain't going to swallow none of it."

She cocked her head and replied slowly, "…but I am not a woman today, I am the Woodsman's Daughter." She squeezed the trigger of her handgun and fired one shot into his right foot. Now he could not stand at all. "Now, take two bites, pretty please with a cherry on top. And swallow them!"

Fuller screamed in agony as he clutched his foot. "You crazy lunatic! You really shot me! I don't deserve this! What did I ever do to you?"

Jennifer cocked her head to one side again. "Yes, I really shot you. Now, I said take two bites out of the bar of soap and eat it, or I will blow a hole right through your family jewels. Not that it would matter."

He hesitated until he saw her start to squeeze the trigger again. "I'm doing it! God, Almighty, I'm doing it!" Fuller took two bites and gagged as he swallowed both pieces. He started to whimper. "Please… please let me go."

Jennifer winked at him. "Now, stay down in that hole, and watch you don't fall and sprain your sorry butt. Do you like the taste of it? It's one of the finest imported soaps. Do you want to call me any more names?"

"No," he said pitifully. "I'll be good."

She looked at him with great seriousness and replied, "...hmmm, *'I'll be good.'* Does that mean you will write a letter of apology to your wife? Does that mean you will finally show Margery your undying love by sending her flowers on her birthday, candy on Valentine's Day? Or my all time favorite," she paused to curtsy, "a trip to New York City to see the lights."

Fuller threw up and started to climb out of the hole. "I ain't dying in this hole!"

"Suit yourself," she said calmly and karate kicked him in the groin. "Now, take off your pants."

Fuller doubled over and fell to his side. He started crying, spittle rolled out of the corner of his mouth. "No woman has ever treated me this way and walked away! I ain't takin' off my drawers!"

She giggled as he squirmed. "Didn't your mama ever tell you to make sure you wear clean underwear just in case you have an accident in an accident? Did you get that one? I love humor, don't you?"

She fired another shot and hit the ground. "I will count to three, and then I will shoot you in the other foot," she shrugged her shoulders, "not that it matters. One...two..."

He started pulling off his pants. "This is humiliating! Why would you want me to take off my pants?"

Jennifer swayed back and forth almost like she was in another world. "Ain't so funny now, is it, *Daddy*? I hated it when you pranced around the house with your undies on. I hated it!! No man should walk around the house with his underpants on while his daughter is trying to concentrate on her studies."

He rolled over on his back and threw his pants at her. "I ain't your daddy! You have mistaken me for your pimp!"

Her eyebrows rose. "There you go again." Jennifer seemed to be in a trance now. Then with grace and eloquence she opened up the sack and three of the most beautiful rattlesnakes fell into the hole with Fuller.

He froze in terror. She stepped back as her face twitched. "Aren't they just the loveliest things you ever did see?" she asked in a hillbilly accent. "I raised them from pups." She pointed to them in an agitated manner. "… the big one is Sugar Mama, the one with the pretty gold specks is Little Sister, and the little one is Clara. I named her after my grandmother."

He started to whimper. "…You are nuts lady. Who in their right mind gives names to snakes?" She was relatively sure that is when he soiled his undies.

She put her free hand over her mouth and then replied with a childish voice. "Now, if you want, I can get that toilet brush for you. You might want to do some scrubbing on your back side before you die. Goodness, when *was* the last time you had a bath?"

He leaned up against the side of the hole and kicked at the debris. "How the hell did I get myself into this mess?"

In a baby-like fashion she said to him, "These are three of my little friends who simply love to play and tell jokes. Sugar Mama shakes, Little Sister rattles, and Clara rolls. Be careful you don't step on them. They are very sensitive to body odor."

The first one, Sugar Mama, coiled up and sat motionless. The second one, Little Sister, struck at his gonads. The third, Clara, was the smallest one but packed a wallop when it came to inventimating her prey. Jennifer was not quite sure if she had procured a rattlesnake when she trapped this one. Fuller was now lying to one side in the hole, afraid to move, and somewhat breathless, he braced himself for the next strike. Nevertheless, Sugar Mama did its job as it struck not once but two times at his face. The second strike was a charmer. "Bingo!" she said as the second strike hit home.

She looked around and found one five gallon paint can, empty, turned it upside down and sat on it to watch Fuller squirm. He really found it quite peculiar that she continued to talk to him as if they were at some family picnic. "How have you been, Uncle Frankie? Been beating on Auntie Margery lately? Done any mean things that would cause her to try and kill your lardy old butt? Are those vehicles you always coveted still in pristine condition? Oh, no. Wait. Didn't I see Donny shoot the windshields out? Dang, if that wasn't the funniest thing I ever did see! Guess you won't be doing any concrete driveways any time soon, huh? And it's really too bad that I can't drop you in a hole full of it."

He fell to one side and whimpered out the words, "You rea…lly need to get help, lady."

Jennifer crossed her legs and smoothed out her dress. "I'm not a lady right now. I'm the Woodsman's Daughter but you can call me, Jennifer. You may have one wish before you die but don't ask for anything to eat. I am fresh out of maggots."

Fuller flinched as his right eye closed. "Whoever the hell you are, you need help."

"I beg to differ with you, Mr. Lardy-butt. You're the one who needs to get help, but I'm afraid I accidentally placed your sign in a position so that it will negatively affect your future. You wouldn't happen to have a cigarette, would you? Usually I only smoke after I have sex, but I will make an exception just this once. Are you having trouble breathing yet?"

Fuller tried to get up. "You are kid-din', right?"

"Yes, I am. I'm a real kidder at times. My papa was a kidder, and a rather good prankster. He was just like you—at times. But he never had any hogs."

He tried one more time to get up, but his attempt failed. She watched him die slowly. Anyone as fat as Fuller had to have heart problems. Jennifer sat and watched him die slowly. It took about thirty minutes for him to take his last breath, and then he coughed up blood.

"That's all she wrote," Jennifer said firmly. "Ain't so funny now, is it?"

She changed back into her camouflage and quietly left the way she came in. The hogs were wandering around the property so she left the gate wide open. She wasn't sure if they were meat eaters or not. They'd get hungry eventually. Now, Jennifer wasn't completely heartless. She would make an anonymous phone call and report it in a couple of days. The sheriff would do his pathetic investigation and call it a day. No need to make any accusations, being he had been stealing money from the contingency fund at City Hall for a long time. He admitted it to Jennifer two months ago. She had him right where she wanted him, and Simms was going to be very angry when he found out one of his cohorts in crime had met their demise.

She looked at "the girls" as they began to root around. She liked pigs. She just didn't like two-legged ones. "I am the Woodsman's Daughter," she whispered.

Chapter eighteen

The news of Frankie Fuller's demise traveled fast through the small town. Paulie Driggers was overly excited about the news of the death of his father-in-law. To think, Frankie had fallen in the same pit he had burned all of Molly's keepsakes in. "Good riddance!" he thought as he threw the paper on the floor board of his truck. Still, it would sadden his wife to know that her daddy was dead, so he decided not to tell her. She would find out soon enough.

He began to drive home when the truck made the familiar knocking sound he knew all too well. "Piece of crap metal!" he yelled as the truck rolled to a stop. "Not now! Not now!" He banged on the steering wheel with his hands. "Not now!" He poked his head out of the window and looked up to the sky, "I need a break! Please give me a break!"

He looked in the rearview mirror and saw a truck come up behind him. A very attractive woman got out and headed in the direction of his truck.

"Got trouble, son?" the lady asked as she took off her sunglasses and smiled.

Paulie swallowed and took a deep breath. "Yes, m'am. It seems she finally gave out on me."

"Are you out of gas?" Jennifer Martin Carter asked.

"No, m'am. Just out of luck," he said with sadness.

"I see you have a lot of tools in your truck. Are you a handyman?" she asked as she inspected the bed of the pickup. "Are you good at fixing roofs?"

"Yes, m'am! But I can't be handy until I have a vehicle that'll take me where I have to be handy at, and my tools won't do me any good this time."

Jennifer held out her hand. "My name is Jennifer Carter. Are you familiar with the area? I live just up the hill. I have found it difficult to find a reputable man to fix our roof. The last wind storm we had made a mess of our guest house. Do you think...?"

"You're *that* Jennifer Carter?" he stammered. "The same Jennifer Carter who donated all that money to the new clinic on Woodbine? Are you that Mrs. Carter?"

"*Am I that famous?*" she asked. "It was supposed to be hush-hush."

"No, m'am. I think my father-in-law's concrete business may have gotten rich off the driveway, that's all. I think I know your husband."

"You do? When did you meet Richard?"

"Well, I don't know him well enough to speak to him, but ain't he the man who used to come over to the diner and order up all those pancakes?"

Jennifer looked down the road. "I honestly haven't a clue as to what you are talking about, son. Are you one of his sons?"

He looked at her blankly. "Well, no, m'am. How could I be one of your husband's sons?"

She almost laughed out loud. "No. That's not what I meant. Are you one of Fuller's sons?"

He looked at her strangely and shook his head before he replied. "No, m'am. I said he was my father-in-law. You couldn't pay me enough money to be any kin to him. That man was a snake."

"You said he *was* your father-in-law? Did he pass away?"

"Yes m'am. He died just the other day."

"Goodness! Please except my condolences. Well, then, would you be interested in working for me? Are you sure he is dead?"

He almost fell over. "Yes, m'am. He's dead," he said, trying to keep up with all the questions. "He had a most unfortunate accident on his property. And no m'am, I mean, yes' m'am, I would like to work for you, but I don't have the money to get this heap fixed, and I sure can't walk there. Besides, I have a wife who is about to pop."

"Excuse me?"

"She's expecting our first baby. We live up on the ridge not too far from here. It's not much, but it's what we call home for the time being."

"Well, not to worry. I have more than enough vehicles, and you're welcome to use one of them and..." she paused, "Did you say you live up on *that* ridge?" Jennifer asked as she pointed to the familiar acreage.

He clamped his hand on the steering wheel. "Oh, shucks, m'am! Is that your property? We sure didn't mean to trespass. Please don't tell anyone. I swear—as soon as I can get back, we will high-tail it out of there."

She smiled pleasantly and responded. "Tell you what I'll do...what was your name again?"

"Paulie Driggers," he said reluctantly. "We didn't mean no harm, m'am. Please don't tell that brainless sheriff we live there. You can go on up there and look," he paused nervously, "we don't litter and the place stays real neat, thanks to Molly. I do what I can but I get home so late."

"Goodness, no harm done! You must love the outdoors if you're willing to live up there. It's my property, but as long as good people like you don't litter, I have no problem with it. You must love it there to have stayed there for seven months."

He looked at her oddly. "Yes, m'am. I do love the outdoors, but I love my wife more. How did you know we been living up there for the last seven months?"

Jennifer got a lump in her throat. She didn't know what to say. "My husband thought he saw you a while back," she lied quickly. "He has a kind heart and didn't want to cause you any trouble. Richard is just that way," she cleared her throat, "Paulie, I'll take you to my house and you can pick up the keys to our truck. I'll take care of the tow. Then you can get back to your wife. Is that acceptable to you? Sometimes I can be very pushy, and I really do need someone reliable. Are you reliable?"

Paulie felt like he was going to faint, or he had died and gone to heaven.

"Son, are you alright? Do you need some water?"

He wiped his brow and looked straight at her. "M'am, do you have wings underneath your jacket?"

She smiled and knew exactly what he meant and replied, "No, son. I was just going in the same direction as you and thought you needed some help. I'm not a guardian angel by any means." He looked at her strangely, and asked, "Are you the guardian angel who left us all those wonderful things?" She looked away, "...no, the woods give me the creeps. It could have been anyone that lives around here."

They walked back to her truck. "Real nice vehicle, m'am," he said. "I never thought I would ever get a chance to ride in a truck this nice."

"Will your wife be alright until you get back?"

"Yes, m'am. We've learned to get by with what I make and..." He paused and looked out the window.

"And what, son?" Her question had sternness in it.

Jennifer glanced at him for one second, and she saw a single tear run down the left side of his cheek. "I guess there is a God," he finished. "I should have never questioned what Molly told me about her angel."

Jennifer cleared her throat again and thought for a moment she might cry, too. "This will sound very forward of me, but my husband and I have a lot of room, and, well, I was wondering if you and your wife would like to live in our guest house for a while."

Paulie almost fell out of the truck again. "Molly is not going to believe any of this. You are a guardian angel! But I couldn't m'am. Besides, you don't know anything about me or my wife! I might be a crazy man for all you know!"

"And you don't know anything about me, either. I might be a crazy woman. Paulie, do you understand what I just said to you? I'm offering you a job and a decent roof over your head."

He stuttered a little and answered, "Oh, m'am, my wife likes it just fine where we are. I don't want to upset her, but I will ask her about it. I will be able to save up enough money to get something decent," he paused, "...I could pay you rent until then. She's kind of funny when it comes to moving around. She doesn't know about her daddy yet, and I just might not tell her."

"I won't tell her, either. It wouldn't be permanent, but it would give you the chance to save up some money to find a place in town. I'll take care of everything! Please, let me do this for you and your wife."

"Oh, no, m'am. I don't want to live in town. There are no jobs, and the ones that are open, well, m'am, they just don't pay enough. I want to get away from here as soon as possible. I want my baby to know what electricity is."

Jennifer cleared her throat. "I can't imagine living in a house without electricity. That must be dreadful. I could offer you eight dollars an hour."

Paulie almost wet his pants. "Whew, m'am! That is more money than I deserve! I don't want to be greedy. You can pay me less than that. I'm not a greedy man."

She smiled and looked to the side of the window. "I'll work you hard. You will earn every penny. We're almost there. Would you mind getting the gate? Sometimes it gets stuck."

"That's what it is," he said out loud. "I have gone and landed right in the middle of heaven!"

There in front of him was a sprawling mansion hidden amongst the trees. "God, Almighty! No one is going to believe this."

If Molly would not come, he would drag her.

"M'am? Do you live here with just your husband? Do the servants live there, too? How many kids do you have?"

Jennifer swallowed and took a deep breath. "My husband and I live here by ourselves. We do not have any servants. We manage just fine without hired help. We don't have any children. I was not blessed with the ability to have little ones."

Paulie blushed. "...sorry m'am, I did not mean to pry. It's just that I saw some place like this in a magazine a while back and there had to be a hundred people living there."

She almost laughed out loud again. "Maybe it was a hotel you saw," she said. "It's our little hideaway from all the troubles of the world."

"Jeez, m'am, you must have a lot of troubles."

Jennifer almost giggled like a school girl.

"Gosh, m'am. I didn't mean that. What I meant was..."

"...Paulie, may I ask you a personal question?"

"Yes m'am, you can ask me anything."

"How old are you?"

"Well, m'am," he paused, "I feel like an old man at times, but I'll be nineteen real soon."

Jennifer did not respond. She pulled up to the front door. "My husband may not be home, but I can show you the guest house. I know you'll like it, but it needs some sprucing up. I have some painting that needs to be done, and I'd like a pathway restored. You can take a look at the roof and let me know what supplies you'll need."

She guided him around the side of the house and pointed to a cottage built amongst the trees. "There it is. You and your wife will make it a home."

"M'am? This is your guest house?"

"Yes. No one has lived in it for a while. I will have to get you to bring some furniture down from the attic."

"Oh, m'am, it's bigger than any guest house I could ever imagine. Does it have indoor plumbing?"

She chuckled. "Yes, Paulie, go check it out. The door should be open, but it may be a little dusty. I don't get up here much. One of the bedroom doors stays locked at all times. I store some of my personal things in there, but there is another room that will be perfect for the baby."

"M'am, it could have dirt floors, and it wouldn't matter. M'am I got to ask you—why me?"

She paused and thought about her answer. "Everyone needs a little help from time to time." He quickly wiped a tear away. Jennifer turned, thinking to herself. "He's hooked. Now I have to convince the mother-to-be."

Jennifer walked ahead of him. "Well, Paulie, anyone who loves the outdoors like you has to have a big heart. I love the outdoors, too." She handed him a set of keys. "Take a look around and leave when you've made a decision. I may be back; I may not. Either way the fridge is stocked. If you need anything else I have left a fifty dollar bill lying on the mantel. Keep the change."

He stammered his words. "Yes... m'am and I'll be real... careful not to break anything."

Jennifer turned and headed back towards the main house.

Chapter nineteen

"Honey! I'm home!" Jennifer called as she walked into her house. A huge fireplace dominated the spacious living room. Leather furniture sat all around. Oil landscapes hung over fine mahogany tables topped with porcelain figurines of birds. A portrait of a rugged looking man wearing an outfit that Robin Hood might have worn focused attention above the massive fireplace. The man held a bow in one hand and, in the other, a quiver of arrows.

Jennifer called out again. No answer. "Honey! I'm home!" she called yet again, only this time with a more dominant tone in her voice. She heard a pan hit the kitchen sink.

"I'm here, love," her husband replied from the kitchen. "I was worried that you wouldn't get home in time for the soufflé to come out of the oven. It is simply wonderful! I have fresh asparagus, and the pork roast is going to be pure perfection."

Jennifer couldn't help but smile when she saw what he had on. There he was, in his 'glory.' 'Glory' being his hand embroidered silk kimono and five and dime slippers. Richard was a handsome man, somewhat girlie, but he was hers. He was thinner than most men but he was very strong. His hair was starting to turn grey on the temples. Richard's teeth were very straight and his fingernails were always manicured as were his toenails. He was a perfectionist in the kitchen. He doted over his utensils like they were his very own surgical instruments. Richard had been a promising surgeon in his earlier years.

She smiled at him. He returned the gesture as he put her purse elsewhere. "...now my dear, you know your purse does not belong in my domain." He picked up her purse and placed it elsewhere.

"It smells divine," she replied. Would you be a love and make me a rum and coke? We have someone looking at the guest house. Come to think of it, you might want to set two more places for dinner. We may have unexpected guests."

Richard Carter looked at his wife as he had so many times before and said, "Please. Not *another* lost soul."

Jennifer reached for the hors d' oeuvres and popped one in her mouth, "...hmmmm, you're lucky you are such a good cook my love," she paused, "or you might be serving up eggs and pancakes down the road."

"I'll take my chances," he quipped, "...you have always told me I am better in the kitchen than anywhere else," he winked at her.

Jennifer ignored his interest in what went on in their bedroom. "He is not lost, and neither you nor I have the ability to know if he has a soul. I've hired him to do the odd jobs that you can't seem to find the time to do. Do I have to get the rum and coke?" She assessed her husband's reaction. "Is this going to be an ordeal for you? Why must you be so inquisitive about who I bring in from the cold? Your business is my business and my business is my business." She giggled.

"I'm getting it, and it's not the cold that I am worried about, and the last time I looked, it wasn't cold outside at all. Goodness my love, you seem much too tense. What have you been up to that would make you so tense?"

"The particulars are not important, Richard," she snapped. A beat passed. "Did you get a chance to go to town today and pick up the strawberries?"

"Don't change the subject. Please, Jennifer, don't start again. We have gone over this too many times, my love. Why do you hire vagabonds to do jobs that we can pay experienced men to do?" Jennifer just stared at him. "Alright. Yes, I got the strawberries. I always get the strawberries and I bought the chocolate, and the cherries, too."

Satisfied she began to defend herself. "He is not a vagabond. Apparently he and his little wife have been squatting on the property over by Shallow Grave. His vehicle broke down, and I, being the person I am," she added importantly, "I offered to help him. It seems he is down and out and, well you know I love to chat with trespassers. By the way, if the conversation of them living on our property comes up, I told him you knew about it and didn't have the heart to make them shoo, and one more thing," she paused, "His wife Molly, well, she thinks there is a guardian angel living on our property."

Richard stood near the sink and tapped his foot. She smirked and turned to him, the familiar look passed between them. "He is not a vagabond. His name is Paulie, and he has a wife who is ready to pop, so get off my back and get the rum and coke before I take your soufflé and shove it up your butt." She adjusted her bra and sighed. "Why must I always be the man of the house?"

Richard's lips tightened and he turned back towards the kitchen whispering ever so softly, "I would like to shove the soufflé up your butt, my love, but you are such a tight ass it wouldn't fit. And if you ever took the time to look, you would *know* I am the man around here." He grinned and whispered again, "One rum and coke, your Highness of the Mountains." He turned to look at her but she was gone. The timer went off and he took the main entrée out of the oven. He practically drooled on the casserole dish, "...*Perfection* at its best."

～

Jennifer walked into the foyer of the guest cottage and did not see the young man. "Paulie! Have you fallen in? Paulie?" she called. She heard his voice, a whisper, almost like he was talking on the phone in secret. "How silly," she thought. "There is no phone." She followed the voice and found him in the far bedroom. The door was cracked. She stood outside and listened.

"Lord, if I am in heaven, would you please go and get my sweet wife 'cause I don't want her to miss out on this. What did I ever do to deserve that lady picking me up? I swear, Lord, if this is a joke, wake me up now 'cause I don't think it's funny," he paused momentarily, "and Lord, thank you from the bottom of my heart for Molly." A beat of silence, "and Lord, thank you for my guardian angel."

Something in Jennifer made her stand back and take a deep breath. She became nervous and started to sweat. All of a sudden she was being pushed backward into the past as if some unknown entity was forcing her to speak. "I've made a terrible error in judgment," she whispered. "How can I tell him he cannot stay?" Jennifer had just realized this young man was wiser than his years. She had come across a male of the species that actually adored his wife. All of a sudden she felt trapped.

The door opened, and Paulie came out into the hall. He was startled when he first saw her, but then he gushed, "When can we move in? I swear we won't touch a thing. We'll sleep on the floor if we have to.

This is the best thing that ever happened to us; well, it's the second best thing that ever happened to me."

Jennifer blinked. "Excuse me. What did you say?"

"I said this was the best thing that ever happened to us…"

"No, what did you say after that?"

"Oh, I meant marrying Molly was the first best thing that ever happened to me." He looked like he was going to cry. "Gosh, m'am, Molly sure has deserved more than I have given her."

Jennifer was dumbfounded and did not know what to say. She had no quick-witted answer, no funny joke, and no snide comment. Slowly, one word came stammering out of her mouth, "What?"

"M'am, are you alright? You don't look so good. Should I go see if your husband is around?"

The room started to fade away, and Jennifer fainted into Paulie's arms. "Hey! I need some help in here!" he shouted. "Somebody! Help!"

~

Richard put his hand on Paulie's shoulder. Paulie nearly fell back. "… are you her husband? She just fainted dead away," he paused for one brief moment and stared at Richard's outfit, a pair of black satin trousers and a shirt that looked like a throw back from a swashbuckler's party and not to mention his hands; Richard's finger nails were manicured and painted a soft pink. Jennifer lay on the floor with her eyes closed. Richard reached down and picked her up like she was a rag doll. Paulie stood in amazement at his strength. "Should I leave now?" he asked. Richard looked over his shoulder, "Get the door, will you? You have come this far, you might as well know what you are in for. You must be the new tenant," Richard stated sternly. "Thank God you were here. She hasn't had a fainting spell like this since…" Richard stopped. He decided not to explain Jennifer's ailment. "She has been doing too much hiking," he lied. "Will you be able to start this week? There are more than enough things to do on the actual property rather than odds and ends. Are you by any chance handy at doing landscaping? I have this marvelous patio that I want to incorporate a fish pond with. Did she ask you about the roof?"

Paulie stammered. "Yes, sir. Well, first I have to go get my wife. We don't have much, but it will have to do." He paused and then hesitantly asked, "Did your wife tell you she was going to let me have a vehicle?" He dangled the truck keys. "Are you sure she would want me to have that truck? Is it your truck?"

Richard shook his head. "Sure, the blue pickup around back. If she didn't think you were worthy, you'd be walking to town by now. What's your last name?"

"Driggers. Sir, can I ask you something?"

"Sure."

"She told me one of the doors was locked. I swear, I wasn't snooping…but, she said you ain't got kids."

A bead of sweat dripped slowly down the side of Richard's face. "We don't."

"…the door was unlocked. I was looking for the bathroom. That room is plumb full of baby clothes! How'd she know my wife was having a baby?"

Richard turned and headed towards the house with Jennifer still in his arms. "…must be ESP, son."

~

When Paulie walked into the living room of the main house he was more than flabbergasted. "…I ain't ever seen anything like this," he paused; staring at the large oil painting of the outdoorsman. "…that looks like your wife," he took a closer look, "…but she's a man," he stepped back, "I mean… it looks like a woman dressed like a man."

Richard did not respond to his comment. "This way. I need to get her to bed." Paulie opened the bedroom door for him. Richard laid Jennifer down with tenderness on the bed. Richard turned, but Paulie was not there. "…Paulie?"

Paulie was near the foyer staring at the oil painting again.

"Listen. Tell you what I will do, son. You don't say anything to her about seeing that stuff and I won't tell anyone you've been trespassing on our property, okay? Are you worthy of my trust?"

"Oh, yes, sir! I am worthy! The wife and me probably won't be back until morning, and I'll be ready to work. I swear, mister. I ain't no thief, and I won't disappoint you."

"Good. Will you wait here for just a few more minutes?" Richard asked. "I have to get something."

Paulie watched Richard walk down the hallway and turn into another room. Paulie took a few steps towards the painting again, and squinted at the signature in the lower right hand corner. "…the Woodsman's Daughter."

He heard Richard open a door. Richard returned to the foyer. Richard was holding two envelopes. "Paulie, you seem like a good kid. Here is the title to the truck. I have signed it over to you. If there is any question about it, I want you to go to the next town and have them call me at this number. Okay?"

"But, sir! I don't understand. I don't deserve this."

Richard handed him the other envelope. "Listen very carefully to me, son. Take this and don't ever come back here—ever! Don't tell anyone that you came here or about what you saw. This place never existed. If you do, I will have you arrested for stealing and trespassing. Got it, kid?"

Paulie shook his head. "Sir, this just doesn't make sense. Was it something I said? Why would you give me the title to your truck?"

"We don't need three vehicles," he was getting agitated but Richard almost chuckled. "Don't worry about it, just go and get your wife. Go to that little camper you called home and fetch your meager belongings. Do you understand? You can come back for a short time, but when the work is done, it's all done with."

"Sir, I don't mean to be ungrateful, but this is a little scary. Is she an escapee from a lunatic asylum?"

Richard almost choked. He decided that maybe the truth would be more than Paulie could handle. "My wife, as you well have seen with your own eyes is much younger than me but we are very compatible. I am her personal doctor and for now she needs my care more than she needs a full time handyman. She has the tendency to bring home many things that have lost their way, and you are not the first one she has taken pity on."

Paulie stepped back. "…sir, I don't need her pity or yours. I should leave now. I may have walked into a hornet's nest. I love my wife too much to bring her here if she is in danger."

Richard sat down on the sofa, now he was agitated at the young man; he had just said three words that caused a red flag to go up on Richard's list of things not to say, the first two being *hornet's nest,* and the third being *danger.* "Son, you seem like a nice young man, full of hope and dreams," he paused, pointing to the bedroom where he put Jennifer, "take this, and leave now before you get involved with *her*. Leave this area and make a go of it somewhere else. Trust me, son, you don't want to work for her. She is a very sick woman, and I am the only one who tends to her. Now, go—or I will change my mind. I mean it. Go."

He looked confused. "Go, as in 'go' and don't come back, *ever?*"

Richard stood up and adjusted his shirt. "*Ever*, the contents of that envelope," he pointed to it, "will take care of all your woes."

Paulie got into the truck and drove off. Richard stood there for a moment and turned to go back in the house.

As soon as Carter's place was out of sight Paulie's curiosity got the best of him. He pulled off the road and stared at the envelope lying next to him on the seat. He finally opened it and began to cry.

It was over two thousand dollars in small bills. As he started to put the bills back into the envelope a note fell out. He opened it and read it out loud. "*Friend, I would hate to disappoint my wife. She looks so forward to having someone to talk with, so if you really are what she thinks you are,*" He looks up, somewhat dumbfounded, and continues reading the note, "*come back with your wife and all is forgiven, but still, I must insist that you not speak of this matter or about the money to my wife or anyone.*"

~

Richard stared blankly at his wife. "I am just so tired of all this shit!"

~

Jennifer opened her eyes. "Daddy?"

Richard looked at her lovingly. "No, it's Richard. Paulie is gone. I will get your medication."

"Isn't he a good boy? I think he will work out fine," Jennifer said, looking up at Richard. "I love you, Richard. I'm sorry for all the trouble I cause. Are we still going for a ride tomorrow?"

"Yes, my love," he replied lovingly as he pulled out a syringe from his pocket. "Close your eyes my love. You have had one of your episodes and now you must sleep."

He swabbed her arm with alcohol and tenderly pushed the needle into her arm. "I have to go out for a while. This will relax you."

He would return in a short while and he would fill the tub like he had done for many, many years. He straightened up and looked out the stained-glass window. "When will I find peace?" he asked. He patted her on the head, "Rest a short while and when I return you and I will take a nice bubble bath together. Would you like that?" Jennifer's eyes were closed. He pinched her. No response, but she did have a pulse.

Chapter twenty

The sun was almost a sliver above the tree line and Paulie was excited. He stopped briefly to pick a few wild flowers and smiled at the thought of arriving in a fancy vehicle. Imagining her reaction when he showed Molly the money excited him, but how would he explain it? Molly might not want him to keep it.

~

As he came around the bend he saw Molly standing by the make shift clothes line. She turned and dropped the basket of clothes. She knew it was Paulie but it sure wasn't the truck he left with. He got out of the truck and grinned. She did not know what to say. He did. "It seems that guardian angel gave us a truck."

She picked up the basket of clothes and replied, "It's so late, Paulie. Please tell me you brought some milk."

"Oh, I didn't forget it, and I have some brand new things for the baby, too. I'm so sorry, but I have some really good news." He saw her eyebrows rise questioningly. "It seems there is a guardian angel watching over the both of us."

"Did you run into Papa?" she asked excitedly. "Has he made amends for all that he did to Mama? Where did you get the truck? She paused, "Oh, please don't tell me you robbed a bank!"

He almost laughed. Paulie shook his head and said tenderly, "No, Molly. That's never going to happen." Her face fell. "I got a job." She looked at him expectantly. "A real good paying job, and by tomorrow night you and I will be sleeping in one of those big city beds."

"Oh, Paulie! Have you been running a still on the side? Don't play jokes on me like that. Please. Where is the old truck?"

"Molly, have I ever lied to you?"

"No—at least not that I recall. But you love me, Paulie Driggers, and you just might say those things to make me feel better." She rubbed her belly tenderly.

He wiped the sweat off of his forehead. "Molly Driggers, pack all that we have in that raggedy suitcase 'cause we're going to live in style!"

She studied his face. "You really are telling the truth. Did you find a pot of gold?"

"Honey that old truck broke down and some lady offered me a job to fix up her house. Then she said I could have one of her vehicles, and then I prayed, and then she fainted dead away and…"

Molly reached for him and hugged him tightly. "It doesn't make any sense, but I'm thrilled anyway." She took his hand and laid it on her ample stomach. "Feel this belly. This is your son, and he's excited, too!"

She hugged him again and felt the envelope with the money in his pocket. "What's this?" she said pulling it out.

"Now, Molly, promise me you won't go crazy, alright?"

He opened it and pulled out the money. "Oh, Lordy be, Paulie! You did rob a bank!" she exclaimed.

"Molly, now, I did no such thing. That woman's husband gave it to me! He told me we could live there until the work is done. I swear Molly…something really strange is going on at that house. Here's the title to the truck. Her husband signed it over to me! He gave me the truck! It's the craziest thing I ever did see. Something's going on at that house, but I don't care."

Something rustled in the underbrush.

Paulie shrugged his shoulders and smiled at Molly. "This is more money than we will ever see in a lifetime. Feel it Molly!" he said as he thrust the cash in her hands. "I love you, and if this doesn't work out, I swear I will take you to your sister's house 'cause I just have to go back there and talk to the woman again." He paused and gently took his wife by the shoulders. "There's something else I have to tell you, Molly. Please. Sit down."

She sat down and saw the same look on his face that he had when his sister died. "What is it, Paulie? Did something happen to Mama?"

"No, Molly, it's your papa. He's dead. The stupid fool fell into that burn pit of his and got bitten by some snakes. Then those dang pigs of his must have been so hungry…well, it was horrible, they said."

Molly didn't cry, nor did she yell or scream or fall down. "…those pigs wouldn't hurt him. I will get our things together right now," she said quietly. "This is an omen. What kind of omen, I just don't know for sure."

"What is? Us leaving this hole on the mountain or your papa dying the way he did?"

She half-way smiled. "I'm going down to the creek and take one last dip in the water. Does this new place have one of those toilets that will wash your bottom while you sit down?" she paused and stopped for a moment, looking back at him, "would you mind gettin' our things together?"

Paulie grinned and watched her walk down to the creek. Then he laughed so hard he thought his stomach would split. "No more cold biscuits!"

~

Molly crouched down and splashed cool water on her face. "I've been waiting for you to die for three years, you bastard. God Almighty, I hope those poor pigs don't die from food poisoning!"

~

Paulie opened the cabinet and took out the one beer he had been saving for a year and popped the top off. It was hot but he did not care. He held it up in a mock salute. "It's hot, but here's to you, Fuller!"

~

Molly stepped into the cool water and grinned. "Mama always wanted to be a widow." She stared up into the trees, almost mesmerized by the beauty. "…things will be different for *you*," she said quietly as she rubbed her belly again.

~

Paulie finished putting the last of their meager belongings in the truck and called for Molly.

He called again. Nothing.

He called one more time. But she could not hear him.

Several minutes pass. "Molly! Let's go. It's no time to be takin' a bath! You can bath in luxury tonight!"

He followed the narrow path that led to the small creek and saw her. He yelled at the top of his lungs. She was lying face down with an arrow in her back. "M-o-l-l-y!" His voice echoed through the trees.

He looked around with desperation, not knowing what to do at first and then shouted into the trees, "Who is out here? Why have you killed my wife? What do you want? I'll kill you for what you did!" He pulled Molly up and held her close, watching the blood trickle through the creek and then he heard the undeniable sound of an arrow leaving its bow string.

He fell to the ground still holding Molly in his arms. The title was destroyed as was the money. The truck was driven away and then purposely put into neutral, then pushed into a deep crevice. There was a storm coming soon and the rain would cause the weight of the truck to wash down further into the fifty-foot ravine, and soon Molly and Paulie would be resting in Shallow Grave.

~

Jennifer woke up. She knew exactly where she was, in the bath tub. It was dark outside. She looked at the clock. It was 1:34 in the morning. She got out of the tub somewhat drowsy and walked into the living room. "Richard?" The fire place was lit and the aroma of something wonderful drifted through the living room from the kitchen.

"Richard…" she said with some degree of grogginess, still he did not answer. She opened the door and saw that his car was not in the driveway. "If he has gone off in the middle of the night, I will…"

"You will what, my love?" Richard queried, coming up behind her.

She jumped.

"How long was I out?"

"Long enough for the water to slowly go down the drain so that you didn't drown and you missed a most fine dessert, my love," he paused kissing her on the cheek, "Just kidding. You know I always save some for you, right?"

"Did they come back?"

"No, they didn't. Are you disappointed? I'm warming up the peach pie for you."

Keeping her balance she didn't answer but turned around and headed for the kitchen. "I need something to eat. Did you give me an injection? Damn you Richard. What else did you do that I don't know about?"

He smiled and followed her to the kitchen. "Sit, Cleopatra, and I will amuse your taste buds."

"Did you scare him off?"

"No, I caught him stealing the silver."

"He didn't seem the type to even know what price silver would bring. Are you telling me the truth Richard? You know I hate lying." She shook her head slowly. "…this just doesn't make any sense. He was so excited about the offer."

Richard rubbed her shoulders. "My dear, you misjudged your lost soul. He didn't even try to defend his actions, but I will admit he might have been a fine handyman. I gave him some money and sent him on his way. You won't be bothered by him again. I had to protect our interests, he put his hand on her cheek, and "…I really am sorry. I'll see to it that you have another chance at finding a new toy."

"…go *stuff* yourself with the rest of the desert Richard. I didn't misjudge him. He spoke about his wife as if he and she were truly in love. He was a keeper." She shrugged away his hands. "Besides, your interests are not the same as mine."

"He was trouble." Richard snapped back. "He would have bitten the hand that fed him. I convinced him not to come back. He will not come back," he said with a note of finality in his voice.

He placed a plate in front of her. She picked up the fork and took a bite. "…yum…this is really good, Richard. What is it?" She reached for the wine glass and took a drink, then two more sips. "…nice, strange flavor though. What kind of meat is this?" Her eyelids became heavy.

"It's the last of the venison. I marinated it in a wine sauce overnight. It's the wild mushrooms that really make the taste come out, don't you think?"

She took another sip of the wine. "Very good, where did you find mushrooms this time of year? At the local market?"

"I came across them at Shallow Grave. It seems they grow well there. Shall I get your bath, dear?"

"...I have had my bath, remember? But I will have a piece of pie while I take another one."

He picked up the plate and put it in the sink. "Are you done with this foolishness for the time being, dear?"

Her vision became blurry. "What did you put in the wine?"

"The usual, my love. It will settle your nerves."

She reached for the steak knife. "I hate you. I wanted to sit by the fire and snuggle with you. Damn you."

Richard took her hand and pushed it away, taking the knife from her. "And I love what my special wine does to your senses, my love. We will do the snuggling in our bed."

He escorted her into the bathroom and undressed her. He eyed her lovely curves, and the simplicity of her beauty. Jennifer had always been pale but she was not sickly at all. She had never been a sun worshiper, and the thought of her letting her skin peel made her sick to her stomach. Richard never questioned her about it. She had one tiny mole right in the middle of her breasts, perfectly round like her perfect breasts. Jennifer knew when to be tom-boyish and she knew when to be feminine. He helped her into the bubbly water, and she slowly sank down into oblivion. "Oh, my bracelet," she whispered and held up her right hand. Richard smiled and replied, admiring the simple lines of the bracelet. He had given it to her on their third anniversary, "Gold and diamonds, you never take this off my love." He looked at her again, slowly pouring in more body oil, "You are so stunningly beautiful when you are all bubbly." His hands massaged her neck. "Do you still hate me, my love?"

She closed her eyes. He placed a tiny white pill under her tongue. She did not try to push his hand away at all. She loved how it made her feel. She loved *everything* when he treated her like a queen, after all, she deserved it and he owed her big time. Richard looked at her lovingly as he poured the last drop of bubble bath into the water. "Damn, she was beautiful," he thought. At times he thought her to be a Hollywood beauty queen. Her auburn hair was flecked with gold highlights, all natural, too, and her eyes were so blue sometimes he expected to see clouds reflect off of her pupils. Of course, her teeth were perfect, too and her legs could have rivaled any Hollywood beauty queen. She was much prettier in real life than the images of her he had plastered on his private office wall. One reason for this was due to how he had drawn on them. The mustaches and blackened teeth did her no justice and she was forbidden to enter this room. It stayed locked at all times and he had the key. She complied at all times and respected his wish. A dart-ridden target hung on the far wall with her picture on it. A deflated blow-up doll hung in the opposite corner attached to another dart board. It was dressed in a black negligee. It, too, had blue eyes, and auburn hair. The initials W.D. were crudely scratched on the forehead of the doll.

Jennifer had bailed him out of jail for some improprieties and they struck a deal with marriage vows that would have made normal people cringe. It was a deal that made Richard a very happy man and for Jennifer, well, she had found a man that worshiped the ground she walked on and then some for the rest of her life.

~

From cold pizza to chicken cacciatore

~

Charlie Holtz was on cloud nine. He was relaxing on his back porch drinking a chocolate shake that his wife had made for him. He popped two aspirin into his mouth and swigged the last gulp. "I have the feeling the other shoe is going to drop. Pinch me." A voice from behind him asked, "And where would you like me to pinch you, lover?" He smiled at her affectionately, and asked, "What is that wonderful aroma coming from the bowels of your kitchen my love?" She giggled, "You have such a way with words," she paused, "its chicken cacciatore, and marinated asparagus. A long way from cold pizza and mid-night indigestion, right?"

It was Callie. She was Callie Holtz now. They had been married for some time. He did get to retire early but kept in touch with Danny still. They were fishing buddies, and from time to time they partnered a client.

Callie handed him a glass of water. "You've beaten the odds, Charlie Holtz. Aren't you glad I asked you to marry me?"

"Yes, Flower Bird," he said. "I just needed a little coaxing," he paused. And don't think for one minute I married you for your money. I had no idea my dearly departed mother had set up a trust fund for me. She always said I was a good boy, and you know most of it is gone.

The girls needed it for college. What's money when I got a rich wife to take care of me, right?"

Callie smiled and took his hand. "I know it was all about wild beer and cheap sex, right? And I have always made it quite clear that my money is mine, and yours is still ours."

He nearly choked. "That is my line, honey."

They watched the sunset together as they did every night. Charlie had fallen ill and had not worked for some time after the ordeal of Thomas Martin's head being found hanging over a mantel. They did not marry until several years after it all got swept under the rug. Callie started taking care of him and one thing led to another, soon they were living together in her cozy little cottage. Jennifer had been sent to boarding school. It had been her one request and last ditch effort to rid herself of her father's death. She was smart beyond her years and graduated early from nursing school, and minored in abnormal behavior.

~

Once Jennifer met Richard there wasn't too much communication between Callie and Jennifer. Their relationship as Aunt and niece sometimes was very strained but they needed it to be this way. It was an agreement they made when Jennifer graduated from nursing school. Callie did not like Richard at all, but she respected her niece's choice. Jennifer had invested her money wisely as did Callie, and from time to time they met for lunch and reminisced. The subject of her father's death never came up nor did they cry over spilt milk. Occasionally Jennifer did mention her mama, but the subject changed quickly by Callie's request and telling Jennifer that her mama was where she was meant to be.

~

Callie stared off into the last rays of the sunset. Charlie looked at her and asked, "When was the last time you talked to Jennifer?"

"I talk to her last month. She sounded tired and is still a little contrite with Richard. I told her if she doesn't ease up on him, he might just leave her."

Charlie sat up and took her hand. "...I would think that would make you happy. You think he is a turd, right? I am sorry that the two of you grew apart. I know you miss her. Maybe we can take a short trip and just drop by to see her, you know, just check on her. Would you like that?"

Callie ignored his comment. "Let's go. I want to get to the cemetery before it gets dark," Callie said as she picked up the vase of gladiolas.

"I sure do miss her."

"Yeah, me, too, Hilda not only was the best darn nurse, but she ended up being a wonderful friend. Don't you think it odd that everything ended up the way it did? Maybe *there was* a reason for us meeting like we did that day."

He looked at her rather strangely and replied, "Yeah, love at second sight. You want to talk about this *now*?"

"I suppose I do."

"…the way everything ended up, like what? Like taking Jennifer out of Mountain View? Or like you running off again to places unknown and you not keeping in touch? I have to tell you I am still a little upset about you doing that."

Callie sighed deeply and replied, "I know. It was not very nice of me to do that to you especially after I had you over for dinner so many times and then…POOF, I left," she paused again, "but I told you why I left."

Charlie got up and leaned into the wooden railing overlooking the hill side. "…yes, you told me and I know and you know that she was never right, *you know*, in the head. The thought of her marrying a man so much older than her just floors me. Why would a young woman like she want to marry an old fart like Richard? The man shaves his legs!"

"…you are an old fart, and I agreed to marry you," Callie chuckled. Richard is older than she but he is good for her. She needed stability in her life, and I am pretty sure they are happy."

"Pretty sure?" he said questionably. "I have one of those gut feelings again. I think you should go for a visit. I will go with you."

Callie patted Charlie on the head. "I know you would go with me, but it is not necessary," she turned her back to him. "I have been in touch. She and Richard are fine. It bothered me at one time that she was so troubled but I am not her babysitter anymore. She knows I care, and you know she always was very distant once it was set in stone that her mama was not ever coming back."

Charlie tapped the railing nervously and turned around. "...and that still drives me nuts. How could someone just drop off the face of this mountain? Nobody found anything. Sorry we had to miss the invite from Jennifer and Richard last month. Did you tell her we would take a rain check? I feel really bad about it. Richard always sounded like he wanted to say something to me in private but would change his mind at the last minute. Ever get that feeling when you talk to him?"

Callie hesitated. "...no, not really, *Richard is odd*. Odd but he is good to her. Maybe when you get your strength back we will make a surprise visit to them, and besides, we all have our little idiosyncrasies that annoy each other. Would you like that?"

Callie picked up her cane and took a deep breath. "I suppose we shouldn't. She was never one for surprise visits so let's not. You know she and Richard are recluses, and they made it quite clear in their last message they preferred we meet somewhere other than their homestead in the mountains. Why do you think that is?"

Charlie followed her to the living room, and they sat down. Callie picked up an album and started thumbing through it and smiled. "She sure was a cute thing even with the hand she was dealt. I am still so very thankful that I was able to help her out and Hilda, too. Hilda was a jewel, and I really must take those glads to her grave site tomorrow," she paused and ran her finger over a photo of Jennifer. "Look at this picture. I swear it's like looking at her mama. Are we old or what?"

Charlie looked on and ignored her comment. Callie turned the page. "Look, this picture is right before we got married. Here's Jennifer in her nurse's uniform. Who would have ever thought she wanted to become a nurse?"

He looked at the picture and smiled. "Who would ever guess that this little girl would grow up to be a psychiatric nurse? Did she ever mention where she worked?"

Callie turned away from him. "Not that I can recall, but why would it matter? I think she went free lance with her RN degree, and if there is one thing those two like being, it's private."

He gave her a stare. "I care because I still have a little guilt about taking your money to shut my mouth. That's why."

"...you most certainly did not do it to keep your mouth shut. You did it to sleep with me in the same bed." She giggled. "Seriously, honey, please, it's too late for that story. I know it's a tender subject, and you didn't take my money to shut up about anything. You would have done the right thing no matter what happened. She was a little girl who needed some help from a man who needed to be loved by me." Then she giggled again, "Besides, we decided to just call it 'love' money, remember?"

"I don't seem to remember it happening that way," he replied. "If I ever found out she was up to any of that weird stuff, I would croak, right now."

"She's not. She's fine, and she's happy with her life now. Granted, she's a little too demanding for my standards, and she treats Richard like a puppet at times, but neither one of them beats on the other. I don't think he has ever raised his voice to her. Doesn't that count for something? He's good to her. She moves to the beat of a different drummer. Always has and the fact that he cooks and cleans without complaining about it, well, yes, he is a turd but a very tidy one."

Charlie chuckled at Callie's comment and then his demeanor changed. "What if he is treating her just like her papa treated her mama? Would she tell you? How would you know?"

"Jennifer is strong willed, and far too independent to let any man push her around. It's an ego thing. I need to go to bed."

"But I thought..."

He looked at her with his big green eyes, and she knew he was tired, too. "I guess the glads will wait until tomorrow."

Chapter twenty one

Charlie could see the kitchen light on when he got up to go pee for the fourth time. Callie had not been sleeping well at all, and he was worried that she was troubled about something. He walked quietly to the kitchen and found Callie reading a letter. On the counter was a shoe box full of more letters. "What are you doing up so late? What's all this?"

He startled her. She jumped and quickly put the letter she was reading back into the envelope. "I was just reading some letters. I'm coming to bed now."

He reached for one of the letters.

"Charlie, they're private. Please don't."

"Since when do you get letters posted to a private box at the post office? I'm a retired detective, remember? What's going on? This looks like Richard's handwriting. What gives, honey?" He looked up at the ceiling with a degree of frustration, "…these had better not be what I think they are."

She looked like she had been caught with her hand in the cookie jar. "They are letters from Richard. Please go to bed. I don't want to bother you with these."

"Why is he writing to you via a post office box?"

"He uses me as a sounding board, I guess."

"May I read one of them?"

"I would rather you didn't," she said. "It will open up a bag of worms. Besides, these are old letters. He hasn't written to me in over six months. I was just making sure I didn't miss anything, you know, like a hidden message to some silent madness."

"Oh, girlie, my curiosity is peaked now! His madness or hers?"

"Maybe both," she replied. "Go ahead, read one of them. It doesn't matter now anyway."

Charlie put on his glasses and sat down beside Callie. He read aloud.

'*Dearest Callie,*

It is midnight and I can hear her. She is outside ranting to the moon about dinner not being cooked to her satisfaction. We had a few neighbors over, and it was a disaster to say the least. I thought it was perfect; the neighbors thought it was perfect. That is, until she slammed her hand into the banana crème pie. It wasn't cold enough, and another friendship went down the toilet along with the most perfect banana crème pie I had ever made. She is getting worse," he paused to sigh, "*…no kidding.*" He continued, "*So far there has not been anyone missing in town. I can't sleep at night, so I close my eyes during the day when she is doing God knows what in the great outdoors. She rants and raves all the time about everything, and it is usually something I have done wrong. I remember when I was a man. I could stand up to her or anyone that confronted me with a problem or even some tiny, little predicament, but I have become a mouse trapped in this house. Me, an out of work surgeon, top of my class, and I made one little mistake. She found out about it, and here I am. Oh God, I almost forgot. Jennifer had the audacity to tell one of our guests that the next time they decided to take a crap in HER bathroom toilet, they needed to make sure they flushed!*' Charlie took a deep breath, "*…oh, lordy.*"

Callie put her hand on his shoulder, he continued, "*Oh, well, don't we all put fuel on the fires we start. You might ask why I stay. This I cannot answer other than she does not cause bodily harm to me. After all she still thinks that some heavenly body is coming down and will pronounce her pregnant. You, of all people, know this is never going to happen, and may I remind you that your promise is your word and is the only thing that very well may be keeping me alive. If she ever found out that I made sure I could not father a child, well, heaven help me, not her…and to think I performed the procedure with my own hands.*' Charlie looked at Callie with seriousness, "You read most of this, right?" Callie cleared her throat, "Yes."

He cleared his throat, "*Last week I got an anonymous phone call from someone. It was a man who said Jennifer was out in the middle of Main Street screaming at the top of her lungs due to some misunderstanding about a man not opening the door for his wife. It never ends! We will have to move. I hear the whispers when I go shopping. I hear the comments then, I hear her when I come home. God help me if I don't have something on her list of groceries! I actually drove thirty miles out of my way just to get fresh fish for her trout almandine; I served it on a silver tray, and then she selfishly threw it out the front door. Why do I do it? I love her, and I remember how she was, and I won't even go into telling you how things are when she has cramps. Listen, I know you both think I am a little off, but I take care of her. She goes nuts every time I buy noodles! I have to hide them, yet she eats my fettuccini all the time. Well, I guess I can't have it all my way, all the time. Silly me, right?'*

Charlie put the letter down, and stared straight ahead, "Pack your bags." He continued reading, *"She is better, in that she tells me she is sorry the next day. I don't know where she goes during the day, and as long as I continue to get the local paper telling me in print there are no missing husbands who mistreat their wives, well, then I do not care. I check her speedometer. She doesn't go far. On Mondays and Fridays it seems she drives just outside the county line and on Tuesdays it takes her all day just to get out of bed. Monday must be a bitch, huh?' So, I ask myself, why does a woman who can get her hands on hundreds of dollars every day want to make my life so miserable. Why not leave me? I have my own money, and you know that she is very generous to me if for no other reason than I am just a nice guy and a marvelous cook. I have to go and prepare a roast duck with orange sauce. Maybe I should just serve it on the ground outside near the picnic table. That's probably where it will end up anyway. Please come up when you get the chance, but call me first.' Best regards, Richard.*

Charlie put the letter down. "Has she cracked after all these years? What kind of trouble did he get himself into that he cannot practice medicine anymore?" he paused, "maybe you should not tell me."

Callie rubbed her eyes. "I think she cracked a long time ago. *This* letter was the last one. Just read it, and keep an open mind. As for what he did, well, he performed an illegal castration on a criminal without his consent. I am not surprised at all that he performed the procedure on himself."

"…you're kidding, right?"

Callie responded with a nod of her head.

Charlie reached for another letter and began to read.

'Dear Callie and Charlie,

'Well, its midnight again, and once more I am writing to you. She is getting much worse. Today she called me 'Daddy' by accident and just missed my head by a hair when she threw a vase at me. I over-cooked her soufflé. You might ask me why she has to have soufflé for breakfast. I am just the cook now. She calls me 'the cook.' Not Richard, not 'the idiot baker,' or, one of my all-time favorites, 'the ass-hole who screws up the soufflés.' I don't mind, really. I have learned to ignore the name calling. What's that they say? 'Sticks and stones will break your bones and soufflés served on silver platters will definitely harm you when they hit you upside the head.' And now if I don't have enough freaking house work to do ... there are leaves in our bed now. She has changed into someone whom I have become afraid of, and that is something I swore to myself I would never let happen.' Charlie paused. Callie looked at him, his eyes were welled up with tears, and he replied, "How could we not have seen this coming after all these years?" He cleared this throat. 'It's the other things that are becoming quite bothersome. She has one room completely stockpiled with baby clothes in the guest house. When she is at home, most of the time she only wears this one particular robe around the house. It smells. I put it in the wash the other day and I should have just let it smell. It shrank. I am now the proud owner of a smashed up Mercedes. Does it matter? Hell, no, when you compare it to what she did to my golf clubs. It's not that I ever use them, but have you ever seen a set of brand new clubs hanging individually from the canopy of a fifty-foot cedar? I asked myself, how did she get them up there? And then I remembered. She's an expert hiker and rock climber. God almighty, she reminds me weekly that she is the Woodsman's Daughter! And did I ever mention just how much I hate that oil painting in the living room? It is hideous! Why would she take an exquisitely painted portrait of a man in tights holding a quiver of arrows, and then hire someone to paint over the face to make it look like her?' She is obsessed with it. I am forbidden to touch it. She dusts it, and then she'll sit and stare at it for hours.' If she dies before me, it will be the first thing I burn in the fireplace.' Charlie straightened up in the chair, "That's for sure."

'She'll buy a new Mercedes for me, and one morning I will find a new set of clubs wrapped up in a big red bow with a note, 'Love to love you.' The one thing that really bothers me is her saying "Alrightie-dietie" all the time!' Charlie looked at Callie, "I remember that phrase. She said it a few

154

times when I came to see her at the clinic when her father was killed."
Callie sat motionless and said, "…finish please."

'And the thing that really causes me to sleep with one eye open is the fact that she hasn't yelled at me for over a week. Yes, she says things that are mean and hateful, but she doesn't yell or say anything that would make me think she's angry. There's no emotion. And thirdly, I found a nurse's uniform in the trash, and it had blood on it. I'm beginning to wonder if that three day a week trek is something I should investigate. God, what if she is moonlighting as a nurse somewhere? I hate to ask you but maybe you and Charlie can come for an unexpected visit. Jesus…it just occurred to me that she could be pregnant, but I keep track of her monthly, and she simply cannot be pregnant.'

Regards, Richard'

Chapter twenty two

Callie looked at Charlie with sadness. "Hilda read most of them. She even wanted to go see Jennifer before she died, but Jennifer said she would come to see her. You got sick, and nothing else mattered. I'm so sorry. I was just hoping that maybe she and Richard would show up at our door step and tell us everything was…" She started to cry.

Charlie shook his head, "That everything was *good with the world*. Hell, Callie, he might be rotting right now under a pile of leaves."

"That's not fair!" Callie said. "I took that child in when she needed me the most, and you knew the commitment I made when I did it! When she and Richard got married, I really thought she would get straightened out," she paused to wipe away her tears, "marrying an older man was the best thing she ever did," she paused and cradled her head with her hands, "It is not my fault that Eileen was never found!"

"No one ever said it was, and certainly I do not blame you for any of this. It wasn't fair but these letters are a big fat red flag screaming for someone to pay attention. Can I go to bed now? I'll think about this tomorrow, but one thing is certain."

Her voice trembled. "What?"

"We're going to take a little ride over there and see what's going on. I want to make sure Richard is alive."

"It's too far for you. Can't we just wait until you feel better?"

"…it's not too far. I said I'll sleep on it. Love you." He kissed her on the top of her head.

"Love you, too," she said.

~

Callie listened for the bedroom door to close and then dug through the pile of letters until she found the one in which Richard wrote concerning the young couple, Molly and Paulie. She would deal with this herself when Charlie got his strength back. She rubbed her eyes and headed for bed. "What have I missed?" she thought.

~

Carter's residence-the following morning

Fog had settled over most of the terrain and a heavy rain pelted the bedroom window. Jennifer reached for a Kleenex and wiped the saliva from the corner of her mouth. "Damn him," she whispered. "He had his way with me again." Even though this kind of weather had a tendency to make her somewhat depressed. The smell of espresso filled her nostrils. "Ah, the cook has prepared my favorite breakfast."

She strolled into the kitchen, half naked and smiling at Richard. "Love, is that the aroma of homemade croissants teasing my nostrils?"

She was correct, but what she didn't know was there was a guest enjoying the espresso, too, and it was not croissants at all. The "cook" had made crepes stuffed with fresh strawberries topped with fresh whipped cream.

Richard nodded in the direction of the terraced garden area and handed her a cup. "We have a guest, Jennifer. Please put something on more appropriate before you go out there, and by the way, I do not appreciate you putting that sign out by the road again." She looked blankly at him, "What sign?" He smirked at her, "*THE SIGN,* don't play games with me Jennifer, the sign that says 'Martin Property' beware of the bears,' not a damn big funny." She shrugged her shoulders, "I have no idea what you are referring to Honey."

She looked out on the terrace, "What is that pinhead doing here? Did he tell you what he wanted?"

"He didn't tell me, and I didn't ask," Richard replied shortly. "It seems he wants to speak with *you*. What have you done now, dear?" The mixed tone of frustration and sarcasm was unmistakable.

She looked him straight in the face, put her cup down, and pulled off her nightgown. "Is this more appropriate?"

Richard picked up her nightgown and handed it to her. "Don't push your luck this morning girlie." He half-smiled, and that is when she decided to go and change. "Party pooper," she whispered.

She chose to put on the silk-print kimono Richard had given her last Christmas. It was black, and on the back was a hand-painted dragon with a pheasant in its mouth. Jennifer did a quick turn in front of the mirror and noticed a bruise on her buttocks. It was definitely a needle prick. She rubbed it.

Her eyes narrowed, and she almost chuckled at the thought of Richard taking advantage of her. It was the only way he could be satisfied. He always enjoyed making love to her when she was unconscious. She had to be unconscious. It kept her from throwing up after he was done. It had always been fine with her. She never could bring herself to look at him cry when it was over. Richard liked to sing when he was overly excited. Jennifer was glad that he sedated her most of the time. He had a horrid singing voice.

She walked through the kitchen and past Richard craning her neck to see the guest again. "You were up to no good last night, weren't you?" She twirled around and flaunted her breasts at him.

"Don't act like a street walker, my dear. It does not become you," he replied with sternness. Richard's eyes narrowed as he watched her walk away from him. "Sit like a lady, please."

She opened the sliding glass doors and walked out onto the garden patio. The sheriff didn't get up, only eyed her up and down. "Good morning, Mrs. Carter. My, you look lovely this morning." He craned his neck to make sure Richard was not standing near the sliding glass doors and continued, "...you look good enough to eat," he whispered.

"He told me we had a *guest*, and then I saw it was *you*. *You are the sheriff*, and will never be a guest in my home." She looked over her shoulder making sure Richard was still in the kitchen. He was. "Did you come here to tell on me?"

He looked past her into the kitchen and whispered. "Easy, my China princess. He might hear you."

Jennifer sat down slowly, deliberately allowing her robe to unfold for his eyes only.

He shifted in his seat. "He's looking out the window at us. Are you nuts?"

She pushed her hair out of her eyes, and cocked her head towards the kitchen. "Yes, as a matter of fact I am, and he is not interested in what you are looking at. He is looking at you looking at me."

She got up and walked past him, whispering in his ear. "Why are you here? Certainly not for a noon-day thrill." She threw her head back and cackled.

Richard walked out casually and was holding a tray with strawberries and whipped cream. Jennifer sat back down and adjusted her kimono. "Be a good husband and make me a plate, will you?" The sheriff smirked at her and looked away. She smiled pleasantly, crossing her legs so that just her lower calves were exposed. The sheriff didn't smile, but he did look at Richard quickly and then licked his lips in Jennifer's direction. "They look real good," he said looking to see if Jennifer caught his double meaning. "Do you suppose I could have some more of this fancy coffee?"

Richard shrugged as he got up. "I'll get it for you. Don't you have some questions for my wife?"

Jennifer looked over her shoulder and watched Richard disappear into the kitchen. "What big eyes you have," she said seductively.

The sheriff tried not to grin. "Better to see you with, Jennifer. You know why I'm here. He's dead, and you killed him. Those little notes have gotten old, and this time you went too far. You have taken away one of my incomes."

"Why, whatever are you referring to?"

He looked towards the kitchen. "As if you don't know. Frankie Fuller. The sleaze bag who owned the concrete business, I found him, Jennifer dear. I must say the snakes were a nice touch, but I wish I had known you had made those plans," he paused, and looked again towards the kitchen window. "I didn't get my last pay check. When one is in cahoots with the local concrete pusher, one wants to get paid before he gets killed."

Jennifer almost laughed. Richard was hovering over the espresso. He stepped back out onto the patio and sat the sheriff's espresso on the table. The sheriff pushed back his hat. "It seems I found some campers up on your property. I just wanted to let you know. Now, I know you are pretty good about sticking those signs around, but sometimes this place is just too inviting. Once in a while they slip through, and it's my job to sniff them out. Ain't that what they pay me for?"

Richard cleared his throat. "We get a lot of campers up on the ridge. As long as they put their fires out, Jennifer and I have no problem with it; do we, Jen?"

The sheriff swallowed a mouth full of crepes and then replied, "You should get a job at the local diner. These are really good, but I said I *found* some campers. I wasn't implying that I chased them off. From what was left of them, they appeared to be city folks, two men, late fifties."

Jennifer's expression did not change. "Where did you bury them?"

Richard looked surprised at her question. "What are you getting at, Simms? Isn't that your job?"

"...I don't bury, I arrest but no, you don't understand," the sheriff said. "The bodies were already starting to decompose. It seems somebody called in and reported the odor. I wasn't aware that an odor like that could travel so far into town. Whew-ee! And did they ever smell? Did either of you happen to run into any out of towners that might have looked like them?"

Jennifer glared at him. The sheriff had no idea Richard knew exactly what he was talking about. "...how could we possibly know what they looked like? Do you have any idea who they were?" Jennifer asked, uncrossing her legs.

Simms tried to nonchalantly eye the view of her cleavage. "...no, but I'll find out soon enough. I got connections down the road. It seems their fancy car was found ten miles down the road, not even close to where they were camping. I find that very odd, and I found out from someone else that one was a lawyer, the other his client, and they were celebrating the fact that the dearly departed wife of the client passed away suddenly and she didn't get one dime of his money before their divorce, and it seems that they were both at the local diner bragging about it, and were quite loud." He turned to Richard, "Don't you frequent the diner from time to time?" Richard looked shocked, and answered him, "I haven't been there in months, and I do not gossip nor do I listen to it." Simms smirked and looked the other way, "Funny that no one around here reported the car until now. Hey, did you hear about Frankie Fuller?"

Jennifer could have kicked him. Richard sipped his espresso. "Funny that the local town's people can't find their front door much less two dead out of towners. Who is Frankie Fuller?"

Jennifer stared Richard down. "Fuller...of Fuller Concrete, he fixed the road for us, remember?" She turned back to Simms. "Where did they find him?" She took a sip of her espresso, "*You* found him, right?"

Richard coughed. "How did he die?"

Simms shook his head as he swallowed the last of his crepes. "Oh, lordy, it was a sight! Someone had stuffed him into the fire pit, stripped him naked, and I think he might have been bitten by a few snakes, but the most peculiar thing was he must have thrown up right before he died. I would swear that it was lye soap!" Jennifer was looking straight at Simms and asked him one simple question. "Shouldn't you be looking for clues instead of stuffing your face with crepes?"

Richard almost spit out his espresso. "What she meant was...we didn't know that man well. He did our driveway, did a good job, too, but I don't think he knew what soap was."

Jennifer looked away, and almost dropped her cup of espresso. "That was a good one Richard."

"I know what she meant," the sheriff quipped snidely. "My point is that he was not liked by many people. It seems he had his thumb on too many people's private business, ya know what I mean?"

Richard stood up. "No, we do not. Are you satisfied with our answers? Can I get you anything else sheriff?"

Simms stood up also. "Would you like to know what else is so weird about all of this?"

"What?" Jennifer replied unconcerned.

"I came across another vehicle not far from here. It was an old beat up pick up, just sitting on the side of the road, no tag, nothing in its glove compartment, absolutely nothing as to who was in it last. I left it and came back. It was gone. Things just keep disappearing around here. Now, why would anyone just leave a perfectly good piece of junk on the side of the road? I gotta tell you, I don't like this at all."

"Why are you telling us this?" Richard asked.

Simms smiled at the both of them. "Well, I guess 'cause you two are the only folks around here that make me feel so welcome," he looked around the garden, "where else can a man of my stature get to eat home made crappies?"

Richard almost spit out his espresso. "It's crepes, not crappies."

Jennifer giggled unexpectedly, and then she straightened up, and smirked at Simms. "Do we look like detectives?"

Richard excused himself and said, "Got to turn the espresso off." He quickly went to the bathroom and threw up in the toilet.

"What's with him?" Simms asked. "Something wrong with the crappies or is it he knows what you've been up to?"

Jennifer crossed her legs again and leaned forward. "...hush, whatever do you mean, sheriff? He's anal about his little espresso machine, and I didn't have anything to do with whatever you are referring to. I'm a respectable woman," she paused to push her hair away from her face, "So Fuller is dead. Frankly, I don't give a damn if he is dead. I hear he was not nice to his family at all. So what if you *found* some misguided campers? So what? Do your job and leave us alone. These mountains are full of weirdoes and lots of things go bump in the night, ya know what I mean?"

Simms cleared his throat. "Oh, sweet Jennifer," he said softly, "*and I don't give a damn* about what goes on around here, but if you cause me to lose more money you will be very sorry."

He looked around and did not see Richard at all. "If you want, I could give you a rub down tonight. Sound good? You look a wee bit stressed."

Jennifer sat back down. He moved a little closer to her and then leaned forward. Jennifer kicked off the silk slipper from her right foot. She rubbed the inside of his left foot and said with a sultry voice, "Want me to play the sheriff and you be the one who gets handcuffed?"

Simms grinned and looked around again. "No, but you can tell me who killed those campers. Just give me one clue, and I will be on my way. Re-election is coming up, and I need a boost."

She grinned and pulled away her foot. "I'll give you a boost later. You best go now before Richard gets jealous besides why would I tell you anything?" She brushed back her hair, and that is when Simms saw the bite mark on her neck, "...did you pick up a vampire lately?" She quickly adjusted her robe, "I had a run in with a fence. You're just jealous it wasn't you that bit me, but there is one little thing I need to warn you about."

"What would that be, Ms. Carter?"

"A little birdie told me you threatened your wife some time ago, and I just wanted to make sure you knew that I knew, so if you still have any intentions of harming her in any way, shape or form, I would advise you against it."

"You of all people are going to warn me?" Simms quipped.

Jennifer seemed very relaxed considering the conversation that was taking place, and she continued, "Yes, me of all people. This is what I want to hear from the little birdie," she paused, "I want you to send her flowers immediately, and I want you to buy a ticket for her. She is going on a trip to New York City, and you will not be going, got it?"

Simms listened intently while he watched for Richard.

Jennifer continued, "If I hear anything that might lead me to even remotely think that you have hurt her feelings, put one bruise on her frail body I will see to it that you are castrated without any anesthetic, got it?"

He was sweating now.

Jennifer stretched, "She might have been poisoned by someone. Anything you might want to add to what I have just told you?"

Simms took out a handkerchief and wiped the sweat off of his face, he stammered somewhat and replied, "She has not been poisoned. I have not poisoned her. I swear to you I have not done anything to her that might cause her to think she has been poisoned. She is a hypochondriac."

"I know that look that women get when they have been mistreated by their husbands. Lilly has that look, so once again I will tell you what you need to do," she paused, "Send her flowers, make her think she is the most important person in the world to you. Clean the house for her and continue to do so. Hire a maid, hell, I don't care. Just do it." He reached for her hand. She was caught off guard and quickly pulled her hand back. "You may leave now, and unless you have some kind of lame evidence to prove that I had anything to do with it, take your pitiful self off my property. Don't call me. I'll call you."

He sat back down, leaned back in the chair, and gave her a kind of half-smile. "I'll do what you said, and I know you had something to do with Fuller's death. I don't have all the pieces, but I will find something. Something that will tie your sweet little tail to it, and then what will you do when you need someone to be your *daddy*? You know, and I know, that nothing is going to come of it. I like my paycheck, and just between me and you, Fuller was a pile of crap. Watch yourself, and see that your little tail stays out of my way. I'll put some pieces together and make them match so you are not part of it," he paused, "and remember one thing, Daddy loves you."

She stared straight ahead. "…you disgust me. Don't be worried about my tail for now. You should be worrying about your hind-end when you no longer have a job. I'm not going to vote for you."

Simms looked at her and cocked his head. "…but I was your *daddy* the other night."

Her face drained of color. She cleared her throat, replying in a different voice other than what he expected to hear coming out of her mouth. It didn't sound like Jennifer. It didn't sound like the voice she would make when they had their secret meetings at his cabin. It was more like a child. *"You're not my daddy."*

Chapter twenty four

Richard walked Simms to the front door. Simms turned to say one last thing to him. "You might want to keep a tight leash on her."

Richard slowly closed the door. Simms would go to the nearest floral shop and pick up one dozen roses. He would do exactly what Jennifer told him to do and even throw in a box of Whitman's for good measure. It would not assure him of an evening of unadulterated joy with Lilly at all. The thought of touching her almost made him vomit, but the thought of these two gestures causing her to have a heart attack made him excited. Still he had Jennifer right where he wanted her, and that was in the corner of uncertainty edged with panic.

~

The Simms Residence

~

"What can I get for you, honey?" Simms asked as he opened the door to Lilly's bedroom. "Are you cool enough?"

Frail and pale, his wife opened her eyes and regretted not having the strength to slip her hand under the mattress and fire one shot into his unfaithful head, but then she remembered what Jennifer told her not too long ago. "Just hang on, sweetie. It won't be long, and, shucks, you haven't missed a thing. He has a trigger finger, if you know what I mean."

Lilly giggled to herself.

Simms looked at her quizzically. "What's so funny, dear?"

It was the first time Lilly had laughed so hard it hurt, but she quickly came up with a lie, "Oh, I was thinking of a show I listened to the other night, just silly stuff." Simms walked into the room somewhat sheepishly. She looked at him, "...what do you have behind your back?"

"Flowers?" she murmured. "You have never given me flowers." The fine hair on her back stood up, "Simms, is this your idea of a joke?" He managed a smile, "No, joke, my dear. It just dawned on me what a lousy husband I have been in the past, and I want to apologize. I will clean the kitchen for you later on, and tomorrow I am going to hire a maid to come and do the house once a week. Would you like that?"

Simms blew her a kiss.

Lilly was speechless.

~

He had no reason to question her again. Lilly listened to the radio all the time. His sweet wife of twenty years met Jennifer not too long ago. As a matter of fact, it was a town picnic, and Jennifer was more than willing to make their acquaintance at that time. There was something about Lilly that reminded her of her own mama, Eileen. They made a connection that no one would ever understand.

Simms' idea of going to a town picnic was to berate his wife behind her back. That was when good old Frankie Fuller used to step out on his wife, too. Fuller and Simms were second cousins.

Jennifer strolled over to Lilly. "May I sit with you?"

Lilly nodded.

"How long have you been in this quaint little town?" Jennifer asked Lilly.

Jennifer knew Lilly was a mouse, but still, there was something in her eyes that told Jennifer to befriend her. She knew somewhere in Lilly's mind revenge was brewing, and Jennifer was just the person to help it along.

"Simms and I have been here about..." she began.

Lilly did not get to finish her sentence because Simms walked up behind her and put a bug down her back. He laughed hysterically before walking away. Others laughed, too, but Jennifer could see the pain in Lilly's eyes as she reached for her hand. Simms walked away. "You okay? Why do you put up with it?"

Lilly whispered to Jennifer, "I'll be fine as soon as he is dead."

Jennifer smiled at her pleasantly, and that is when they became friends for life. It was a secret pact. No one knew about it except

Jennifer and Lilly. It bonded them like peanut butter between two slices of white bread. One piece was Lilly and the other was Jennifer.

"Isn't this the most beautiful place in the whole world?" Jennifer asked Lilly. This was a phrase that she had heard her mama say so many times when she was on the edge of madness. It calmed her.

Lilly looked at the backdrop of the mountains and sighed, "It would be if I could get rid of his dumb ass."

Jennifer almost cackled. "If you want to remain friends with me, Lilly, I must ask you to refrain from using bad language, okay?"

"How long do you plan on living here?" Lilly asked.

"For about as long as you need me, does he beat you, too?"

Lilly did not look surprised at her question at all. "No. He has never laid a hand on me. He just bad-mouths me. But he is a good man sometimes," she paused to take a sip of tea.

"…sometimes?" Jennifer whispered.

Lilly giggled childishly. "When he's unconscious."

Jennifer smiled. "Does he cook for you?"

"Does a honey bee like vinegar?"

Jennifer giggled. "Does he make it a habit of putting bugs down your back?"

"No, not really. Lately he has been slowing down. I think he is having an affair."

"I think you're right."

"She can have him. I'm a sick woman, and I really just don't care. If I knew who she was, I'd shake the woman's hand." Lilly did not take her eyes off of Jennifer. Their eyes met.

Jennifer looked straight ahead. "Have you ever done anything to him? You know, like put things in his food that normally wouldn't be there?"

Lilly giggled in a childlike fashion again. "I have baked him some special cornbread on occasion. How odd that you of all people would ask me that!"

Jennifer looked away. "You know, *don't you?*"

Lilly patted Jennifer on her hand. "You're my kind of woman, Jennifer. I have known about you for some time. Does it surprise you that I don't care?" She settled her hand on Jennifer's. "It's alright, really. He is so stupid, but he does have good taste in women! But I am surprised it is you of all the women who live around here that he chose," she paused, "you are smart and pretty, but it is alright with me. I am a very sick woman, but I'd like to know that he will suffer just a little bit when I am gone."

Jennifer looked very seriously at Lilly. "No, it's not alright. *He is stupid*, but he still has no right to treat you like this. I asked about the food because my mama used to put things in my papa's food all the time."

Lilly was now serious. "*Yes, it is alright* if it's you he's fooling around with. I know you will keep him in line. I hold no grudges against you. Will you do something for me?"

Jennifer was speechless for a moment, and then she cleared her throat and answered Lilly. "Sure. Does it involve having a little fun with pranks?"

Lilly smiled. "Kill him for me. I won't hold it against you. I'd be grateful. It doesn't matter if he never laid a hand on me," she looked over her shoulder. "I can't pay you much, but I am a wonderful seamstress. He is cruel with words, and words leave wounds that don't heal as good as bruises."

Jennifer was not shocked at all, but she did look around to see where Simms was. "You want *me* to kill him or hurt him really bad? How do you know I won't tell him about this offer?"

Lilly relaxed and sipped her tea before she replied, "Hmmm, the thought of him being in pain makes me want to jump for joy. On second thought, play with him a little longer. Then you can kill him. Could you give me a clue as to what you might do to him? I lay in bed at night and think of things I would like to do to him. He catches me giggling from time to time. He thinks I'm nuts."

Jennifer put both elbows on the table and adjusted her sunglasses. "…join the club. Are you sure you know what you're asking me to do? I could be one of those 'undercover' spies."

"Good choice of words, Jennifer, but you wouldn't waste your time on that business when you can be part of the excitement, right?" Jennifer nodded. "Are you sure you can handle the job?"

"Oh, I can handle the job," Jennifer replied. She looked Lilly straight in the eye, "When did you get diagnosed?" Lilly looked off into the crowd, "…one month, give or take a week."

Jennifer patted her on the hand, "…you were diagnosed a month ago?" Lilly shook her head slowly "No, I meant I have about one month to live."

Jennifer looked nervous, "Wouldn't you like a few more nights of putting wigglers in his spaghetti?"

Lilly slapped her knee. "I hadn't thought of that! Good one!" She became serious again. "I can't pay you much, really, but anyone who lives in a fine home like you do does not need my jar of pennies. Is it possible to put something like this on layaway? But you might want to take my seamstress offer for now."

Jennifer almost spit out her tea. "Layaway!?! Honey! This one is on me!" They laughed, but then Jennifer became almost sinister. "I have to tell you something very important. If you turn on me, I'll come get you next."

Lilly simply smiled and looked over to where Simms was standing. "…yeah, right, like you of all people are going to take revenge on a wife that has been mistreated most of her married life. He's been killing me for years. It's his turn now." Another sip of tea. "Did you know my mama knew your mama?"

Jennifer sat up straight. "You're kidding, right?"

Lilly shook her head. "I don't kid about things like this. They were friends at one time. I know all about how she was treated by your papa. **Did you kill him**? You can trust me with the answer. After all, I just hired you to kill my husband."

Jennifer stared straight ahead unmoving. "We don't know who killed him," she said simply. Her body relaxed. "You do know my mama was never found."

Lilly put one elbow on the picnic table and rested her head on her hand. "Too many people think I am just another country bumpkin, but you and I are very much alike." She paused. "My mama was just too sick to do anything about how my papa treated her. What is it with this place? Do all the husbands treat their wives like crap? And now I'm too sick to do what I need to do. Frankly, I think he has poisoned me, but there is no proof."

Jennifer was touched by Lilly's words. "Have you ever wondered what happened to old man Spencer? Or that slime ball, Hanson? It's been over ten years, Lilly, but there were a few husbands who died of unnatural causes. Those men were not nice to their wives either."

Lilly smiled nonchalantly. "I remember old man Spencer. Didn't he die right after your mama disappeared?"

"Yes."

Lilly stood and stretched her legs. "Mama never did like him. He and Papa were fishing buddies. Spencer used to come over a lot. I never liked him. He always smelled fishy. He always wanted me to sit on his boney old knee. I didn't like the smell of fishy knees."

Jennifer giggled. She was intrigued. "Was he ever 'mean' to you?"

Lilly seemed nervous now. "Yes, and Mama told him to never come to our house again. Papa was very angry at her. Mr. Spencer was very mean to me at times." She paused and sat back down. "I think she told your mama about it right before she died."

"Did your mama ever tell anyone of importance that he was mean to you?"

Lilly seemed surprised at her question. "She didn't have to."

"Why is that?"

"Mama marched right up to his house and told his wife about it!"

Jennifer's face became flushed. "Tell me more."

Lilly seemed amused. "It was so wonderful to see her finally stand up for me."

"You went with her?"

"Well, of course."

"What happened?"

"Well, at first he was shocked that she would even have the nerve to come to his house. She was so brave. Then all hell broke loose."

"Did he hit your mama?"

"No. I kicked him right where he peed."

Jennifer tried not to laugh. "Then what?"

"His wife stepped out on the porch."

"Oh, crap, what then?"

"His wife was a very large woman. I could not imagine him pushing her around. He was more of a string bean with big feet."

"What happened next?"

"She did something I could not believe. Mama was flabbergasted."

170

"She hit him over the head with a flower pot. He fell to the ground and cursed at her. I never saw so much blood in my whole life. I screamed."

"Then what?"

Lilly giggled. "Well, I'm not sure what happened to him after that. His wife dragged his ugly butt into the woods, and Mama followed her."

"Why didn't you go with them?"

Lilly giggled like a school girl. "His wife told me to stay put and go into the house and take the cake out of the oven. I did. She said it was her birthday."

Jennifer giggled, too. "Did his wife come back with your mama?"

"No, just one of them came back."

"What do you mean?"

"His wife came back, but Mama didn't."

"Did you go into the woods and try to see where she was?"

"There was no need to."

"What do you mean?"

"She came back eventually but without him. There was so much blood on her dress! I just figured he had a very unfortunate accident."

Jennifer was really listening now. "What do you think happened to him?"

Lilly looked at her oddly. "You're kidding, right? I reckon she killed him! Then we all sat down and had a tea party. That was the best tasting cake I ever had."

"Lilly, listen to me," Jennifer whispered. Have you ever told anyone about this before?"

"Do I look crazy? We understand each other, right?"

Jennifer nodded and looked away. "I understand more than you know."

Lilly reached for Jennifer's hand.

"Weren't you the teensiest bit curious as to what your mama did? Didn't you hear him yelling?"

"Yes, and you must know this, too." Lilly paused and looked over her shoulder.

Jennifer stared at her intently. "Yes?"

"I know your mama isn't dead, so if we can just agree with your taking care of my cheating husband, I can get on with my life. But do understand this, Jennifer."

Jennifer stood up. "Don't even try and blackmail me, Lilly. You need me on your side, but I have to ask you," she paused, "...how can you get on with your life if you have been told you only have one month to live?"

Lilly looked like she was going to cry. "...I never said I was diagnosed with anything. You did. Simms has told me he plans on killing me in one month. He has told me a hundred times I need to die because I am useless, and you have misunderstood my intentions! I respect you, and wherever your mama is, the secret is safe with me! I can tell you more if you want to hear it."

Jennifer nodded and kept an eye on Simms. "I don't know if I want to hear anymore. I am flabbergasted, but very intrigued. I think I know enough about your mama. I would have admired her."

Lilly shook her head slowly. "Oh, no, it's not about my mama. It's about yours."

"What do you mean?" Jennifer asked.

They both turned at the same time in the direction of Simms. He was pointing their way laughing. The crowd dispersed as fast as his laugh ended.

Jennifer tapped her fingers on the picnic table. "It seems one of us is the butt of his joke."

Lilly just smiled pleasantly. "He's the butt! Oh, how I hate that man!" She waved and blew a kiss to her husband. "Your mama had more backbone than any woman I ever knew."

Jennifer watched Simms spit and walk off in the other direction. "I don't understand. Mama never stood up to Papa. Granted he had his fill of bugs in his food, but she only back-talked him once that I know of. So, just what do you mean?"

Lilly pushed her plate to one side. "Oh, your mama was a strong woman at one time. My mama used to tell me some of the things she used to do."

"Like what and to whom?" Jennifer asked.

"Well, there was old man Dickerson. Dickerson owned the five and dime at one time. He was nice enough to the men, but for some reason he just didn't like women, especially your mama. Your mama was so smart but she never showed it around your papa. No, Dickerson didn't like women with spunk, that is, women like your mama. She used to come to town on a bicycle. She could drive but I recon your mama didn't want anyone to know she could. This was right before you were born, I think. She had parked her bicycle up near the entrance to the door of his business. He came out and started yelling at her. 'I told you not to park this dang thing near my door!' Your mama asked him why, and he just went crazy! He picked up the bicycle and threw it in the street."

"What did Mama do?

"She asked him to please get it out of the street. He told her to leave."

"Did she?"

"I suppose she did, but some people thought she came back later."

"Why would they think that?"

"Old man Dickerson lived alone. He had a wife once, but she ran off with his brother." Lilly paused. "Hmmm, that would explain a few things. Anyway, the next day the town was in a stir with what happened to him."

Jennifer tapped her fingers on the table again. "Did he die?"

"He didn't die that day, but later he did."

"So they thought Mama had something to do with him dying?"

"Maybe and maybe not, most everyone loved your mama but they did not like your papa at all. But everyone knew old man Dickerson was scared to death of snakes. It was one of those phonias, you know… when you're scared of something real bad."

"I think you mean 'phobia'."

"Yes, it seems he was taking a midnight bath and someone slipped into his house and put a rattler in the tub with him. The rattler was not what killed him. He hit his head on the floor when he slipped getting out of the tub, and he died two days later. They never did find the snake."

"They wouldn't have. Anything else you feel the need to tell me about my mama?"

"I suppose you know more than you let on, but for now I will tell you some things you might not want to hear at all."

"I have all the time in the world."

"Your mama and my mama were two peas in a pod when it came to pulling pranks on people who were mean and nasty to others, but they did it to avenge..."

"...the mistreated wives on this mountain?" Jennifer finished.

Lilly nodded her head in affirmation. "Did you know that for a long time some of those mistreated wives left flowers for your mama up near Shallow Grave?"

Jennifer looked stunned. "No, I didn't." Jennifer wiped a tear away.

Lilly smiled tenderly at her. "Your mama overheard a conversation one time about a husband who had mistreated one of her friends. Well, one thing led to another...it was just awful."

"What was?" Jennifer responded. "The conversation or what happened to the husband?"

"Well, the husband of course," Lilly answered in a tolerating tone. "It seems he beat the poor soul so bad she couldn't walk. Your mama went to pay her a visit, and he wouldn't let her in the house. So...one thing led to another." Lilly's voice trailed off.

"Is that when he paid his dues?"

"Yes, if you mean is that when he had a horrible accident with an outhouse?"

Jennifer grinned. It was not a silly grin at all but more of an evil grin. "Tell me more," she urged.

"Oh, goodness! That man was so tight he made her wash dishes in the creek, but they had two outhouses—his and hers. Weird, don't you think? He told her he didn't want her rear end sitting on anything he sat on," she paused, "Whew; he was the nasty one, not her. Anyway, one night he went to his outhouse. He had a habit of smoking a cigar while he did his business. It seems there was an unfamiliar odor in the outhouse."

Jennifer smiled and crossed her legs. "Do tell."

Lilly giggled once again. "Are you familiar with the smell of gasoline fumes?"

"At times I am."

"Well, he lit that big old cigar up and then...poof! Up went the outhouse with him in it. It was an awful sight, they say."

"And smelly, too, I suppose."

Lilly started to giggle. Jennifer laughed out loud. Neither one of them could speak. Jennifer slapped her knee. "…and no more business for him!"

Lilly was the first to regain her composure. "They never did find his head!!!"

Jennifer looked at her seriously. "You really have to stop. People will think we're nuts!"

Lilly giggled again and then looked over Jennifer's shoulder. "He's coming over here." She caught Jennifer's eye. "Just between you and me, I like being nuts. If it weren't for the boogers I put in his food, well, life would be pretty dull. Putting boogers in a husband's food was passed down from your mama to my mama and then to me."

Jennifer turned around and waved at Simms with a welcoming smile on her face. He walked up to the picnic table and stared at his wife. "You two are making spectacles of yourselves," he growled in a low whisper. "Are you talking about me?"

Jennifer stood up and leaned into the table, pulling her gaze away from Lilly. "If you make a spectacle of yourself, who would know the difference? I'll tell the whole town you and I are having an affair."

Lilly looked at Simms lovingly and then got up and left. Simms sat down, and Jennifer sat down. Simms rubbed his foot up against hers. "…shit. Jennifer. Did you tell her? She just might believe it."

"You are such a moron!" Jennifer spat. "Told her what? That you are a pervert? *They* already believe you're having an affair with the mayor's horse."

He looked blankly at her. "You didn't tell anyone that did you?" She threw her head back and laughed.

"Damn you, Jennifer. Your sense of humor is revolting!"

She took a deep breath and wiped a tear from her eye. "I only told the horse." She cackled.

Simms kicked at her under the table. "I hate you when you tease me like this. That kind of gossip is not a damn bit funny! I have a reputation to uphold!"

Jennifer snickered. "So does that horse," she said snidely. "Personally, I hate it when you have horse breath!" Simms glared at her menacingly.

"Goodness, Simms, you're such a tight ass! You used to like my humor." She thought he was going to hit her, but instead he calmly got up and she replied, "You excite me when you lie."

He almost answered her until he felt a hand on his shoulder. It was Lilly with a piece of apple pie. "Here," she said as she set the plate in front of him. "I thought you'd like a *piece*." He grinned at Jennifer and replied, "...see, this is how a woman should treat her man."

Lilly pulled out a tissue and wiped her nose. "It's my special apple pie. I made it just for you, honey," she paused to look at Jennifer, "would you like a piece?"

Jennifer knew what she meant. Simms looked at her then Lilly and said, "Go get her a piece. Maybe she'll ask you for the recipe."

Jennifer looked at Lilly and said, "No, no... thank you, Lilly. I am sure you made it special just for him."

Simms gobbled the pie down and picked the plate up. "I think I might just go get another piece. Now, don't run off Lilly, okay?"

Lilly stared off into the mountains. "I wouldn't dream of it dear."

He walked off. Jennifer half-smiled at Lilly and said, "What did you put in the pie?" Lilly turned her head very slowly to look at Jennifer. "Absolutely nothing but what the recipe called for, I wouldn't want anyone to get sick if they had a piece, right?"

"Right," responded Jennifer.

"However," Lilly said pausing to see where he was. I did make him his usual breakfast this morning," she paused again, "as sick as I felt; I made him eggs and bacon, all the fixings."

"What kind of fixings?" Jennifer asked.

"The usual," Lilly replied. You know the kind, boogers, spit, and a pinch of shit."

Jennifer patted Lilly on the hand as she got up. "Keep up the good work."

Chapter twenty five

Later that afternoon

Simms opened the bedroom door. "I hope you did not believe anything that lunatic said at the picnic. She has a history of mental problems. Are you sure I can't get something for you before I run errands?"

Lilly tried to hide her excitement about him leaving. "...nothing, dear. I just want to listen to the radio. You go do whatever you have to do honey; I paid no mind to her."

He was pleased at her answer, and he really was very tired and decided not to say anything to her mean or contrite, after all, he still had plans to kill her very soon. He wanted to go to his retreat. No, he needed to go. It was a pleasant little cottage just off the interstate, hidden away and locked up tight like a drum. It had been bought with money Fuller had paid him. Jennifer paid him, too, but for his silence as to her gallivanting. Inside his little "estate," as he called it, were his toys. The girlie magazines and his black velvet pictures, so gaudy and pathetic, were his special collection. Jennifer let on that she liked them because she adored his cooking. Simms was an excellent up-scale southern cook. He never screwed up her omelets. Alas, poor Simms did not know how many talents Jennifer had.

For example, Jennifer had already made friends with his dogs. Dogs not hogs. She actually kept dog treats under the passenger seat just for them—tasty little tidbits of prime rib sautéed in olive oil. They would lap them up with excitement. Yes, Simms was anxious to get to his hideaway, a hideaway that was not the secret he thought.

~

He opened the door to the bedroom again and sweetly asked, "Are you sure there is nothing I can get for you?"

177

Lilly wanted to shoot him right then, but why waste good bullets when she knew his fate? "Take your time, honey," Lilly said sweetly. "And listen. I don't believe a thing that woman said," Lilly assured him about Jennifer. "Everyone thinks she's a little off."

"Isn't she though?" he replied. "There's talk that she was locked up in a nuthouse at one time."

~

He grinned as he stood in the kitchen and dialed the private line. He whispered when he heard that voice he loved to hear at the other end of the line, "Your place or mine?"

It was Jennifer. "Yours, of course. Shall I bring the wine?"

He took a deep breath in anticipation of their brief two hours together. "I'm sorry I had to talk to you that way. I had no choice. You know I have to keep up the tough guy appearance."

She looked at the sack lying on the floor. "I know, sweetie. It's alright," she purred. "I'll be there as soon as the cook finishes up with the kitchen detail. You know how he is. I'll be driving the junker. It's less conspicuous." Jennifer couldn't resist. "How's the wife? Shall I bring some leftovers?"

He paused again. "Just bring the wine. I have my own leftovers." He chuckled. "Who needs leftovers with you as the main dish?"

The line went dead. Very quietly she took the sack and set it outside near the front door. She was not at all worried that Richard would see it. He was in the kitchen stirring a special sauce that only he knew what was in it.

~

White silk sheets, windows decorated with stained-glass, and a Persian rug that had blue flowers that matched the paint job on the walls. She was wearing a loose fitting dress; her auburn hair was tied back with a silk bow. The room smelled of lilacs. This was one of those times when being feminine was important.

"Are you going out?" Richard asked. "Am I to spend another lonesome night on the couch by myself?"

She looked at him sympathetically. "I'll be home soon. Leave the light on for me, and we'll have a night cap when I return, and I will make it up to you, too."

He knew exactly what she was up too, but she did not know that he knew. "Are you really going to leave me here by myself after the day I have had?" he asked.

"Exactly what kind of day have you had, dear? Was your cake a flop?" She could feel her face begin to flush and she knew it was no time to get him riled.

He tried not to show his aggravation and decided to toy with her a little. "The police came by early this morning. I made the decision not to wake you. You looked so peaceful lying spread eagle with your mouth open. Must've been something you ate, huh? Anyway, they wanted to know if we had seen the two young people who were staying up near Shallow Grave. Have you seen them by any chance? Are you sure you want to leave right now?" Richard was taking a big chance. His facetiousness was more than she could handle right then so she choose to ignore his question. "No, I thought I'd pack a bag and pretend to stay overnight at my own house," she said sarcastically. "Will you be alright with your recipes and cookbooks? See if you can pick up the house while I am gone, love."

For one brief moment he almost told her where to put her overnight bag but decided not to. "Have a good evening, dear. Do I need to wait up for you? You know it worries me when you take off like this. There are too many nut cases out there who would love to hitch a ride with you." He paused for a second. "Oh, by the way, I told the police you had Paulie over for tea that day." Her face flushed. Was that something I should have told them, my sweet?"

Her face drained of all color. "You told them what?"

He grinned. "Just kidding, my love. It was a joke. Have you forgotten how to take a good joke?"

She smiled and winked at him. "Funny. I'm a big girl. I'm just going for a drive. Besides, I don't pick up hitchhikers, only husbands who have lost their way."

He moved out of her way. "Would you think about staying here? I made a lovely dessert. We could play one of your games."

She ignored his expression of interest in any game and stepped out the door. If she had put on her regular shoes, she wouldn't have tripped. Instead she had on high heels. She lost her balance and stumbled down the steps. One of her two-inch heels got hung up in a crevice of the stone steps. Down she went, her left foot twisted like a pretzel.

Richard rushed to the door and found her lying on her side. He reached for her, and she screamed. "My blasted foot is broken! What the heck did you leave in the doorway?"

He stepped back and looked at the sack. He saw the shoes. "Since when do you wear those kind of shoes when your are just going for a drive?" He kicked at the sack. "I think that's yours, Jennifer. You really need to keep track of how many pills you take, honey. What's in here?"

"Crap Almighty!" she yelled. "Get me up, and see if you can remember any of that handy doctor work! Just wrap my foot so I can get out of here! And who the hell do you think you are reminding me of how many pills I take?" She kicked at him, "Get out of my way!"

Richard stepped back. "I think it might be sprained, Lovey. Try and get up."

She grabbed at her foot. "Oh, you are so funny, Richard. Are you enjoying this? Just wrap it up! I need to go, and I'll take one of those pain killers, too."

"Jen, hon, you can't be serious. It's already starting to swell. Let me help you back to bed. You know, you should not mix those lovely pills with alcohol. Let me help you slip into something more comfortable, and we can play a game or maybe two. I'll give you a massage. I'll start with your foot."

"You sad little pervert. It hurts like a steam roller has run over it! Just get me something before I go mad."

For once in their married life Richard finally had one up on her. She was his now, and God help her. "Too late for that, my dear. You have been mad for some time. I'll get you to the bedroom. Do you want me to call an ambulance or do you want me to fix it myself?"

She whimpered. "Oh, it hurts, just fix it, please."

He looked at her sympathetically. "Do you want a nightcap? Do you want me to put a cast on it? Do you want me to kiss it and make it better? Do you want me to put you out of your misery?" His tone began to change. "Do you want me to cut it off? Do you want me to marinate it? Just tell me what you want me to do so I can get on with my chores. I really am sorry you can't take your drive. Was it by any chance close to where Simms has his little cottage? Or shall I just go ahead and call to tell him you won't be there tonight?"

"What? Are you nuts? I have no idea what you're referring to," she said indignantly. "And don't you dare raise your voice to me. Just shut up, and while you are tending to your chores," she wheezed out a very unladylike groan, "make me something yummy."

He stepped back. "I didn't raise my voice. Jennifer, I love you so much. Why can't you tell me the truth? One day you are going to be a shriveled up old woman and I am not going to be around to take care of you."

She tried to bite his arm. "You want the truth? You, of all people, want the truth after all this time? You, the very person who got me hooked? It's entirely your fault that I'm this way." Her face continued to turn red. "I hate your silky shaven legs, I hate your manicured fingernails, I hate your straight teeth, and I especially hate the way you smell all the time," she took a deep breath as Richard stared at her, "Why can't you smell like a man, just once?"

His face drained of all color this time. "My fault? My dear, let me remind you that I found you this way and if it wasn't for me, you'd still be rotting away at that pathetic little cottage near the goat farm, and I will not apologize for shaving my legs, or for my nails, and I was born with straight teeth," he almost grinned at the anticipation of her next rant, "and I always smell this way. Goodness, Jennifer, you are the one that has always insisted that I wear this aftershave. You pathetic female! You bought it for me!"

She reached for him, and yelled, "...I did? *It was a dairy*, and it is *your* fault!"

"So *it's my entire fault* now, is it?" He paused for a moment. "I suppose it is, hmmm, I suppose it is," he folded his arms with contempt, "I will still wrap it if you want. Hey, I've got a marvelous idea! If you want me to cut it off, I can do that, too! Just tell me what you want. I am your humble servant."

"You can **cut** the crap Richard," she snorted, "just make a list of things you need and do what you do best," she paused and looked at him with restraint, "making my taste buds quiver."

He looked at her lovingly. "I'll help you up and get some ice on it, but tomorrow you and I are going to sit down and talk about how things are going to change around here. You, my dear Woodman's Daughter, are going to go into rehabilitation right here in our quaint little home."

She almost cried at the thought of his kindness and replied, "Crap. Richard, I had something planned. I was going into the city to get something special for your birthday."

She started to cry.

He did not respond, only helped her up and led her into the bedroom. "There, there, my love, just lie still while I get my little doctor's bag. You may have to have something for the pain. As your faithful doctor, I must tell you I think this is a very unwise decision to be out on the road tonight."

"Oh, you do, do you? You twit!! I'm going! Just wrap it up tight and get me that crutch in the hall closet. You ought to know by now I'm one tough broad."

Richard walked out of the room. "One minute and I'll see how tough you really are." His voice drifted down the hallway, and she was not sure exactly what he meant. He came back with a medical kit and pulled out a syringe. "This will take care of the pain. I don't think it's as bad as you think," he paused to look at her ankle, and then poked at it. She screamed. He withdrew his hand, "It's not broken, just sprained."

"Thank you," she whimpered. "Do me a favor?"

He looked down at her and smiled. "What would be in it for me, my love?"

"A foot up your ass!" she yelled, trying to kick him in the groin. "Take my little bag and just empty out the contents down by the ravine, will you? One more thing, call Simms and tell him I won't make it tonight." She cringed with pain. "There, now you know. Are you happy? You have your retreat and I have mine! You know he and I have been having an affair, but what I cannot figure out is who you are having one with."

He turned to her with no expression on his face and answered, "I'll think about it, but I'm serious. What do I get in return?"

She tried to reach for him. He stuck the needle in quickly, pushed the plunger, and backed away. "There, how does that feel now?"

This time when she reached for him she grabbed him and scratched his arm. "Damn you! You know I don't like shots!" Her eyes started to roll. "Hell, Richard, you didn't have to give me that." The pain killer had already started to kick in. She sighed and fell back onto the bed. "Stupid ninny. I hate… you."

He smiled at her and pulled her boots off. "Don't you mean, '*I hate you, Daddy*'?"

The darkness folded over her eyes, and the last thing she remembered was Richard pulling off her stockings.

He could have done away with her right there, but he loved her too much. "Another time, another place." He stepped into the foyer and picked up the sack. "You fellas get a reprieve for now."

With Jennifer snoring loudly in a rather unladylike position, he closed the bedroom door and wondered if she would wake up if he poured honey on her and rolled her in flour. "Probably not," he said aloud. "I would be the one who had to clean it up."

He chuckled.

So without any hesitation, he changed into something more appropriate for what he was about to do and grabbed his keys and walked out the door. He was going to the market before he paid a visit to the sheriff. How wonderful it was to be a midnight traveling chef! His thoughts returned to his wife. He knew Jennifer was not going to the city. The city was two and a half hours away, and his birthday was one month away. Rehab would be quite interesting and he would enjoy the hell out of it. He had already made up the extra bedroom in the guest house, padded of course, and he was the only one who had the key. It was sound proof.

He really hated it when she lied to him, but he did agree with the statement of it being his fault, well, at least a little. He would take responsibility for some of it.

~

Chapter twenty-six

Simms' cottage

It was amazing how quickly Simms' dogs passed out.

Each delicious raw meatball had one pain killer in them. The dogs readily gobbled them down, and Richard took his time attending to his 'stainless steel' layout. "No need to sterilize them," he thought and stuffed the untraceable sack in his bag.

⌐

The look on Simms' face was priceless when he opened the door and saw his rival standing in the doorway. Simms stepped back. "What are you doing out this late?" he paused to study Richard's outfit, "Better, yet, where is your note from Jennifer? Don't you have a permission slip?"

Richard stepped forward. "I don't need a slip from my wife. I've known about your affair for quite a while. I'm here to ask you politely not to see her anymore or come to our home. After tomorrow she will not mess with you, dabble in your affairs, or travel on these country roads. She is going into rehab. Will you do that for me?"

Simms smirked at him. "So…you know. Does Jennifer know you know?"

"Jennifer is indisposed for the evening. I can make it easy, or I can make it painful. What's it going to be? I would suggest you choose the easy way out. After all, you have been known to be a coward."

Simms laughed in his face. "You will be the one that takes the easy way out, friend. Turn left at the road and take your sorry tail out of here. Your wife is who I am leaving my wife for. Jennifer has told me what a sicko you are. She doesn't love you. She wants a man. If I thought you might give me a good fight, I'd take you on right now," he looked down at Richard's legs, "...what kind of man shaves his legs?"

Richard cocked his head. "Oh, I was hoping you'd say that. I've been itching to use my new knife. I do not take lightly to being insulted for being a clean-shaven man, legs included; besides Jennifer has no complaints about how my legs feel against hers, and it is quite odd that she has said the opposite about you, in regards, to what pleases her."

...And then Simms did something extremely rude and revolting. He opened his kimono and flaunted his masculinity at Richard. "Does this look like something she would give up?" Simms laughed hardily, and made the mistake of becoming too relaxed in his stature so with great precision and steadiness Richard sliced at Simms' stomach, cutting through to his lower intestines. The kimono was just like the one Jennifer had, but Simms' had the face of a warrior on each side.

Simms dropped to the floor like someone had pulled an imaginary plug out of his leg and Richard smiled as he finished what he came to do. It was more difficult than he expected, but at the same time it all happened so quickly Simms did not even have time to put his dukes up. Richard tied him up and then rolled him in netting. Simms became more entangled the more he struggled to get loose. "My dogs will eat you alive...my dogs will de..." He stopped yelling long enough to regain his thoughts, "What did you do to my dogs?" Richard smiled at him. "You're pets are fine. I came here for you not them."

It was *bird* netting. Richard thought it amusing that he found a different use for it rather than the peach tree he had bought it to put over. Somehow it looked better on Simms.

Simms looked like a cast member in a horror movie struggling to get out of the alien webbing. Simms had become swiftly convinced that he was going to die. The cut on his stomach was so precise and the pain was "exquisite," and the netting was working like a Chinese finger puzzle to keep him immovable.

So when Richard started pulling things out of his bag, Simms thought it had to be the worst nightmare he had ever had. For an instant Richard wished he had strapped on his gun before hand. "This is downright absurd," he thought. His last words of wisdom were 'You are heartless.'"

Simms cocked his head and said, "Me, heartless?" It happened so fast Simms didn't even have a chance to run, not that he could, much less fend off the maniac wielding the small, strange shaped knife. Simms frantically tried to move away, and Richard had to admire his tenacity…really he looked more like a six foot inch worm wrapped in a fish net than a side-kick sheriff caught by a cartoon villain. He fell straight back, paralyzed in fear. Richard leaned down and looked him straight in the eye, "I am not the one who is heartless," he paused, "I have put all my heart into your demise. Your escapades with my dear Jennifer are over with. Understand?" Simms attempted to shake his head. Richard continued his barrage of contempt for Simms. "I blame men like you for her unhappiness. You made yourself available to her with your crudeness, your rudeness, and inability to treat your own wife with respect. Shame on you, for it is men like you, and I use the word *men* lightly that make men like me have sleepless nights." Simms' body started to shake. Richard pulled out a lighter. Simms' eyes bulged out. Richard smiled. "…that's right, I don't smoke, so you are probably wondering why I have a lighter," he paused and giggled like a kid finding a special treat, "I am going to light you up like no woman could ever do."

First, Richard smeared a batter mixture all over Simms. Then, he pulled a one gallon container of melted vanilla ice cream out of his sack. Richard stood back for a moment and admired his handy work. Next came the egg whites.

Simms tried to scream, but nothing came out of his mouth. As soon as his jaw dropped, Richard stuffed it with marshmallows and a gag. Finally, the fun came. Richard got to do what he did best, sewing. He stitched up Simms' mouth with the finest of surgical steel wire. He hadn't had this much fun since he watched Jennifer beg for a fix.

He loved her so much.

"I'm not heartless, **Simms, baby**. Isn't that what she called you at times? Why would you want to mess with my wife when you had one of your own?" Richard looked puzzled for a moment. "I've wanted to make baked Alaska for quite a while. Simms' eyes bulged again. "It's too bad Jennifer will not be here to enjoy it. I think she has wanted to devour you for some time, but finally, I have one up on her. Won't she be surprised?" he grinned and looked at Simms straight in the eyes. "You made a deal with the Devil when you messed with my wife."

Simms wanted more than anything to curse Richard. He would never have the chance.

Richard pulled out a pack of matches. "These are more traditional, don't you think?" Simms squirmed to get free. Richard pulled out a tin and unscrewed the cap. Simms smelled it and squirmed again. Richard stepped back and opened the door, emptying the contents of the tin all over Simms. "Baked Alaska with a side-order of sheriff," he mused.

~

The fire consumed the quaint little cottage, and, just like Richard said, he was not heartless. He moved the dogs to a safer location and called the fire department, anonymously, of course. It would all be blamed on carelessness. Simms loved to light candles when Jennifer was coming over. Old wooden cottages like this one had been known to go up quickly if a candle was accidentally overturned, and once anyone saw what might be left of his hideaway knickknacks, well, things would all fall into place.

One day the authorities might figure out what really happened, but Richard would be long gone by then. He already had his ticket and his bags were packed. The Caribbean was calling his name, and most likely some beautiful tanned young woman who was just itching to tend to his fantasies, also.

~

Morning had come too early. Jennifer rolled over only to find a breakfast tray next to her. It was the aroma of the espresso and hot cinnamon rolls smothered in cream cheese that awakened her. "My head hurts," she said to the room. "Richard? Is anyone home?"

She screamed at the top of her lungs. "Where are you, Richard? I have a big fat bone to pick with you!!"

Richard was sitting in the chair near the window staring at her. "Would that be a chicken bone or a human one, my dear? Your head is not the worst of your problems, my love. *Simms is dead.* It seems someone saved you a trip to your little den of iniquity."

"Do I look like I care? What are you talking about?" she said impatiently.

"Jeez, Jennifer! Do I have to spell it out for you? Your lover is dead!! I killed him...rather, I baked him."

Her head sank more deeply into the pillow. "Please get me something for this pain in my head," she paused, "and a glass of milk." She moved too quickly and hit her injured foot on the bed post. "Oh, my God! What have you done to my foot?"

Richard remained in the chair. "You tripped last night, remember?"

"*Oh*, I forgot and I honestly don't care what you did to him. He deserved whatever he got. But really, Richard, you took away my fun."

"I'll get you another pill, and put some chocolate in that milk," he said. "By the way, your handyman and his wife are dead, too. Simms confessed. Not to worry, I have everything under control."

She looked at him with sadness and replied, "*Oh*, I liked him."

"I got a confession out of Simms, and I had him sign it."

Jennifer tried to get out of bed and grabbed at him. "I hate you!" she screamed. "You're supposed to be on my side!!" He stepped out to go to the kitchen.

She was sitting on the edge of the bed when he returned. He pushed her back on the bed and held her down. "That was one couple you were not to mess with!" he replied. "I warned you not to bring anyone to this house again. Don't you remember the last time? It was a disaster! I had to cancel my dinner party. You ruined it! The one time I have a few friends over from the city and you decide to walk in stark naked!"

She giggled. "It *was* funny. It was a misunderstanding. I said I was sorry, and you are a meanie."

He looked at her with disgust. "Funny? I invite the very few friends I have on earth over for a quaint little dinner party after you tell me you are going to go visit Charlie and your aunt for the weekend, and right in the middle of smoked salmon and stuffed mushrooms, you stroll into the dining room with your birthday suit on and ask 'Anyone want desert'! he stood up, "You ruined my evening Jennifer!"

She screamed an obscenity at him. "Oh, boo-hoo!" she mocked. "You had no right to tell Paulie he had to leave. I found him! I made a mistake. I know I did, but he was a good kid."

He stood up and moved away from the side of the bed. "He wasn't your property!" he replied. "I thought it best to send him away. He was more than happy to leave when I told them you off'd Fuller," he lied.

The expression on her face was priceless. He blew a deep breath. "Jennifer. Jennifer, do not exert yourself. I've made a few calls. Someone will be here this evening to tend to your needs, and then, my dear, you are going to the psychiatric ward. It seems while you were doing all those nasty things, I was not attending my cooking classes."

She glared at him. "What are you talking about?"

"I have catalogued and taken pictures of most of your gallivanting. Some I could not take pictures of, but I have enough to put you away with the rest of the nut cases at Mountain View. Fuller was the best, but you really shouldn't have killed those last ones. Shame on you, Jennifer. You've had every opportunity to get help, and you blew it. The last little episode with you almost cost me my life. I have the evidence put away for a rainy day. I want a divorce and all that goes with it."

She chuckled. "You'll get nothing. It is all in my name and besides you told me 'I have my own money.'"

He cleared his throat. "But, dear, you've told everyone for such a long time that I was the *wife*."

She almost fell out of the bed. "If you hadn't stuck your nose in my business, none of this would have happened. I am very discrete."

"Hell, Jennifer! You can't go around killing every husband who treats his wife poorly."

"Why not?" she asked incredulously.

"By the way, remember Ray?"

She did not answer.

"I know you do. Did it ever occur to you that his wife lied to you about all those things she told you?"

"Well, no. That doesn't matter now anyway?"

Richard stood in the hallway. "I have a postcard that you need to see. Don't go anywhere."

She spit at him.

A few minutes later he returned and handed her a postcard. "Read it," he ordered.

She read it out loud. *'Hello, Friends and Neighbors, here I am in Florida having the time of my life. Too bad the wife couldn't come. Have her over for dinner. She is really ticked off at me for leaving her at home. My best, Ray B.'*

"...so what? He went out town," she mumbled.

"Jennifer, it's dated two days before she said he locked her in the closet for two days. He didn't return until three days after her accusation. Don't you think this might have been a set up? You've mouthed off too many times to too many wives about how you feel about husbands who don't live up to your standards! He is dead!"

"Oh, doo-doo," she pouted. "I messed up, didn't I?" Her tone became disdainful. "Still though, he was a jerk. It was only a matter of time," she paused, "Did you know he made her scrub the toilet with a tooth brush?"

Richard didn't smile. "...you are so gullible. You are a sick, sick woman, Jennifer, and I can't stand by you anymore."

"If I could get up, I'd stuff you in that oven you drool over," she slurred. "You are just as guilty as I am because you knew it and did nothing.   She became very quiet and seemed to ponder for a second. "Besides, I am a sick, sick woman—remember?" She started to sob. "You knew. You knew I was sick when you married me. You will not be able to prove any of your accusations. Aunt Callie will get me out of it."

"No, I doubt that. She has my letters. I'm not as stupid as you think I am, dear. I've learned to forge your handwriting quite well. I am not all 'meanie' as you say I am. I have seen that you will be taken care of quite well." He looked at her and realized she was having trouble keeping her eyes open. "I think I may have given you too much pain medication. Listen, Jennifer, I'm packed and ready to go on an adventure without you, my dear. I don't need much because if you remember, you have been very generous with trusting me with your finances. I have not left you penniless," he paused, "All I have to do is make one phone call, and they will be here to take you away but if you promise me you will behave until I am long gone, well then, I may very well have a change of heart. I know you'll probably hire a full-time cook, and they don't come cheap. You could continue to live here, but only because I have chosen not to be a tattletale."

She tried to stand up. "You sack of crap-filled crepes! You had better sleep with your eyes open."

"Now that was a good one, my dear." Richard replied sarcastically. "You can't actually think I'm going to stay in this house one more night with you. My bags are already in the car, and I have my ticket. Here are a few numbers you might want to dial if things get rough."

"You better hide and take all those kitchen tools with you, because if I get my hands on any of them, I will personally stuff them where the soufflés will never shine! I will find you, wait and see. No man leaves me and lives to talk about it."

Her sudden recovery took him by surprise. "My dear Jennifer, I was the only man who ever took interest in you, remember? And don't you mean, 'no man lives if they ever talk about you'?" Tears fell from his eyes. "Jennifer, what happened to us? We were so much in love. I gave my heart to you. Even when it became obvious you were insane, I kept taking it and taking it. You need help. If you had just gone to those doctors…, we would…we might have had a family by now."

She looked away. "I know that's not true. I know what you did and I understood. I forgave you. Go. I've caused you enough pain. Like you said, I'll be fine." There was a beat of silence. "Can I have one little kiss good-bye for a parting gift?"

He took her hand and bent over to kiss her on the forehead. "Good-bye, my love. It has been a wild ride on this mountain of yours. Anyone as independent as you will do just fine."

Most doctors' wives never paid attention to their talented husband's expertise, but Jennifer was very smart. She knew eventually the time would come when this opportunity would be presented to her, and she took it.

He flinched, but Jennifer was very strong and not nearly as immobilized by the pain killers as he had thought. Truthfully, she never swallowed all of them, only occasionally when she needed sleep. "Stupid, stupid, Richard," she whispered in his ear as she stuck the filet knife into his groin with her free hand. Her grip was stronger than he could ever imagine. "Stupid, stupid Richard," she said louder. "I'm a hiker, and a rock climber. I will not go to any hospital unless it is to identify you at the morgue. And one more thing, Richard, my love," she twisted the knife to one side, "I AM THE WOODSMAN'S DAUGHTER!"

Getting up from the bed was painful. She found her pills and took one before she started dragging him to the back of the house. She had already placed a layer of plastic under the Italian rug where he fell. "Papa always said I was smart," she said out loud, "But where is Mama when I need her the most?"

It took her forty-five minutes to get him outside. Putting him in the trunk was more than difficult, but she was amazed how well a dolly came in handy. Richard was not a big man. He weighed in at one sixty-five soaking wet. With his head cut off he weighed less. And with his legs cut off at the hip bone everything was falling into place, literally.

The pain killer was kicking in. It would take another forty-five minutes to get to Shallow Grave. "No problem," she thought. "I'll sleep it off in that little shanty those lowlifes lived in. No gratitude."

She shoved the dolly into the back seat and puked when she slammed the door shut.

Chapter twenty seven

Charlie Holtz was feeling much better. His nightmare about being forced to eat macaroni overlooking a precipice made him a little worried, though. It always drove him crazy when he had a weird nightmare and couldn't figure it out. As always, he had to backtrack and figure out what someone had said to him or what he had seen on television. Maybe it was something he read. Whatever it was, he was going to figure it out. "What have I seen or heard that would make me afraid of eating mac and cheese?" he thought.

~

The phone rang too early for Charlie. It was Danny. "Hey, you old vagabond sleuth. How are things going?"

"That's too personal a question this early in the morning. Don't you ever sleep?" Charlie said with a chuckle. "I suppose you want to take me fishing."

"You read my mind, old man," Danny replied. "I'll pick you up at 8:30."

"How are the kids?" Charlie asked.

"Danny, Jr. is good to go, but Charlene had a bout with a cold so right now all she wants to eat is chicken noodle soup. Ain't it weird? She hated noodles when she was a baby, and now she can't get enough of them!"

Charlie stared ahead and blinked. "What did you say about noodles?"

"I said, she hated noodles when she was a baby and…"

Charlie interrupted him. "Hey, this is going to sound really weird, but can you do me a big favor?"

"Anything, man."

There was a pause on the line. "Can you get your hands on the report that we did together on the Martin case? I just want the inventory that says what was in the kitchen."

"It's a closed case. Why would you want to know what was in the kitchen? I'll be lucky to find the evidence box! That was close to fifteen years ago." Charlie remained silent. "...are you there?"

"Yes, I am here. I really need to look at it if you can be so kind as to look for it."

Danny sighed. "You've got to be kidding. The report probably has mushrooms growing on it by now—or worse!!"

Charlie sat down. Danny heard him groan. "Danny, I know you have it somewhere. You're the only person that I know who packs things up in his attic about cases that were unsolved. I know you kept copies of the unsolved cases, so cut me some slack and just bring it over. I'm very serious. I need to see it. Please, just do it so I won't have anymore nightmares. Thanks."

The phone line went dead. To Danny that meant old Charlie was up on his horse again, and the trail was about to get blazed over some case that happened some fifteen years ago.

~

Callie walked in the room and saw the tackle box. "Crap, Charlie! Are you going fishing?"

"Want to go?" he responded. "They might be biting."

"No, you silly old man," she said teasingly. "Make sure you take your medicine, or I will kick your butt. Want me to pack you a lunch?"

"That, my dear, would me marvelous. And may I say how lovely you look in my shirt!"

"Thank you, kind sir. Somethings never change, huh?"

~

Jennifer thought she was going to vomit again, but one last push and the cook was over the edge. Shallow Grave was now the grave of her husband. She began to cry, but she knew it was the pain killer, not grief. She decided not to stay at the little bungalow Paulie and Molly shared and drove back to her house. She was just about to turn onto the road that led to her house when out of the blue; Curtis Duffy pulled up and blocked her way. She slammed on the brakes while yelling through the window, "What do you want?"

Curtis Duffy got out of his car and slammed his hand on the hood. "I've got proof that you were the one who set my shed on fire! What are you going to do about it?"

She revved the engine and replied, "Run your sorry butt over if you don't move. I didn't do any such thing! I'm having a really bad day, Duffy, so if you don't mind, move!! Richard isn't home right now. He's on a business trip."

He cocked his head. "You look like you missed one of your salon treatments. What are you doing out this time of the morning? Women shouldn't be out on this mountain by themselves. Don't you know there is a killer on the loose?"

She almost spit at him but decided not to. "...I pay no mind to rumors but I might ask you the same thing, Curtis. Were you here to see me or Richard?"

He smirked at her and turned his head. "Don't flatter yourself, Jennifer. I wanted to talk to Richard about some missing people, and no one can get a hold of the idiot sheriff. Hell, the last time I was here you made an ass of yourself."

She stuck her head out of the window and vomited again. Duffy looked at her with some degree of concern. "Are you up to answering a few questions? Damn, you look like you haven't slept in days."

Her head hurt, and now her foot was throbbing like it was on fire. "Ask me, and please just move out of the way. Richard is waiting for me."

He cleared his throat and stepped closer. "I thought you said he was out of town."

She started to sweat and pulled on the door handle. "Who are you, Sherlock Holmes? He's at the house!! Get out of the way! For the last time, I had nothing to do with your shed or those blasted eggs!"

He smiled at her. It was one of those smiles that your mama would get when you were a kid just after you lied to her. "There was nothing in the papers or any report stating anything about eggs. So why did you do it, Jennifer?"

She giggled like a school girl. "Oops. I guess the jig is up! You got me after all! Honestly, Curtis, don't be such a pansy. I'll write you a check for the damages. After all, I seem to remember the case was closed, and you signed off on it!"

He stepped in front of her, blocking her way. "Are you still mad at me because I made a comment about your cookies?" He looked over his shoulder and then back at her, focusing on her nightgown. "Is he *really* out of town?"

"*Oh, god, please tell me he is not making a pass at me?*" she whispers. Jennifer rolled down the window.

Jeez, he was more than good looking, but his breath was that of the south end of a north bound skunk. "Did you eat a dead skunk this morning for breakfast, or is it your after shave?"

He blinked. "You are quite the bitch. You need a lesson from a man on how to speak to your elders."

She laughed so hard spittle came out of the corner of her mouth. "Oh, Lord, please tell me you are not the one going to give me that lesson!! Vicky told me about how you like to be tied up and ..." He slammed his hand on the window. She jumped.

He grabbed her so quickly she almost thought her head would jerk off. "The last time any woman talked to me like that I slapped her so hard her teeth rattled."

She winced and tried to grab his hand. "Let me go, or I will cut off your family jewels." Her head was really hurting now. He grabbed her arm, but only to keep her from falling on the ground.

He let her go and shoved her against the door. "You're not worth the effort. Come and see me when you don't smell like vomit," he smirked, "I am really curious about what makes you tick."

She got back in her car, then stuck her head out of the car window and threw up again.

Curtis Duffy turned around and walked towards her. He said something unforgivable according to Jennifer Martin's standards. "Are you pregnant? Usually when a woman is cranky and moody, she's pregnant."

Jennifer became very stiff and wiped her mouth with her hand. "*What did you say to me?*"

He actually looked concerned. "I asked if you were pregnant. Hey, you know what? I'm sorry I roughed you up. Sometimes I get cranky, too. Let's call it a day, shall we?"

Jennifer threw back her head and got out of her car. "No, I cannot call it a day, not now. I can't have any children. Thanks a lot for reminding me."

He started to get back in his car. "Hey, I'm sorry, but someone saw you light the match. It was pretty brazen of you, don't you think?" Jennifer's color turned ashen. "What's your problem? You don't look so good." Then he noticed her foot. "Jeez, what happened to your foot? Did you get it caught in the washing machine?" He laughed. He glanced in the back seat, "Why do you have a dolly in your car?"

Her head started throbbing. "You just don't know when to stop do you?"

She slammed her hand on the hood of *his* car. "I dropped a cake on it. Case closed. Case closed. I don't feel so good, and as you can see, my foot is killing me," she paused to adjust her nightgown, "Could you drive me home?"

He looked at her strangely. "You're fifty yards from your driveway. Are you on drugs? Where were you coming from anyway with your night gown on? I didn't know there was a road up this way."

She took a deep breath and turned back to her car. "I need to get to a doctor, so just help me in the car. Richard is a doctor. He can help me, and I just might tell him you made a pass at me."

He giggled like a school boy. "Richard couldn't win a fight with a dead chicken." He opened the door for her. "What you need is a real man...someone who will keep you in your place." Curtis took her arm. He glanced at the side of the car and saw the blood. "Did you hit an animal or something? Whew, Jennifer, what have you been up too?"

Jennifer moaned. "...or something."

Curtis walked around the car. "Something really weird is going on here. You look like you have been put through a ringer, your foot is injured, and..." he stopped in his tracks and pointed to the passenger side of the car. "There's more blood!" he said almost hysterically. "What's going on? Did someone get injured in your car? Did you hit a deer?" He scratched his head. "...seriously, where is Richard?"

She looked at him rather unconcerned and pulled out the pistol, shooting him in the stomach. He looked at her and then looked at his stomach. "You shot me?" It sounded more like a question than a statement. "Why have you shot me?"

She stepped back and tried to aim at his heart. He swayed and fell forward. She pulled the trigger again. Curtis Duffy was dead now. She shot him right through the top of his head!

"Bullseye!" Jennifer watched him as he fell forward. It looked like it was in slow motion. She decided against cutting off his family jewels. Instead she tied his legs up to the hitch and dragged him toward her house. How convenient it was that there was a culvert half-way to her front door. It had been Richard's idea to keep it that way for drainage. Duffy rolled down the culvert slowly and landed perfectly as if the Grim Reaper himself had planned it.

The Woodsman's daughter had always planned ahead. She walked to the shed and got the chain saw. She was oblivious to the pain in her foot now. It was her head that was killing her. Cutting the tree was a piece of cake. Getting it to land perfectly on top of him was more than she had anticipated, but she did it. No one would ever suspect that Curtis Duffy met his demise due to his disrespect of the Woodman's Daughter.

Chapter twenty eight

With Callie putting some lunch together for Charlie and Danny, Charlie watched for Danny. He had left to go find what Charlie had asked him to find. It was now nine o'clock. He was sitting on the front porch when Danny drove up and shouted at him. "I found it! Do you still want to dip your line in the water?"

"Always," he said.

"Here's your lunch," Callie said. "Make sure he takes his meds, okay?"

Charlie stood up and put on his fishing hat. He kissed Callie good-bye. "See you later, love. Could you make some of that potato salad for dinner?"

Callie smiled and kissed him tenderly on the cheek. "I've already made some macaroni salad, but I'll do it for you, stud."

Danny grinned. "Ain't love grand?"

Callie patted Charlie on the shoulder. "Yes, it is."

Charlie picked up his tackle box and tipped his hat at Callie. "I bid you farewell, my lady. Let's go before the fish find out we're coming. Danny-boy, bring that folder with you."

Callie glanced at the file lying in the back seat. It was marked 'T. Martin (deceased) Eileen Martin (still missing)

~

A half- mile up the river Charlie cast his line and stared past the ripples. "Let me see that report, will you? I need a break. If I read it now, that means the big one will bite your line."

"Jeez, Charlie, I thought you retired. What's so important about looking at it right this minute?"

"You're a dream boat, Danny-boy; just give it to me before I fall asleep."

Danny looked at him and smiled. "You know, I don't like that kind of talk."

Charlie grinned. Danny handed him the report, and Charlie started thumbing through the pages. "Put on your thinking cap, Danny-boy."

"What are you looking for?"

"That's a loaded question! Hmmm, what *am* I looking for? A one night stand with the Queen of Sheba would be nice, but I'll take something regarding 'what's for dinner?'?"

"What's for dinner?"

"Just fish, will you? Pull in the big one so I don't have to. Did you bring any beer? Callie only lets me have two beers a week."

"She told me you'd ask, and the answer is no. I love you, too."

"And I hate *that* kind of talk."

Charlie thumbed through the pages and read out loud, "*One large pot sitting on the side board…green beans in it. Clean dishes in the sink. Table set for three, one table setting on small table near dining room. The house is dust free. We could eat off this floor. Three wine glasses, one small metal cup. Uneaten apple pie…apparently must have been taken out of the oven before incident happened, residue of apple pie drippings on oven liner. Uneaten salad in wooden bowl with serving utensils lying on top of the salad, a mixture of salad dressing in a mason jar and four t-bones seasoned and sitting near the kitchen door on a plate. Four baked potatoes wrapped in foil with butter on the side. Wish my wife would make a dinner like this for me! One loaf of French bread, not buttered, one meat loaf sitting on the side board and one very small casserole of mac and cheese and a very expensive uncorked bottle of wine, breathing heavily.*" Charlie paused. "Stanley wrote this. He always had a sense of humor. Is he still alive?"

Danny cast his line. "No, he took a bullet right after the Martin case was closed. So what did you find out that you didn't already know?"

Charlie stared off into the distance. "It'll come to me. Just fish and I'll let you know. Think back, Danny. Was there anything that you can remember that might have been out of place other than his head?"

"Nothing," he said. "But it was a long time ago, brother. My memory is not as good as yours, and you're an old man!"

"Can you just close your eyes and think for me?"

Danny closed his eyes. "Okay, but if I get a bite, it takes precedence over a fifteen year old case."

"I got that gut feeling again."

"That's old age or gas. I can think with my eyes closed but not with you talking." The two fell silent.

Danny reeled in his line. "I thought it was odd that the grill had been stoked up and never used. I thought it odd that such a wonderful dinner did not get eaten. I often thought if I had planned on killing someone, well, I might have eaten the dinner, ya know, one for the road?" he paused, "I thought it kind of strange that even a killer wouldn't have taken a bite of the food, ya know, made themselves a bite to eat? The husband, I think, was wired a little too tight. Why would he have put charcoal on the grill and leave it? The little lady had a nice dinner set for the three of them. There was a meat loaf. He must have ticked her off big time. Maybe she was supposed to make pecan pie and the apple pie pushed him over the edge. Maybe she didn't make enough mac and cheese. We'll never know."

Charlie pushed his fishing hat back on his head. "Go back about the mac and cheese and tell me what you said about there only being three of them."

Danny watched his line. "I said maybe she didn't make enough mac and cheese. I said the wife had a nice dinner planned for the three of them."

"Crap!" Charlie said loudly. "Listen to this. *Table set for three, one table setting on edge of small table near dining room… Three wine glasses, one small metal cup …four baked potatoes, and baby makes four!* Damn it! I knew we had missed something."

Danny got a hit. "This is the big one!" Then he turned around and asked Charlie. "Did you ever see that movie about the guy who came to dinner?"

"Tracy, Hepburn, and Poitier, 1965," Charlie replied.

"You're good, but did you ever see it?"

"Yes, of course, many times. Getting back to the subject at hand— someone either came to dinner that night at the Martin's, or they were expecting a guest who didn't show. Or maybe they did show and …how the heck could we have overlooked it?"

"It was Stanley's handle, not ours. Remember? He handled the dressing; we did the salad."

Charlie shook his head. "I never understood that line. I understand my dream now, though."

"What dream? Are you having nightmares again?"

"Hopefully not anymore, but it's because of something little Jennifer told me when I interviewed her."

"Man, you have a mind like a steel trap! How do you do that?"

Charlie chuckled. "I eat my veggies and let's go get some beer and not tell Callie anything about it."

Danny giggled. "I'll take you to get a shake and that is all. Callie is one mean lady when you do not do what she says."

Charlie flipped through the pages again. "Jennifer told me she hated macaroni and that her folks weren't too fond of it, either. So, I was thinking, who did the little wife cook the mac and cheese for?"

Danny fiddled with a lure and did not look up. "So the kid didn't like macaroni. What's that got to do with anything? Nobody would kill for that. Would they?"

Charlie did not respond. He flipped through the folder again and said, **'one very small casserole of mac and cheese,'** he said slow and loud. "Three wine glasses and they wouldn't have let the kid drink wine, hence, the kid's cup off to the side. Someone was coming to dinner; someone… who was special. Someone that did not want tight-ass to know anything about it, perhaps someone who might have wanted to jump out and say, 'Hey, it's me. I came to cut your head off!'"

Danny laid his pole down with the cast in mid-air. "Or someone who came too late for dinner and left very quickly. He or she could have been scared and did not want to get involved. Crap. Somebody was coming for dinner. Somebody Eileen was very fond of or Jennifer. Maybe it was a business acquaintance of the hubby's."

"Some how I just don't see the old man having an acquaintance with one of the three stooges. I'd kill for a beer right now. I don't see the business acquaintance invitation at all. He'd have to have a lot of anger to do something like that to him." Charlie put the folder down. "Somebody who loved macaroni and cheese was coming to dinner. It was going to be a celebration…a celebration of Thomas Martin's death. Well, maybe…maybe not."

Danny picked his pole up and cast again. "This case will not be revisited over a technicality about a menu. Besides, Eileen was never found, and Jennifer is almost twenty seven by now, isn't she?"

"…something like that, maybe older, it doesn't matter though. I sure can ask her some more questions. Maybe the wife and I will go on a little vacation, ya' know….up the mountain?"

"Will you just fish, Charlie? And I believe it is down the mountain and then up."

Charlie put on one of his favorite lures and cast his line out past Danny's. The tip of the pole went down, and the lure took off. "That's how you do it, son."

"How the heck did you do that?" Danny asked.

"It's all in the wrist Danny-boy."

Chapter twenty nine

Callie packed the last of her personal items and checked the animals. She put her small suitcase in the back of her pick-up truck and took a deep breath. "It will all be straightened out. I have got to believe that." She climbed in the truck and began to drive away.

She turned on the highway that would eventually lead her to Jennifer's house, but before she did, she made sure she had enough gas. The drive would take her a little over two hours, but she could do it. Her arthritis was killing her but no matter. She had to be the one to confront Jennifer.

Richard would make a fuss and dance around like some kind of frantic tap dancer, but he would see to it that she ate like she was in a queen's palace. He was more than prissy at times, but he was good to Jennifer. He had promised Callie he would keep an eye on her niece. He had made sure that anyone looking for her headed in the wrong direction, and it was out of respect for Callie that he did this. It also had to do with the fact that Jennifer had been an innocent child, and he felt like she needed his protection. She did.

The only thing Callie didn't like was Richard's hollandaise sauce. It made her nauseous. She knew when he went off to bed, just like always; she and Jennifer would sneak off to the local ice cream parlor and stuff themselves with hot fudge sundaes. They would talk about the past and make plans for the future. Jennifer would cry. Callie would cry over the loss of her sister. Callie would comfort her and make sure all was well with the world.

Many times it made no difference if it was or not. Jennifer had her meds, Richard had his kitchen, Callie had her secrets, and Charlie loved Callie. Callie loved Jennifer. Jennifer did not love anyone, but there were times she cried for her mama.

~

"I'm getting tired, Danny," Charlie said. "Do you mind if we call it a day?"

"No problem. Want to hit the local chili parlor?"

Charlie rubbed his stomach. "Not unless I can find somebody to tie a bucket to my butt! I can't handle spices of any kind. I'll have some of Callie's homemade potato salad. I need to speak with Jennifer. I got that gut feeling again. Something is amiss with the niece. Want to come?"

"I'll swing by tomorrow morning. Do you remember how to get there? I'll give you a call. We can drive up there together."

"I'll pack my pole just in case she is not home. It's funny how some things stick with you, and then the next day you can't remember where you put your shorts," Charlie replied. "Even though it's an old case she might remember something now. It would make my day to find out who killed her papa. I wonder if Crockett is still alive."

Danny started rowing the boat and headed towards shore. "I remember what I can, and I can only hope that the things I forgot are not that important."

~

Danny pulled into the driveway. "I don't see Callie's truck. She must have run to the store. Let me come in and use the facilities." When he was finished, Danny came into the kitchen and saw Charlie staring at a note. "You don't look so good, partner. What's wrong?"

"She's gone to Jennifer's. Crap almighty! I feel like crap, and she runs off."

"I'll stay with you, man. What's the big deal? You forget how to cook soup?"

Charlie managed a smile. "No, *Lucy*, I have some splaining to do," he said with his best Ricky Ricardo accent. He told Danny all about the letters. It took Charlie about ten minutes to get his meds, pack a small bag, get back in Danny's car, and head for Jennifer and Richard's home.

"You sure are quiet. Afraid of what you might find?" Danny asked.

"No, I'm afraid of what I didn't bring with me."

"You have your meds, right?"

"Yes, and my underwear, but I don't have a weapon."

"Not to worry, old man. I'm packing, and I have my little shortie strapped to my left ankle."

"Wonderful, Tonto. Let's ride."

Danny turned to Charlie. "Are you real close with her?"

"I was at one time. She and I would sit on the porch and talk until the fireflies went to bed. How is it that my grandkids turned out peachy even with all they were dealt and Jennifer is still struggling to keep afloat?"

Danny spoke softly, "Charlie, I think it all has to do with how the cards are dealt and you have to know when to fold." Danny cleared his throat and turned onto another road. "It's been a long time. What do you think you're going to accomplish? She was exonerated."

"Peace of mind. I feel like I owe her mama something. Callie swore to me she had nothing to do with it. There were two affidavits as to where she was right before she found Jennifer."

"Well, Callie *was* a suspect," Danny replied.

Charlie stared out the window. "Is it possible ..." He paused, "Do you think it is possible for a kid to carry a trauma around for fifteen years and not know it? And then it suddenly pops up one day and screams 'boo.'"

Danny kept a close eye on the road. "Yes, it is possible, and there is a name for it. I'll get back with you on that one."

Charlie turned to Danny, "Callie was a suspect at the time, and then we got married." Charlie paused and said quietly, "There was no way Callie had anything to do with it. She is the most passive person I have ever known."

Danny wondered who he was trying to convince.

~

Jennifer popped another pill and hobbled up the path to the back entrance of her home. She was looking forward to some leftover fusilli with gorgonzola and mushroom sauce. "Dang," she thought. "I will miss his cooking."

She opened the fridge, eyed a jar of Marsala cherries, and grabbed the whipped cream. "Oh, Richard, you were such a thoughtful man.

Too bad you had to end up at Shallow Grave…right where all this mess began."

Jennifer did something out of character. She flopped down on the floor and ate every last cherry. Then she ate the fusilli stone cold, and then she threw up. A sudden chill caused her to crawl into the living room and stoke up the fireplace. The thought of a nice hot bath made her feel a little better, but more than that, the thought of her having the whole house to herself made her feel even better. She most definitely would take up the offer of calling those numbers Richard left. She would hire a cook, and it could be someone from the local town. It did not matter to her at all, and she would go back to the clinic where she had worked and collect a few things. She had written a letter requesting a leave of absence, and maybe it was time she got back to doing what she did best.

~

As she peeled off the last of her clothes and was about to slip carefully into the hot bath trying very hard not to fall in and get her disabled foot wet, the door bell rang. "What now?" she whined. She reached for her kimono, and the bell rang again—this time over and over until she screamed at the top of her lungs, "I'm coming you nit-wit!! God almighty, if you are a salesman I will shove whatever you are selling right up your sorry butt!"

She opened the door. It wasn't anyone selling door-to-door items. There, standing in front of her, was someone she knew quite well. The look on the woman's face left Jennifer wide-mouthed and a little scared. It wasn't anyone from the neighborhood; it wasn't Duffy's' x-wife looking for him, nor was it the state police, and it sure wasn't Lilly. Lilly would be on her way to New York City by now, 'bless her heart,' Jennifer whispered. It was none other than Mary Morella, the head honcho at the clinic where Jennifer had worked part-time.

Mary Morella was five feet two, well-endowed, and looked like she had just stepped out of the beauty parlor. Hot pink lipstick adorned her lips, and her eyebrows looked like they might have been stolen from Joan Crawford. "Good Lord, Jennifer," she said softly. "Where have you been? I thought I'd never find your place! It is beautiful, but seriously, could you have made it anymore isolated? Why haven't you been at work? It's been months since you were there. I got your letter, but seriously Jennifer," she paused to take off her shoes, "I simply cannot give you a leave of absence." She looked down at Jennifer's foot, "Jeez, what happened to your foot? You look like hell. Is Richard here by any chance?"

Jennifer was speechless. The rapid fire questioning made her head hurt. She knew right then and there if this woman came up missing, she would have the authorities on her door step quicker than a fly on a hambone. "Mary," Jennifer said with a considerable degree of slowness, "You should have called. I've been a little under the weather. Richard isn't here. He decided to take a little trip, and well, it seems everyone in the neighborhood has taken a hiatus. I was just about to take a bath. Maybe you could come by later; like next week? And you need to put your shoes back on."

Mary showed no emotion and shouldered the door open a little further looking into the living room. "Hell, honey, you look like you have been under a rock! What a hideaway! Richard was right."

"Right about what?" Jennifer asked politely, trying not to show her agitation.

Mary looked her up and down. "My goodness, dear, have you gained weight? Maybe, you really do need a vacation. I find it quite odd that a man like Richard would leave you in the state you are in."

Jennifer leaned against the wall, too tired and hurting too much to argue. "Why have you graced me with your pleasantness, dear?"

Mary ignored her. "This is simply marvelous! To think, he helped decorate it as busy as he was tending to all your needs."

It was more of a question than a statement. Jennifer's head was spinning. "I did the decorating, and he does not tend to all my needs. Mary, what brings you here anyway?"

Mary stepped forward and looked in the kitchen. "Honey, what happened to your foot?"

"I tripped over a sack of snakes," Jennifer answered with a great deal of seriousness.

Mary laughed loudly and walked into the living room. She placed her large leather purse on the love seat. "Ooh, nice fire. You have such a sick sense of humor. Why haven't you come back to work? Things aren't the same without you, dear. Richard wouldn't have cooked anything really good before he left, would he? I'm starving! You are the luckiest woman alive to have a man like him. He cooks, he cleans, and he is so devoted to you." Mary paused. "So, where did the master chef run off to?"

Jennifer cringed at the thought of having to listen to her conversation. Mary's voice was somewhat high-pitched and had a monotone air about it. "I really have to get off this foot, Mary. Please, have a seat. Richard doesn't tell me where he runs off to. As long as he meets most of my needs," she paused, "I don't care where he goes."

Mary flopped down on the leather sofa. She spread herself out like a flounder on a platter. "Oh, honey, I won't keep you. I was just wondering what you wanted me to do with those things you left in your locker. I had to open it," she paused, "...the tight-asses demanded an inventory. Sorry. I hope you don't mind. Lucky for you I had already cleaned out all those pills."

Jennifer felt like she might throw up. "You opened my locker? You had no right to do that! I told you I was coming to get my things. You have overstepped your authority, Mary."

Mary acted non-responsive to Jennifer's remarks and reached for her purse. "May I smoke?"

Jennifer shook her head. "Yes, you can. Do you mind if I throw up in your purse?"

Mary giggled. "I called and called," she paused to light her cigarette.

Jennifer's eyes lit up. "I said no smoking."

Mary put the cigarette away. "Now, don't get angry, but I did some backtracking, and I found your number in a file. You really shouldn't leave your personal things in your locker. I still have the items I found in the locker. Richard promised me he would tell you. Did he mention anything to you about it?"

Jennifer was intrigued. "No. What things? I don't remember leaving too many things in there. When did you talk to Richard?" She would have jumped on top of Mary and beat her with a fireplace poker, but her head hurt too much. "You spoke to Richard... when?" she repeated.

Mary chuckled. "Hon, are you alright? You look like you've had too many shots of tequila or a wild ride with some ranger," she chuckled, "Have you been taking the wrong meds again? Goodness, you really do look like crap warmed over. I could get you some of those under-the-counter pills if you'd like. We 'nurses' have to stick together, right?"

Jennifer leaned back and stretched her arms across the back of the sofa. "I feel like crap, but do I really look like crap?"

Mary sensed the sudden upscale attitude in Jennifer's reaction. "Now, honey, I swear he didn't seem upset at all. In fact, he was delighted that you got out of the house, but you really should rent a safe deposit box for the unusual items I found. I took the liberty of making a list." Mary pulled out a folded slip of paper and handed it to Jennifer. "Here, let me show you. It will be our little secret."

Jennifer started sweating profusely. "I don't care to see any list right now."

"My...you have a lovely home. Do you plan on coming back to the clinic? We seem to be a little short this time of year, what with all the nutcases that live on this mountain. It really is difficult to get good help. You fit right in."

Mary glanced at the oil painting hanging over the fireplace mantel. "Is that a real fake Van Gogh?"

Jennifer rubbed her temples. God, she hated this woman. How she ever managed to get the job at the clinic amazed Jennifer. Jennifer had wanted the job. She didn't need the money or the aggravation. She needed the exposure. She needed a place to hide, as silly as it sounded.

Mary stared her straight in the face, and pointed at the list Jennifer had laid on the coffee table. "You really should leave these kinds of items where no one would ever find them."

Jennifer wiped her forehead. "Is it hot in here to you?"

She reached for the list that had been in her locker for over one year. Jennifer's face drained of all color. "Where is the picture? Did you touch any of the other stuff?"

Mary smirked. "Of course, I touched it. She really was photogenic, wasn't she?"

Jennifer didn't look surprised at her question. "Yes, many have said it odd that we looked so much alike. What's your point?"

Mary stretched out her legs on the coffee table. "Not odd at all to me. Not one little bit."

"And why is that?" Jennifer asked impatiently.

"I know exactly who that is in the picture." She chuckled. "I should know. She was in the nuthouse for some time until someone checked her out!"

Jennifer tried not to show her sudden fear. "There are several women in that nut house that could have resembled …me. That picture is just a memento of a patient I liked."

Mary sat up straight and reached into her purse again. "Oh, silly me, I have all the items that I thought you might like to keep. I put them in an envelope." Mary handed the envelope to Jennifer. Jennifer opened it and emptied the contents out onto the coffee table; a gold ring worn thin lay next to a faded black and white photo of a woman and a young girl. The backdrop was the north end of Shallow Grave. It was Jennifer and her mama, Eileen.

Jennifer ran her finger across the photo. "So pretty, so…." She paused and said with sudden perkiness. "This was a picture of…me and someone who was at the clinic for a short time. My mama took the picture. What point are you trying to make?"

She picked up the third item. It was a gold inlayed heart-shaped locket. She opened it with her fingernail to expose another photo. "Papa," she whispered.

Mary leaned forward and picked up the photo. "*This* is your mama," she said, pointing to the woman. "*This is you,* so if this is *your* mama and this is *you*, who took the picture?"

Jennifer shrugged her shoulders. "I don't remember. It was a long time ago. It could have been Callie that took the picture."

Mary picked up the ring. "I found it quite odd that the woman in this photo looks to be the identical twin of the nutcase you were so fond of." She cleared her throat. "This is your mama's wedding ring."

Jennifer decided to play along with her questioning and looked up at the oil painting. "Yes, it is a real fake, too. Richard bought it for me. He was…is always buying me things. Are you familiar with Van Gogh's portrayal of what he thought the world should be?"

Mary stood up and walked over to the painting. She ran her finger across the painting. "…cut the crap princess. No. No, but I am familiar with your portrayal of how you thought Richard's world might be. It's a good thing he isn't here. I have some things I need to tell you. Let's get back to this ring," she said, holding it up to the light.

"Put it down, please," Jennifer said with restraint.

Mary put the ring down. Jennifer picked it up and placed it on her pinky finger. Mary picked up the picture. "How important is this to you, dear?" She moved closer to the fire place.

"Put it down, please. It's the only one I have."

"You tell me right now what's been going on or I will put this in the fire."

Jennifer simply stared at Mary and did something that not even Mary would have thought Jennifer would have done under the circumstances. Jennifer stuck her tongue out at Mary. Mary did the unthinkable. She threw the photo into the fireplace. Jennifer thought she might be having a heart attack and gripped the sofa arm rest. "No!!! You didn't just do that!!" She scurried to the fireplace and tried to retrieve the smoldering photo, but it was too late. She turned slowly to confront Mary. If there was ever a time Mary wished she had been a marathon runner, it was now.

Mary turned around slowly keeping one hand on the fireplace mantel. "...I am so sorry I did that. Why do you work at all? I was working two jobs just to make ends meet. Did you know I worked as a part-time real estate agent up until my mother got sick? You threw a hot poker into the whole mess!"

Jennifer's eyes became glazed. "...tell me I am having one of those seizures...tell me you did not just throw that picture into the fireplace? That was the only photo I had of her." Mary misunderstood the quickness of Jennifer's eyes glazing. Jennifer felt like she was sitting on a pitch fork, but with great restraint she answered, "As you know, Mary, my paycheck goes straight to a charity, and no, I wasn't aware you had training in real estate. Maybe when Richard and I decide to sell this place..." her voice trailed off. Jennifer's temples throbbed.

Mary walked around the sofa, running her finger across the leather. "You may have under estimated what I am capable of doing Jennifer. I figured out how much this place is worth. I think my commission should be more than I deserve, but then again I didn't deserve to lose my second job. I trusted you. I'm sure you're aware of the time and money it takes to care for a sick mother, and when those tight-asses found my prescriptions in your freakin' locker, all hell broke loose. Do you have any idea how humiliating it was for me to have to pack up and leave that place?"

Jennifer was quite certain she didn't know what Mary was talking about. "Not really." She had to move. "Would you like some wine?"

Jennifer stood up, regaining her balance. Mary stopped and turned to look at Jennifer. "I didn't expect this kind of attitude, Jennifer. I'm being audited at this very moment. Richard must have been really ticked off at you because of the way you treated him."

Oh how she hurt! Every bone in her body screamed for something illegal to pop into her veins. "I never hit him, you twit! Do you want some wine or not?" She fell back on the sofa. "Help yourself to whatever is in the icebox as you can see my foot is out of commission. Fix yourself something to eat. Just do something other than running your mouth!"

Mary got up and looked into the kitchen. "Oh, this place is really, really nice. I should have taken up Richard's invitation."

"What invitation?"

Mary smiled and showed off her perfect teeth. "He and I had a lot in common. It seems he and I liked to cook together. Did you know that?"

Jennifer could feel the blood rush out of her head. "Crap," she thought. "Here it comes. She's going to tell me Richard cried on her shoulder while he spooned cherries jubilee into her mouth."

Mary was short, but with her hair down around her shoulders she was rather cute. The clinic rules clearly stipulated that all hair be off the shoulders, and it was the first time Jennifer had ever seen her with make-up on. She looked like a brunette Marilyn Monroe with big teeth. Mary smoothed the front of her dress and stepped closer to her. "I might know what you're thinking. You might be thinking I'm a cow, or you might be thinking straight-laced Mary would never do anything sleazy or out of character regarding her career, by the way, where is Richard?"

"I…" Jennifer started. "What are you talking about?"

"Hush now, sweetie," Mary said putting her finger to her lips. "Isn't that what you called the lady who was moved to the clinic a while back? Isn't that the name she called you when you got upset during your visitations with her? What's her name? Better question, Jennifer. What's her real name?"

Jennifer thought she was going to vomit. "You need to leave now, Mary. I've had a really bad morning. If this is some kind of visit to blackmail me for something, you've come to the wrong house," she paused to elevate her foot, "better yet, just let me write you a check and then get the hell out of my house."

Mary responded by going into the kitchen and did what any professional health care nurse would do. "Here, love, put this cool towel on your head," she paused and looked at the open jar of cherries on the floor, "and I'll get you an icepack, jeez, were those cherries? Too many pain pills will do that to you! Now, back to the problem at hand," she said with perkiness.

"Don't..." Jennifer pleaded. "Do you have any meds with you?"

Mary's voice seemed to echo down the hall. "No, not today, honey. Richard and I were having an affair. He's going to divorce you and I'm going to tell the authorities what you've been up to...unless you can hand over a stack of hundreds, but you can tell me how long ago he left. We had a rendezvous not too far from here."

Now Mary had her attention.

Jennifer tried not to throw up as she slowly pulled herself up. "What... do you think...I have been...up to?" Jennifer asked hesitantly.

Mary opened the ice box and eyed what might have been an apple pie. "Is there any whipped cream?"

Chapter thirty

If Mary answered her last question correctly, Jennifer would have to drag her sorry butt up to Shallow Grave.

Mary walked back into the living room and stood by the fireplace. "…that woman. That pathetic, slobbering woman you were so attentive to. The one you looked in on when you could have been on a break. You know…your mother, Eileen. Jeez, Jennifer, you have the same bone structure!! Did you really think that nit-wit of a night nurse, Hilda, could protect her from my loyalty to the clinic?"

Jennifer could not speak; she could not move either, and if she could have had one wish, she would have wished that Mary would turn into stone the very second those cruel adverbs describing her mama, however accurate, came out of her mouth. "Do not speak poorly of those you do not know personally." Jennifer growled, and wiped the spittle from the side of her mouth.

"She was the most pathetic psycho I ever had the pleasure of pushing in a wheelchair, but she was pretty. I knew she understood every word I spoke to her. She did not fool me for one minute. Want to know what really ticked me off, Jennifer?"

"No, but I have a feeling I'm going to have to listen to you anyway."

"How come my mama couldn't have the same attention your mama had? Was it because you had money and I didn't? You rich broads have got it made," she paused pointing to the painting above the fire place, "with your paintings, and fine clothes," she paused, and waltz back into the living room, "…jeez that is a hideous portrait."

With every synapse firing, Jennifer said the words that Mary did not expect. "It is a portrait of my papa …what did you just say? Never mind, so, I like to visit pathetic patients? It keeps my spirits up. What's wrong with that? You know I always loved the weak ones. They were

215

my specialty, somewhat like your mama. I took the oath just as you did. I did my job well and I have the paper work to back it up."

Now Mary was four inches away from Jennifer's ear and said so very sarcastically, "I want what you have, and I will take Richard, too. You never deserved him."

Jennifer took a deep breath as Mary's cheap perfume filled her nostrils. "I don't believe you. Richard is not an adulterer. I would know."

Mary stood back and adjusted her brassiere. "Let me refresh your memory, Mrs. Hoity-toity. He has a tattoo of a butterfly on his hairless butt," she paused to stoke the fire.

"What...?" Jennifer whispered.

Mary's voice got louder. "I said he has a tattoo of a butterfly on his hairless butt! Ask me how I know. Go ahead, ask me!"

Jennifer felt weak and closed in. "How do you know?"

"Because I love to shave his hairy butt," Mary mused. Mary cackled.

Then Mary deliberately nudged Jennifer to the sofa. She tried to get up, but Mary's nudging became a push. Jennifer started to cry. "Let me up, please! So what if I had my mama brought there? I loved her. So what if I wanted to see that she had better care. I even tried to see that your mama and my mama shared the same room! It's not a crime, and I don't give a crap if you and Richard were having an affair. Guess what? You just admitted to me that you and he were having an affair! Why is that my wrongdoing? Besides what does this have anything to do with you losing your job? Are you sure you don't have anything for a headache?"

"You don't get it, do you?!?!" Mary said stepping closer to the fireplace again. "Richard is leaving you for me!! Plump little Mary!! Mary, who could never get a date, and Mary, who everyone felt sorry for."

"I suppose I don't get it. Tell me, please."

Mary folded her arms. "I have done a lot of fact finding. It seems your mother killed your daddy, and you have been covering her tracks and your past ever since you figured out how to write all those checks to cash to pay off those people who helped you cover up all this mess. I also know that Callie is part of it, too. It wouldn't surprise me if she was the one who really off'd your daddy. God, did she really put his head on the mantel?"

216

Jennifer shook her head. "What did you just say?"

"...damn Jennifer. Are you going deaf? Are you hooked on that crap again? Never mind," Mary said. "Your mama is a fugitive of justice. You and that other person will have some explaining to do when I make a few phone calls—unless, of course, you make it worth my while, if you know what I mean. I have been eyeing a lovely piece of property about fifty miles from here, and I seem to be a little short of a down payment. Oh, hell, I want the whole amount. You have it. I'll take a check."

Jennifer struggled to get up. "Mama is...was sick. You can't be serious about this! It was all but swept under the rug when I left that clinic. How the heck do you know all of this anyway? I know Richard didn't tell you. I never talked to him about it, and Callie sure didn't tell you."

Mary chuckled. "Eileen Martin is sick? She stopped being *your mama* when she started eating the toilet paper. You belong in the nuthouse with her, and by the way, just where is dear sweet Eileen these days?"

"That's none of your business, and you had better leave Callie out of this, so shut your mouth," Jennifer replied. "She's dead. She was tormented by my daddy for years and never did anything to deserve it. He was the reason she lost my baby brother."

"And you should have been her roommate," Mary spat back. "What happened to your mama? What happened to Hilda?"

Jennifer managed to get up and move closer to the fireplace. She might have pretended to be in great pain, but there was no need. She really was. Jennifer gripped the edge of the mantel. "You're so smart. You figure it out. It's none of your business! You really need to leave now. I'll tell Richard you came by when he returns, and when he left he left with empty arms," she grinned at Mary, "...you want the truth? He told me all about you, and he made the decision at the last minute to back out."

"Wha...aa...t?" Mary stuttered.

"What's the matter? Is your heart breaking?"

Mary stepped closer to Jennifer, "You are making this up. He loved me."

Jennifer decided not to laugh. "I am sorry...this could have been avoided. He wanted to break it off some time ago, but I pleaded with him not to call you. I did not want you to get hurt."

Mary's eyes welled up with tears, "You are so cruel. You are not capable of wanting anyone to have happiness but yourself, and I do not believe you." Jennifer had almost convinced herself with what she had just said.

"I have in my possession two tickets to Hawaii. His name is on one, and mine on the other. The reservations were made two months ago. How's that for proof, sweetie?"

Suddenly Jennifer started getting cramps. She doubled over. Mary's eyes widened as she looked down. Blood started to trickle down the inside of Jennifer's legs. "Hell…you're bleeding! My God Jennifer, are you pregnant?"

Jennifer grabbed at the pain and saw the blood on her hand. "I can't be." Another sudden jolt of pain and Jennifer fell to the floor. "You should leave now. It's nothing. Go."

Mary poked Jennifer in the chest with her manicured finger. "I'll leave when I am good and ready. Maybe I'll move in when you're gone," she leaned down and looked at the blood. "You are having a miscarriage. You could bleed to death," Mary stepped back, "…how convenient."

Jennifer screamed as the last wave of pain was released in the form of a push. Mary stepped back. "…my goodness, girlie, you were pregnant."

Jennifer took a deep breath and slowly pulled herself up against the mantel. "You can have Richard."

Mary regained her composure, "Now wouldn't that be a riot? Me and Richard sittin' in a tree…k.i.s.s.i.n.g"

At this point Jennifer did not know if there were two Marys. Mary moved towards the fireplace and reached for the poker. It was not there.

"What are you doing?" Jennifer asked.

"Making myself at home…I will wait here until Richard returns. You may start hemorrhaging. I am sure Richard will want to see the afterbirth. Can I help you to the bathroom?"

~

Jennifer was not quite sure how a fire poker could get stuck in a human skull so quickly, but it did. Mary's head was stuck in between the fireplace and the steel grate that held the firewood. Jennifer looked down at her. "You told me we were friends. I trusted you."

Mary kicked at Jennifer, but it was only a reflex. Jennifer pulled the fireplace poker out of the side of her head and placed it back in the holder. She stood there for what seemed a lifetime, until urine ran down her leg. Jennifer heard that voice she loved to hear when she was little. It wasn't the little voice in her head that she tried to get rid of so many, many times, but the voice of Callie. "I'm here, baby. Aunt Callie is here."

Jennifer gasped. "Oh, Aunt Callie, what are you going to tell the police? Have you come for dinner? Papa has gone to the market and Mama...well, where the hell is Mama? I think Richard has gone, and I don't know how to cook macaroni and cheese. Will leftovers be alright with you?" She looked down at Mary. "She threw Mama's picture in the fire. I asked her nicely not to do it. She is a bad girl."

Callie looked at the blood and knew immediately what it was. She went into the kitchen and came back; carefully cleaning up what could have been her great niece or nephew. "Oh, honey, I am so sorry." She paid no mind to Mary at all and attended to Jennifer for the time being.

Callie knew exactly what frame of mind her niece was in now. She was the young girl Callie had tried to protect when she was there that dreadful day. It was as if time had swept them up and they were there again, right in the middle of all the turmoil. "Aunt Callie, are you going to stay for dinner?" Callie drifted back to that fateful day and cradled Jennifer in her arms...

Thomas stood with his fists right up in Eileen's face. Poor Jennifer had her face pressed against the outside of the window looking in. "Aunt Callie!" she yelled through the glass pane. "Papa! Don't you dare hurt my mama!" She ran to the kitchen door. It was locked. She ran to the front door and it was locked, too.

Again she went to the window. "What are you doing here, Aunt Callie? Were you and Papa arguing?"

Astonished at what Jennifer had just said to her, she replied, "I was invited. Stay out there until one of us lets you in."

Thomas screamed his question at Eileen. "You invited someone for dinner and didn't tell me about it?"

Eileen had replied in quiet terror. "My sister is not 'someone'. It's her birthday. I missed her. I didn't think you would mind. I've cooked all your favorites. Please, just this once, be nice to me."

He laughed and stepped forward holding his fist up. Jennifer became wide-eyed and yelled at him through the window, "Never will you hit my mama!"

Callie stepped forward. "You need to leave now, Thomas."

Thomas did the one thing he never, ever should have done as long as he was alive. He slapped Eileen across her face. She fell against the kitchen chair, hitting her head. Callie reached for her, looking up at Thomas. "This is the last time you will ever, ever hurt any of us."

He chuckled. "I'm really scared," he turned to look at Eileen. "Is *she* going to stop me, 'cause you sure as hell are not." He reached for her again.

Callie stepped forward. "Oh, yes I am."

Jennifer came around to the kitchen door again, and looked through the window, "Will someone let me in, please!"

~

Callie had been there for some time. She walked over to the kitchen door keeping an eye on Thomas.

"Honey, sit on the stone wall. I will come and get you when Mama and I are done cleaning up the dinner dishes." Jennifer looked bewildered. She had not eaten dinner at all, but she did what her aunt told her to do and waited while sitting on the stone wall.

"But I don't remember eating dinner," Jennifer said to herself. "I feel like I might throw up."

Thomas had already stepped back into the living room. He stared intently at the deer head, tapping his right foot. "You're worms, both of you."

The sting of the needle made Jennifer twitch.

~

Callie's head jerked and she was back in the land of reality. She had to clean up this latest fumble of Jennifer's. She helped her niece to the bathroom and put her in a hot bath. Then she went back to the living room and started dragging Mary outside. She was heavier than Callie thought. It took her thirty minutes to get Mary's body into the bed of

220

her truck. Pushing her out was the easy part. Callie was dumbstruck for a few minutes when she looked down into Shallow Grave.

She knew poor Molly Driggers was there with her husband and others, too. Then she saw it. It had to be one of Richard's slippers. She kicked it into the dense underbrush.

Callie heard something behind her, the soft crushing of leaves, and then her lights went out. The last thing she remembered when her face hit the soft earthy leaves was the sight of pink bedroom slippers. "Oh, my god," she murmured.

~

"Anyone home?" Charlie called as he pushed open the door to Jennifer and Richard's home. "Danny, go around to the back and look in a window. I don't see Callie's truck at all. Richard's vehicle is gone, too.

Danny went around and reached for the doorknob. The back door was not locked. He smelled it, not a woodsy kind of smell, but something he was familiar with, way back in his mind. It wasn't dish soap, not hair spray, but much sweeter. The kind of smell you smell when you open up a bottle of girlie shampoo and wonder how they got all those strawberries in one bottle. "What the heck," he said.

Then his memory danced as he followed the smell of bubble bath. Keeping his hand on his weapon, he stepped into the hallway that led to the master bath. "Ms. Callie? Jennifer are you hiding from me? It's me, Officer Danny and I am here with your Uncle Charlie. I don't want to hurt you. Callie?"

Charlie stepped into the hallway. Danny jumped. "You scared me! Do you smell that?"

Charlie pointed in the direction of the bathroom. Not quite sure what they would find, he slowly pushed the bathroom door open. The window was fogged up, but he did smell strawberries. There she was. The Jennifer Charlie had known as a little girl. "Are you taking a bubble bath?" He asked. "Where's Richard? Have you seen your Aunt Callie?"

"Uncle Charlie!" Jennifer screeched. "Who's Richard? Did you bring me something? Do you know it's my birthday in three days?"

He couldn't believe his eyes. It was Jennifer naked from the waist up and having the time of her life in the tub.

Danny stepped back out in the hallway and sighed. "Sorry. I'll wait out here."

Jennifer splashed water at Charlie. "Have you ever seen so many bubbles? Where's Mama? Are you staying for dinner? Aunt Callie told my papa he had to leave right then and now. Why would she say that to my papa? Why would she leave and not tell me? I don't think daddy is coming back at all, but Mama is hiding in the woods so the bears won't eat her."

"Crap almighty," he whispered, motioning for Danny to come in. "Forget what you see, okay?"

"This place has gone to hell in a handbag," Danny whispered to him. "You better go find your wife, and where is Richard?"

"Where's your Aunt Callie, honey?" Charlie asked.

"This isn't good. What the heck happened to her foot?" Danny whispered again. "Am I seeing things or does she think she's a little girl again?"

Charlie wanted to cry but replied, "I am going to find something for her to wear. We need to find Callie. Can you keep an eye on her while I take a look around?"

Danny nodded and grabbed a towel. "We need to call an ambulance," he said looking down the hallway. "This is really giving me the willies." Charlie reached for a light blue chenille robe hanging on a hook behind the door, "Put this on her and stay with her."

Danny looked around for a few minutes. He picked up the phone sitting on a small table near the bathroom door. "The darn phone lines are dead. Did you ever see any of those movies that had those sound effects you never wanted to hear if you were in the same situation?"

"Not sure. Are you referring to the screams or the groans?"

"Both. I'm hearing them now."

Charlie looked at him funny. "This isn't the time to bring up a Boris Karloff movie. I'm going to look for Callie. Lock the doors, and don't let anyone in, and that means me, Pilgrim, unless I show you my badge. I think Richard is a goner."

Danny wasn't sure if he should crap in his pants or smile; he did the latter and unlatched the holster on his firearm. Jennifer smiled and blew bubbles from her hand. "Are you staying for dinner, too? It isn't wise to be a guest in this house if you plan on being rude to the ladies."

Danny stepped back and leaned against the wall. "I am a nice man, honey, and I like my ….." He almost said 'noggin' but decided it was not appropriate. Charlie grabbed a small hand towel from the edge of the sink and blew his nose. "Stand by the bathroom door, and if she comes at you with anything sharper than a toothbrush…hell, do what you have to, but I would rather you didn't hurt her if you don't have to."

"I won't hurt her, Charlie. I know how to rock a kid to sleep. Hurry back, please. Do you think there might be anything in the fridge to eat?" Charlie gave him a funny look, "You're kidding, right?"

Charlie pointed in the direction of the kitchen. "Leave it to you, Danny, to be hungry at a time like this. Help yourself, but eat it in here, will you? She ain't a kid in body, just in spirit. How the heck did I let this happen? I swear if Callie is hurt I'll…"

Jennifer stood up. Danny helped Jennifer put the robe on and then looked at the water. "Charlie," he said slowly, "There is blood coming from her woman parts." He turned away. "Put the robe on honey."

Charlie's head felt as if it were going to burst and looked at Jennifer. "Honey, what happened? Is it that time of the month? Are you in any pain?"

Danny had a shiver. He looked back at Charlie. "That doesn't look like any monthly I ever saw."

Charlie took Jennifer's arm. "Honey…can you tell me what happened?"

Jennifer sat down on the edge of the bathtub and sighed. "Could I have some ice cream now?"

"Go find your dream girl, partner," Danny said.

Charlie high-tailed it out the front door. Danny turned back around and Jennifer stood up, letting her robe drop to the floor, "I am all grown up now." Danny turned his head. It was difficult not to look, but out of respect he didn't. Jennifer was gorgeous, not a pound of fat on her body. No tan line, no visible scars or stretch marks. There was just one very small tattoo on the inside of her right ankle, "Daddy's Girl."

Danny smiled at her and picked the robe up; helping her put it on again. "Is there any ice cream in the ice box honey?" She giggled. "Of, course there is silly boy. What respectable girl doesn't have ice cream when a boy comes calling?" Danny suddenly felt nauseous.

Chapter thirty one

Charlie did not see Callie's truck anywhere. The garage had two cars in it, one Mercedes and Jennifer's pick up truck. He heard something hit the ground behind him and he turned. There was one of Richard's golf clubs. He looked up and saw the rest of them. He couldn't help himself and replied, "...four."

Then as if some little green man crawled into his brain, he remembered. "Shallow Grave might be where she's at. What are the chances?"

A chill ran through his very being. He rushed towards the path when he got out of Danny's car and started making his way up the trail. His legs ached. His heart pounded, and now he had to relieve himself.

"I'm too old for this," he said aloud. "A cancer survivor, if anybody might ask, buried my daughter just before her nineteenth birthday, had to adopt my grandkids, loved it, love them, met the girl of my dreams when I thought Cupid had forgotten me, and now look at me, strutting myself up an embankment looking for God knows what. Callie, if you are up here somewhere in this God-for..." Fifty more paces and he would be at Shallow Grave.

"Isn't this the most beautiful place on the face of the earth?" a gravely voice from his past asked. It shot through him like a bullet. He didn't turn around. He was too afraid, but somehow the voice did not seem threatening. He took off his hat and turned around very slowly making sure he still had the small handgun Danny had given him. He did.

As he turned around slowly, he was out of breath. "This just isn't worth it."

Charlie thought he had heard someone say something. It certainly wasn't Callie's voice, more raspy, more "I can't breathe without my respirator" kind of voice. Charlie looked to the left and turned around again, facing Shallow Grave. He almost lost his balance. Before him was an old woman, someone who could have been his mother, perhaps his grandmother. "This woman, by the looks of her, should be at the pearly gates right now," he thought.

She was not an old woman by any stretch of the imagination. She just looked old. This woman had to be a throwback from a silent film, or a sidekick of Bela Lugosi, perhaps, but she gave him the creeps. She was wearing a hooded goose-down jacket from what he could see, it was pulled down past her forehead, pajama bottoms, pink granny slippers, and a pair of bright blue gloves, and if that wasn't a sight for his sore eyes, she donned a coon-skin hat on her head. "Howdy!" she quipped.

"Madam, who the heck are you? And what are you doing out here on this mountain all dressed up and no place to go? Could I assist you down the mountain?"

The mummified-looking granny adjusted her coat and pulled back her hood. "...I love a man with humor. So, there really are a few gentlemen left on this God-forsaken mountain. Who are you and what are you doing on my mountain?"

If it was possible for him to crap out a green apple, he would have. She *was* the Mummy from the 1932 Boris Karloff movie but she didn't have any wrappings. "Madam," he managed to say with deliverance that even Boris himself would have been proud of. "I'm Charlie Holtz, a retired detective, trying very hard to solve a case I may be sorry I ever stuck my nose into again. May I be of some help?"

Without hesitation, but certainly with trouble breathing, she quipped out a one-liner, "Got a cigarette, honey? What's a stud like you doing walking around all by your lonesome?" She paused to take in the view and replied, "Ain't this a pretty place?" Charlie did not expect to see sledge hammer in her boney hands. It had to weigh more than she did.

It seemed like the scenery was slipping by him in slow motion. He looked past the old woman and saw Callie heading for the two of them holding a rock over her head. She was headed straight towards the drop off of Shallow Grave. Her eyes were wide open, and fear spread across her face like nectar on a bee's behind. "Move out of the way, Charlie!" she screamed. "Drop the hammer or I'll drop you!"

Eileen raised the sledge hammer at him. "I said I wanted a cigarette."

He froze. "I don't…"

He thought it not wise to tell a two-hundred year old mummy he was flat out of cigarettes. "Let me see. I may have one left. Let…me… just…"

He could picture her falling apart, but the vision of Callie falling over the cliff got his attention more. "One minute, please," he said as he fumbled through his pockets. "I know it's here somewhere," he said as he held up his hand motioning for Callie to stop. "Madam, you might want to sit down."

Callie was wide-eyed and still moving in their direction. Her words seemed to come out of her in slow-motion. "Char…lie get out of the… wa…y!"

Then the mummy did something unthinkable for someone needing a cigarette. Charlie thought it quite odd that an old, old broad could even lift a sledge hammer up that high, much less swing it up so high. Then as if someone had stuck him with a hot poker right up where the sun doesn't shine, it dawned on him like a train coming out of a tunnel. "She's going to kill me! God, almighty, you're Eileen Martin!"

Too late, not for him, not for Callie, Eileen Martin swung the sledge hammer. The momentum was her down fall, literally. She and the sledge hammer went right over the drop off as Charlie grabbed her by the tail coat.

"That is my sister!" Callie moaned, slipping on the loose gravel. "She hit me on the head with a shovel! I had no idea! I swear!"

Eileen yelled something along the lines of, "Get off my mountain!" And then she was gone.

Charlie sat down. "Okay, it might be possible, but can elevation cause one to go nuts?" He shook his head. "I had to pee, but I don't now." He caught his breath. "What were you thinking? I mean… what are you doing up here? Better yet, what the heck is she doing up here? How did she get up here? Have I lost my mind, Callie? Was that your sister?"

Callie sat down and breathed deeply. "I had her moved out here a long time ago. Jennifer knew it, just us. I found her ten miles from here right after she killed Thomas. I couldn't have Jennifer dragged through all that mess. I thought I could take care of her, and she would get better. She did get better. All those prying eyes made it more difficult. Too many people asking too many questions that I couldn't or wouldn't answer. It seems this is entirely my fault. Eileen became the patient without a name. Will you promise me one thing, Charlie?"

"...I didn't bring a change of underwear, so the answer is no, but seriously, *anything*," he said. "Just get me off this mountain."

"Promise me you'll see that Jennifer gets real help this time. They may want to come and get me, too."

"Why would anyone be coming to get you?"

"Because I have been hiding a fugitive from justice all this time."

He put his arm around her. "I promise, and no one is going to come and get you or anybody else. I promise I will take care of both of you. This never happened. I'll take some of that guilt, Callie. How the heck can a person that old get up this mountain and club her sister on the head? How old is she?"

"She's a little older than me, but she's much younger in spirit," she said. "Jennifer still took her on hikes. Eileen was a mountain goat. What are we going to tell the authorities?"

"How did she get here? She didn't walk!"

"I think Jennifer must have gotten her. I just don't know right now."

"I saw the blood on the fireplace. Did Richard get cracked over the head?"

Oh, how she hated lying to him. "She told me they had a dreadful fight. He has left her. He ran off with the head of the clinic Eileen used to reside in, well, at least I think that's what happened. Richard had his own money. I guess he had all he could take from her, too. I suppose it's best we don't try to contact him."

Charlie took hold of Callie's arm. "You have to see that Jennifer gets help. You do it, or I will. She is back at the house taking a bubble bath. Danny is with her. Something is amiss in all this bliss."

"I won't do it," Callie said. "I'll move here and take care of her. I'm not that decrepit that I can't take care of her. I saw to it that my sister was taken care of, and I will care for Jennifer again. She is a child with a tormented soul inside of a woman's body."

"Let's go," Charlie replied. "I'll figure out something."

Callie smiled. She knew he would not do anything to jeopardize their love. Charlie was a good man. He had grown to love his life with her. She knew that.

~

"Find or see anything unusual?" Danny asked.

"Found her," Charlie answered pointing to Callie. "And she is very unusual, and I found the mystery of the missing woman."

Callie walked past Danny slowly and mumbled, "…what does it matter?" Danny followed her into the house.

Callie stepped into the living room. "Thank you, Danny. I was looking for Richard."

"Is she still in the bathtub?"

"Ah, no, she led me to the guest house. Go take a look see."

"What the heck is she doing in the guest house?" Charlie asked. "I thought I told you to watch her."

"I did!" Danny protested. "I watched her walk to the guest house. She is asleep in that room with all the baby things."

Danny tugged at Charlie's jacket as Callie headed towards the guest house. "I'm not sure, but if she stays the way she is now, no one is in any danger. What are you going to do?"

"Not sure right now. Do me a big favor," Charlie replied.

"Anything," Danny said.

"Take your car and leave. Callie and I will get back later, okay? I have some figuring to figure out."

"You got it. Are you sure everything is okay?"

"Sure as rain."

Callie walked towards the guest house and motioned for Charlie to come with her. "I suppose it is time. I can't do it anymore."

"Maybe you should just stay outside for now. I will go in and check on her."

"No, she is my responsibility. I will get her some things for now so she can come with us. Would that be alright for now until we think of something else?"

Charlie shot a glance at her that seemed to say, 'that hurt.' He opened the door to the first room and wondered why a rusted pot and an old chair would be sitting in the corner. It smelled of stale cigarette smoke, and then he knew why it smelled like that. The second room was decorated in an art deco style. There was a full-size bed, and in the far right hand corner was a small table with a palate of pastels. A large a-frame stand stood near the window with a blank canvas, and from the ceiling hung a piñata. Charlie shook his head, "Don't ask Charlie," he said to himself. Where did he say she was?" he said loudly.

"Look in here," Callie said quietly, pointing to a door with a pink bow nailed to it.

Charlie walked in and saw Jennifer asleep in the last bedroom. It was a four-poster bed with more frills than any little girl could want. Piles and piles of baby clothes were stacked up against the walls, some to the ceiling. A rocking horse sat in the corner near the window, and what Charlie could not believe was the portrait of Thomas Martin hanging on the far wall.

"Crap almighty," Charlie mumbled. "Would you look at that? Why in the world would she want a picture of her papa hanging on a wall where she sleeps?"

Scribbled across the portrait with finger paint were the words, "The most beautiful place on earth."

Callie had stepped into the room. "How could I have been so selfish? How could I have let this continue? I should have seen this coming with the training I had."

"Just go, Callie, just go," he said. "I'll sit here and wait to see if she wakes up, and then I will figure out what to do."

"Alright, I'll go make some coffee. Please don't call anyone, promise?"

"I promise," he said as he picked up the teddy bear and sat down in the rocker. "This is one big mess, but I'll figure it out."

He looked up and noticed the large shelf hanging over the bed. It was lined with all kinds of stuffed animals, and they all had wings. "Angels amongst us, little one," he said out loud. He ran his hand across her forehead. "Say, good night honey. Your nightmare is about to come to an end."

Jennifer shifted in the bed. Charlie started to get up but she turned over and started humming. It was the same tune she had hummed in the bathroom that first day he met her, and the only reason he remembered it was the fact it was the very song his father used to sing when he was working on his little projects right before he died of cancer, "...*somewhere over the rainbow.*"

Tears ran down his face as he pulled out the syringe that would take the pain away from Jennifer the woman and leave Jennifer the child with sweet memories only.

He had planned ahead a week ago in anticipation of finding Jennifer in this state. He had thought for sometime she was hooked on something really bad but had no way to prove it. He had found what he was looking for in Richard's office. Who would have known that Richard kept his 'stuff' hidden in a hollowed out cookbook? Charlie would. He knew what was in the syringes. He only took two. It would be enough. No finger prints, at least, not his.

He took down all the angels and placed them around her before he stuck the needle into her arm. She flinched for a second, and then her head jerked back. "She's gone," he thought. He was very careful not to leave his fingerprints on the syringe, and then he dropped it on the floor right after he made sure Jennifer's fingerprints were on both of them.

~

Jennifer didn't move or open her eyes as he gently injected another amber liquid into her arm. He thought she was already gone, but she opened her eyes slowly, looking at him with her puppy dog eyes. "Thank you, Uncle Charlie," she whispered. "I always knew I could depend on you to do the right thing."

He waited a few moments. He checked her pulse. No pulse at all.

~

He and Callie went to Shallow Grave and stood on the very spot where Eileen had fallen. Callie made sure Jennifer had no pulse. Gently, they let her slide down the precipice to her grave. She was wrapped in a gingham quilt, and she still had her mother's ring on her pinky finger.

Callie leaned forward a little as she held on to Charlie's arm. "Can you see anything?"

"Nothing but sadness and death," Charlie said sadly. "Let's go. It's going to rain real hard. We best head back."

"Shouldn't we say something?" Callie asked, looking up at him with tears in her eyes.

"What do you want *me* to say, honey?"

"Tell me you'll stand by me."

"I will. I'm too old to find another Flower Bird."

Two months later

"Why are you going to sell it?" the real estate person asked Callie. "Didn't she leave it all to you? This is a really, really lovely place. It is so immaculate, and well taken care of."

Callie nodded. "Too many memories, too many miles on this old woman's bones, and who could live with this quietness? I would go stir-crazy. I'm used to roosters crowing and cows mooing in the morning, but I sure will miss his cooking."

"Whose cooking?" the woman asked.

"Never mind. You might have a problem selling it. The press has gotten a hold of her past. Oh, well, do the best you can. If you can't sell it, I'll move in and bring my roosters and cows with me."

"Do you mind if I ask you something, Mrs. Holtz?"

"Ask away dear."

"How could she have left the house to you if she is considered missing?"

"Well," Callie pondered, "the dear girl was quite sane when she signed over her properties to me. I was the only relative she had. She suspected her husband was going to do something to her, and it was always her wish that he never got his hands on anything that was hers. Trust is what it is all about, don't you agree?"

The young woman nodded. "I suppose anything is possible."

Callie started the engine of the Mercedes. "I have to go pick up the hubby. Give me a ring if you get any bites. I'll go down on the price if need be."

The agent smiled with glee. "I'll be in touch. Do you mind if I take a few more pictures? This is one of the loveliest places I have ever seen."

Callie smiled and replied, "It most certainly is."

"Have a good day," the young woman said as she waved and returned to her car.

Callie looked up at the mountain. "Alrightie-dietie."

~

The real estate lady took a few more pictures and didn't notice what she had stepped on. It was weather worn, but it would have been the clue to lead authorities to what happened to Paulie and Molly Driggers. It stuck to her shoe and managed to fall off just as she lifted her foot to get into her vehicle.

A Polaroid of Paulie and Molly looked up at the sky as it faded into the leaves. The two of them were smiling, and in the middle was an old woman holding a sign, "Home at last." These were Molly's last words just before the Polaroid was snapped. "Don't go and be tricking me, okay, Paulie?"

At the time, the amateur photographer had been very pleased with the picture at the time it was taken. Richard had many talents; photography was just the tip of the iceberg. He had cooked a zucchini pie and for dessert were Valencia caramel oranges. He did not share it with anyone. He had learned to hide his gluttony and still keep his slim figure while Jennifer was out gallivanting across the Woodsman's paradise.

⁓

Two miles down the road, Charlie stopped to relieve himself. He finished and admired the view of the hillside's blanket of colors. "Always beautiful," he mewed.

Callie smiled at him affectionately as they got back into the car. "It is the most beautiful place on earth, isn't it?"

Charlie leaned over and kissed her on the cheek. "Yes, it is, but I don't want to live here," he paused to kiss her on the cheek again, "… ever."

The End

Synopsis

Revenge can take on many forms. It can be served as three meals a day, or it can be served by someone you least expect, or it can sit in the darkness until the right hands crack it open, causing an emergence that will sneak up on you, and then ...

The Woodsman's Daughter is set in the foot hills of the Smokey Mountains. Jennifer is a young girl who may have witnessed her father's murder, but her memory of it has gone. Her father made a past time out of playing tricks on people, some of these tricks ended in tragedy, and Jennifer reached her breaking point when one of his 'victims' died.

Jennifer is admitted to the Mountain View Hospital for observation, but her aunt sees to it that her stay is short lived, and takes Jennifer in her care.

A retired detective has one last case to look into and it ends up being the murder of Jennifer's father.

Her mother has disappeared into the mountains, and is never found. Charlie Holtz, the detective takes an interest in Jennifer, and visits her in the hospital, and soon finds out that her aunt is someone he had a past with. Cupid shoots his arrow.

Time passes. Charlie and the aunt marry. Jennifer has a life of her own now, and is married, too, but her past has followed her in the form of a serious mental disability that goes haywire.

This mental problem goes unchecked for sometime until some letters are read by Charlie that lead him to believe all is not well with Jennifer.

It seems Jennifer has another side, and it is called **Revenge**. A revenge that crept up on her through the years, unchecked, and misguided, but very much a part of her life as a woman set on making life miserable for men who mistreated their wives.

Charlie decides to pay her a visit only to find out that Callie, his wife, has already left before him. Mayhem and murder has already shown its ugly face in the guise of several deaths, a local business man, a nosey neighbor, a disgruntled employee, her husband, and the sheriff, who Jennifer has had an on going relationship with.

Charlie arrives at the home of Jennifer and Richard. Jennifer is there, but she is not what he expected at all, and he cannot find his wife either. He goes to a place where it all began, Shallow Grave. He finds his wife, but not before someone from the past tries to kill him.

Charlie returns and goes to the guest house, only to find another side of Jennifer, the side he tried to interview when she was a child at the Mountain View Hospital. Saddened by all the events, he does what he thinks is necessary to take her pain away.